AWAKES MY HEART

Delia Grayson's childhood sweetheart Keith suddenly decides to marry the superficially charming Susaline, leaving Delia broken hearted.

However after treating herself to a beauty treatment her employer Sir Timothy Nodeleigh starts to look at her with new eyes. But she isn't in love with him and neither does she see the true value of Paul Faversham's adoration. For her heart – not yet awakened – is still with Keith.

AWAKES MY HEART

Awakes My Heart

by

Kay Winchester

Magna Large Print Books
Long Preston, North Yorkshire,
BD23 4ND, England.

British Library Cataloguing in Publication Data.

Winchester, Kay
  Awakes my heart.

  A catalogue record of this book is
  available from the British Library

  ISBN   978-0-7505-3654-7

First published in Great Britain in 1949
by Ward, Lock & Co. Ltd.

Copyright © Kay Winchester 1949

Cover illustration © Mohamad Itani by arrangement with
Arcangel Images

The moral right of the author has been asserted

Published in Large Print 2012 by arrangement with
The executor of Kay Winchester, care of S. Walker Literary
Agency

Magna Large Print is an imprint of Library Magna Books Ltd.

Printed and bound in Great Britain by
T.J. (International) Ltd., Cornwall, PL28 8RW

CHAPTER 1

'I *wish* they weren't coming today!' Delia Grayson burst out, passionately, then, catching her aunt's eye, she smiled ruefully and bit her lip. 'Well, of all days, did it have to be today that Keith brought her home for our inspection?'

'I suppose you don't *mind* me having guests to tea in my own flat?' Miss Grayson put in, mildly.

Delia flicked a look in her aunt's direction, and coloured a little. 'I always suspect that mild tone of yours, Aunt Cora, and I suspect it more than ever at this moment. They're my guests, Keith and Susaline, and you know it! Just the same, today of all days—'

'Sit down there and I'll bring you an aspirin and some water,' the older woman said, carefully and slowly enunciating as was her habit. 'I never care for guests on Saturdays, personally. You're always too done up after rushing around all the morning in the wake of that mad idiot of an employer of yours, that you're usually fit for nothing, the rest of the day. There, now, a cushion behind the head – that's it!'

'You are a darling, Auntie,' the girl murmured. 'But I do wish you weren't right *every* time!'

Miss Grayson went carefully out of the room, hiding the grin that lurked round her very slightly made-up mouth, and giving her carefully dressed white hair a pat as she passed the mirror in the small hall. Something, she told herself, as she shook out two aspirin tablets into a teaspoon and carefully filled a glass with cold water, would have to be done about Delia. Regretfully, it would have to be herself, she decided, and the decision was regretful because Miss Grayson had learned during her forty-five years that it was much better to let life take its course than to attempt to interfere.

After she had given Delia the tablets and ordered her to keep her head back and her eyes closed, Cora Grayson went back to the tiny kitchen and carefully loaded the tea-trolley with tiny bowls of fruit and cream, jelly and blancmange, plates of minute sandwiches decorated with triangular flags on which was printed the contents of each pile, and a chocolate cake with pink and white icing. She did everything carefully, not because she was in any way infirm, but because by nature she abhorred quick movements, because it was so seldom that quiet and efficiency accompanied them. She herself was a most restful person to live

8

with, as Delia had often told her with gratitude, after the hectic days the girl spent in that big, noisy office in Town.

Delia was dozing when she went back. Softly the older woman moved around, setting out the dishes, and completing the table by getting out pale green china with white spots, some of the delicate old pieces of silver from the now broken-up Grayson home, and finally a slender cut-glass vase in which were half a dozen early daffodils fringed with some delicate fern stuff. She stood back to survey the table and liked the effect.

Delia opened her eyes and sat up with a jerk. 'Ouch! My head!' she gasped, clapping a hand to the temples and leaning back again.

'When will you learn the art of moving slowly?' her aunt murmured, going out to the kitchen with the trolley.

'Auntie! Why this marvellous spread?' Delia expostulated, when her aunt returned some minutes later with the tea-pot and hot-water jug. 'I just thought ... a cup of tea and some toast...'

'My dear,' Miss Grayson murmured, carefully avoiding Delia's eyes, 'I told Keith it was my wish that today would be something in the nature of a celebration, so you don't need to feel personally guilty about it. After all, I have also known the young man since he was five!'

'Yes, but–' Delia protested, flushing.

'I thought it might look less – er – odd, shall we say, if both of us were enthusiastic about all this,' and Miss Grayson let it go at that.

'Am I *awfully* obvious about the way I feel about Keith?' Delia asked, fiddling with her handkerchief.

'Well, not to *me*,' Miss Grayson replied, carefully. 'I'm used to it. I've seen you both together for twenty-odd years – every day since you both started school together – so I'm used to it. But this young woman he's bringing home might not think it looks so natural. With a name like Susaline…' and Miss Grayson broke off with a deprecating shrug of the shoulders.

Delia grinned, partly to cover her confusion, partly because she had been waiting to hear what her aunt would have to say about that very unusual Christian name. 'I think she must have thought it up herself. She wants to be a dancer, you know. It would make a good stage name, wouldn't it?'

'Possibly,' Miss Grayson agreed, rather absently. 'Delia, what's happened to that nice young man who brought me some sugar for my tea, the last time I visited you at your office? That tall young man with the dark hair and nice eyes, and the rather old-fashioned manners? I liked him!'

Delia effected to look puzzled for a second, then said carelessly, 'Oh, Paul Faversham! He's only one of the clerks in the counting-house. Why?'

'Oh, nothing, except that if Keith is going to make a habit of bringing this young woman home here I thought it would be rather nicer if you had someone your own age to bring, too, to make a foursome.'

'We do make a foursome, Auntie, with you.'

'You're being deliberately tiresome, Delia! I meant a foursome of young people, as you knew very well. Aren't you going to put on something less casual than that suit? It looks as if you've come straight home from work.'

'Well, I have – practically,' Delia grinned. 'I thought you'd appreciate this lack of dressing up, in case the successful female thought I was setting up in opposition.'

'Well,' Miss Grayson said, composedly, 'it's too late to do anything about it now. Here they are,' and she went to the front door herself without another word. She was aware that Delia would fly up, prink anxiously in the glass, and wish frantically that she had changed into her new blue wool frock, but perhaps it was as well as things were.

The flat was the downstairs floor of Miss Grayson's own house, and the tiny hall was but a fraction of that once spacious lounge

11

hall, before it had had a chunk taken off it to serve as an extra room. The door was still large and handsome, with its stained glass window of a stag leaping through the forest, and it still opened out on to a flagged path and a quite attractive garden.

Miss Grayson allowed the fraction of a second to elapse after the door bell had pealed, to give her niece time to regain her composure. Then she flung wide the door, to admit a tall fair young man with an anxious face and sensitive mouth, and beside him a petite little blonde with an already possessive way of holding his arm.

'Ah, Keith, my boy! Come in, do – we're waiting tea for you both,' she cried, putting out her hand to him in a businesslike manner. He took it and shook it warmly.

'Aunt Cora, you are a pet,' he murmured. 'May I present Susaline Baird – Miss Grayson.'

'How do you do?' Miss Grayson said, coolly taking the girl's limp plump hand, and not keeping it more than a second.

'Miss Grayson isn't really my aunt, Susaline, but she's been a better friend and counsel to me than a good many real aunts are!'

'Thank you, Keith,' and the older woman flushed with pleasure. 'Now, hang your things up and go and see Delia, while I take Susaline into the bedroom to take off her things. You don't mind, my dear, if I call you Susaline from the start? I like to be informal with young people – they look so strange these days when addressed formally, I find.'

Susaline looked doubtful at this, and flicked an uncertain glance at Keith, but was saved the trouble of answering because Delia herself came out then.

'Keith, I've one of my wretched Saturday headaches – do forgive me if I'm not very bright and entertaining! Oh, is this Susaline? I'm so glad to meet you at last.'

There was warmth in Delia's voice, and a certain eagerness. 'How does she do it?' Aunt Cora wondered.

'I've heard a lot about you,' Susaline said darkly, and rather obscurely.

She didn't seem to mind leaving Keith and Miss Grayson when Delia offered to take her to the bedroom, and Aunt Cora hid a smile as she went back to the sitting-room with the young man eagerly behind her.

'Well,' he began, as soon as he had closed the door, 'what d'you think of her? Isn't she pretty?'

Miss Grayson racked her brains to think of something kind to say about the plump little blonde she had just met. There was something set and stupid about the little plump face, with its flawless skin beneath the surface of careful make-up, that the look in the china-blue eyes belied. Susaline Baird was

13

by no means the innocent child that Keith obviously took her to be. That she had brains was obvious; for a girl just under five feet she dressed cleverly and had a good sense of colour. She carried herself well (didn't Delia claim that the girl had dancing ambitions?) and she kept her rather common voice at a low, careful pitch. So much Miss Grayson had taken in in that first rapid glance of acquaintance. Why, she asked herself, irritably, did the nice young men pick out young women such as these?

'She's pretty,' she allowed, and looked hard at him.

'Oh, Aunt Cora, don't you like her?' he protested, like a hurt schoolboy whose treasure has been examined and tossed aside as worthless.

'My dear Keith, I've hardly seen the young woman for more than a second or two. Now, tell me, how've you been getting on at the bank this last week?'

'Oh, awful! The chief clerk's got his knife in me, since the new manager came. Of course he's sucking up to him like anything. Oh, Aunt Cora, it's such a damned dull job. I think I'll have to change. Susaline says I'll get to be old before I've had any fun if I stay there.'

'Nonsense!' Aunt Cora said, crisply. 'A job is what you make it, and if you stop to think, a conventional job needs more character to hold down and do well than does an unconventional one. I suppose you're dreaming of becoming a crooner in a dance-band, or some such nonsense? Well, it's a phase. Most young men go through it sooner – your time is coming later. How old are you?'

He grinned under her censure. 'You know perfectly well I'm twenty-eight. Two years older than Delia. I hope she doesn't get chivvied all the week like you chivvy me at weekends.'

'She survives,' Miss Grayson said, dryly. 'Ah, here they are. Come along, you two. I've just poured out the tea. Do you take sugar, my dear?'

'Oh,' Susaline eyed the tea with dismay. 'Didn't Keith tell you? I have Russian tea: no milk, just a slice of lemon.'

There was a little, tight silence, and Delia noticed Keith's look of agony at Susaline.

'Well,' Aunt Cora said, with a smooth smile, 'it's common or garden tea or nothing, because I haven't a lemon in the place.'

'Well, just for this once–' Susaline capitulated, and Keith ludicrously dropped his agonised expression and looked happy again. Miss Grayson was amazed at the sweetness of the girl's smile, once she let that set expression relax. Delia, who had had five minutes of the girl in the bedroom, replenishing her make-up, thought with the dispassionate judgment of twenty-six years: 'What an ass he

15

is to fall for that little bit of goods!'

Keith ploughed happily through all the sweet things, and talked happily, superbly unconscious of the strained feeling between the three women. Susaline delicately bit through two minute sandwiches and had two cups of tea, refusing the rest.

'What, not even a bit of jelly or fruit?' Delia asked, eyeing her aunt's spread with dismay.

'Of course she won't,' Aunt Cora exclaimed, unaccountably. 'If I'd known beforehand that Susaline was hoping to become a dancer I wouldn't have embarrassed her with the sight of so many sweet things! It's your figure you must look after, isn't it, my dear?'

'Oh, I *knew* you'd understand!' Susaline breathed, vehemently. 'As soon as I looked at you, Miss Grayson, I said to myself, Now there's someone who under*stands!*'

'Yes, my dear,' Aunt Cora murmured, and flicked a glance at her niece, whose mouth was gaping rather foolishly.

'How's the bank these days, Keith?' Delia asked, as Aunt Cora quietly cleared away the tea-things. She never allowed visitors to help, on the grounds that they didn't really want to (as they were invariably in unsuitable clothes for domestic tasks), and she loathed people making duty offers or showing off how domesticated they were.

Besides, she said, it was the best china and glassware.

Susaline digested all this with pleasure, and settled herself daintily in the corner of the settee beside Keith.

'Cigarette?' Delia offered, but Susaline shook her head.

'I never smoke. A most disgusting, unfeminine habit, *I* feel! Oh, but don't feel–' she floundered, as Delia arched her eyebrows. 'I mean, you work in an office or something, don't you? With such an awful job, well, you must feel you *need* a cigarette!'

'It's not a disgusting job, no more than Keith's bank job – which he doesn't seem eager to discuss,' Delia smiled.

'Oh, but I thought you and Keith saw each other a *lot* during the week,' Susaline murmured, sitting forward and watching them both closely.

'Oh, on and off,' Delia said, carelessly.

'If you must know,' Keith said, at last, as he packed his pipe to his satisfaction and stuffed it between his teeth, 'I'm hating the bank job as I've never hated it before, and I'm seriously considering taking Susaline's advice and getting something less prosaic.'

Susaline watched Delia's dismayed face with pleasure. 'It's not really my doing,' she purred. 'Keith told me he was fed-up to the eyebrows with it long before I started advising him to chuck it.'

'*Long* before?' Delia was puzzled. 'But I thought you two had not long met?'

'Oh, we knew each other ages ago, didn't we, Keith?' and she treated him again to that heartbreakingly lovely smile, that had something of the quality of a tiny baby's – joyful, with no reservations.

Keith grinned, entranced. 'Yes, she's a "dropper,"' he told Delia, without taking his eyes off Susaline's face.

'What's that?' Delia asked, with a lump in her throat.

'A ravishing young woman who isn't capable of shutting her handbag, or of holding it tightly. Result – it falls, spills contents, which roll in all directions, while said young woman makes ineffectual but highly interesting efforts to grab everything at once, to the annoyance of irascible old gentlemen who are too old to appreciate her youth and beauty and, anyway, are in a hurry to get by!' Keith said.

Susaline gurgled with pleasure. On Keith's face sat that partly imbecile yet entirely happy look that a young man has when he desires (yet dare not put into practice) the entirely cannibalistic pleasure of eating his young woman.

Delia felt hot and uncomfortable, and experienced for the first time that utterly lonely feeling which comes to the third person, the odd man out.

18

She cleared her throat. 'Oh, and that was some time ago, I suppose?'

'A year ago,' Keith said, still not able to tear his eyes away from Susaline's face.

'Jealous,' Susaline said, with a quick glance in Delia's direction, yet still that gurgling note of laughter in her voice which removed any sting from the word. 'You've got the advantage of me, anyway, because you've known Keith all his life. I should have liked to know you, darling, when you were a little boy.' This last sentence was delivered in a soft, pathetic little voice that brought Keith a shade nearer to her on the couch.

Delia got up. 'I'll see what Aunt Cora's doing,' she said, and went out, but it is doubtful if either Susaline or Keith noticed her going.

'Well, dear,' Cora Grayson said, as she took off her apron and carefully hung it on the peg behind the door in the kitchen. 'I'm just going to take these back into the sitting-room.'

'I shouldn't,' Delia said, savagely. 'They're probably petting by now!'

Cora Grayson's eyebrows delicately arched.

'Oh, no, rub that out, what I just said, Aunt Cora! I'm a catty wretch. It's my headache, I expect. It's just that – oh, why, why does a nice fellow like Keith have to fall for a dopey little Jane like *her!*'

'If you weren't in love with him yourself,

19

you wouldn't notice it, or care if you did!' Aunt Cora shrewdly observed. 'Come along, now, my dear, open the door for me and I'll push the trolley with a little more noise than usual, to give them warning!'

As it happened, the length of the room was between them when Delia looked in. Keith was thoughtfully going through gramophone records at the radiogram, and Susaline was patting her thick gold hair into place and trying to fix an already immaculate curl into better position.

'Susaline's going to show us her new exhibition dance,' Keith said, with a fatuous grin. 'I'm to be her unworthy partner.'

'Unworthy nothing!' Susaline said, stoutly. 'I've been telling him for ages that he ought to get a job as a dancing partner. He'd be simply marvellous. With his fair hair and thin face he'd be a tremendous "draw," because he doesn't look villainous like the rest of the fellows at the Starlight Hall. The girls would come in droves after him!'

'Would you like that?' Delia asked, curiously.

Susaline smiled smugly. 'Oh, I don't mind him dancing with other girls – nothing much can happen on a dance-floor – but it'd be me he'd be taking home!'

Delia could have slapped Keith for looking so pleased. Never, she thought savagely, have I ever seen him acting such a complete idiot before.

Aunt Cora came in with her knitting, a fair-isle pullover for Delia, and settled herself in her favourite armchair. 'You young people going to dance, then?'

'No, Auntie, Susaline's giving an exhibition,' Delia said, with the faintest trace of distaste in her voice. 'You don't mind?'

'No, not at all! In fact, I'd rather like to see what she can do. Keith will, of course, see that the furniture's not damaged.'

Susaline pouted. 'I'm not doing a hulahula or an apache turn – it's a dance that can be done on a square foot!'

'Incredible!' Aunt Cora observed.

Keith said, 'Should we practise a few routine steps first, darling?'

'Oh, no, it isn't necessary,' Susaline told him, in a new, businesslike voice. She was the professional dancer. The coy little-girl act was for a moment abandoned. Delia marvelled at the change, and it struck her that this quality alone might have a lot to do with endearing Keith to the girl. She certainly wasn't just a stereotyped little blonde.

'Samba rhythm – you've done it before,' Susaline told him, and to the others she explained kindly, 'I do the complicated steps while Keith stands poised on one toe.'

'I hope he can keep his balance,' Aunt Cora murmured, and when Keith smothered a laugh Susaline shot the older woman a furious glance.

'May we put the top light off, and just keep on the small lamps?' Susaline asked briskly.

'Oh, dear,' Aunt Cora murmured. 'Well, I'll have to keep on my small lamp, because of doing fair-isle. I don't want to go wrong!'

'Put your knitting down, Auntie, and watch what may be a new sensation in the entertainment world,' Delia said, and was conscious that she was being catty, and that Keith had directed her a quick, incredulous look.

To partly atone, she got up herself and switched lights on and off for them, to try out the effect, and Susaline proved her sense of showmanship by picking out two lowish lights that flung her silhouette into high relief each time she passed them, but almost made Keith into a shadow in his dark suit.

Delia watched incredulously. The girl was no doubt a good dancer, and knew her personal points, making no attempt to reach beyond them. The record music throbbed and vibrated, and into the prosaic sitting-room of Miss Grayson's flat, in a quiet road on the outskirts of Chiverstock, crept the heady rhythm of the Congo tropics; the sensuous movements of the two bodies on the centre of Miss Grayson's fawn and brown carpet, moving (as Susaline had said in truth) over a very small space, conjured up for Delia the South American scene – the damp heat of the tropical night, and the unspoken passions of the moving couples. It merged in with the fanatical light in Keith's eyes as he took Susaline into his arms, it echoed itself in the soft, snakelike movements of Susaline's soft body, and it was heightened to fever pitch by the absence of sound, owing partly to their dancing on carpet. Delia was glad when it was over, and Keith turned the gram off and put up the lights. The magic was over, the hideous spell broken. She felt she could breathe again.

The dancers seemed to relax, too. Susaline flung herself into the corner of the settee and Keith perched himself on the arm beside her. 'Well, Aunt Cora, Delia, what'd you think of it?'

Delia made a helpless gesture.

Aunt Cora murmured, 'Well, personally, I don't care for that kind of dance. I prefer the graceful ballroom dancing of my youth. But, of course, I am quick to recognise and acknowledge merit, and I believe Susaline has a gift for dancing.'

Susaline looked pleased. 'You see, Keith, I knew it'd be all right! Now all you have to do is to give your silly old notice to the bank, and we'll practise like hell, and be ready for the championship in six weeks' time. Then – the halls! I'll have my name in lights before you know where you are!'

'I think you're wonderful, darling,' Keith murmured.

Delia was frankly alarmed. 'You're going to chuck up your job at the bank to go on the *stage?*' she gasped.

'What's wrong with that?' Susaline was surly.

Keith looked alarmed. 'Oh, now, hold hard, I didn't say I would! What I *will* do, though, is to practise with you, darling, and if by any good chance we did happen to come anywhere in the championship – *if*, remote as it may seem – well, then, I would seriously think about it. But frankly, darling, I'm no dancer. I'd spoil your chances.'

'But, Keith,' Delia objected, ignoring the warning pressure of her aunt's hand on her knee, 'your job – you can't be even *playing* with the idea of giving it up. After you've worked up in it all these years, and at *your* age – Keith, you're not a boy, you know! If you failed on the stage the bank wouldn't take you back!'

Keith flushed with annoyance. 'Really, Delia–'

'Yes, really, Delia,' Susaline purred. 'Keith *isn't* a boy. He can make up his own mind what he does!'

'Keith and Delia are like brother and sister,' Aunt Cora said, 'so you mustn't be surprised if Delia is apt to take the liberties a sister would take, in her brother's interests.'

Pouring oil, Delia thought savagely, cross with her aunt for once. For two pins I'd smack that silly little idiot's face for messing up Keith's career. Dancing!

Susaline measured the older girl's turbulent face, and did a bit of quick thinking. 'Keith, you know what we were talking about, coming along? You know what you wanted, and I wouldn't agree?'

'Yes,' he murmured, doubtfully.

'Would you do this for me if I altered my mind and said "yes" to your idea?'

He leaned over her. 'Susaline, do you really mean that? You're not just saying it?'

She shook her head up at him, and gave him again that bewilderingly lovely smile of hers. 'Then we could practise all the time, and try for a job on the halls despite the championship,' she said softly. 'We could, you know ... *then!*'

'Well, all right, then, I will! I'll give in my notice tomorrow!' Keith said, enthusiastically. 'May I tell them? Now? Oh, how marvellous that this happened in Aunt Cora's flat, the day she invited us home to tea to meet her!'

Susaline nodded again at him.

He turned round, pulled Delia to her feet and hugged her, and bent and kissed Miss Grayson.

'What's this in aid of?' Miss Grayson asked, with a quizzical smile, and a lift of her immaculately plucked brows.

'You knew all the time, you old fraud,' Keith laughed, turning to pull Susaline to her feet. 'Aunt Cora – Delia – Susaline is going to marry me! We're engaged!'

CHAPTER 2

Delia Grayson was private secretary to a manufacturer in Chiverstock. The main building was at the back, where theatrical cosmetics were made, but the offices occupied what had once been a fine old house in pure Georgian style, and still occupied its old position in King's Square in the centre of the town.

Delia loved the town and the old house. It seemed to her to be sheer sacrilege turning a house of that kind into an office building. The stairs had carved balustrades and the walls were still covered in the fine old wood panelling which had been there when the family had had it – that family now died out, the last heir having been killed in the 1914 war – and there was still, in the centre of the big entrance hall, the magnificent old fireplace. A great china urn had been placed in it to save it looking quite so bare, and all the people who went through – employees and customers alike – seemed to think it was there for the purpose of an outsize ashtray.

Delia's boss had a room overlooking the square, and when he was out, or in the factory, she would have the place to herself, tidying his desk and sorting his letters, using the private filing cabinet which he kept in there between the two tall windows, and occasionally looking out into the sunshine. Across the square was the King's Cinema (built to match the pillared Georgian houses still standing), Richenbor's select coffee-house (also pseudo-Georgian), and Kirby's, the gentlemen's outfitter, which actually occupied a fine old piece of early Georgian architecture which drew artists from the surrounding counties to paint the upper part of it. Kirby, it is true, had a feeling for architecture, and would allow no advertisements to intrude in his window-dressing; but then it was part of his own personal advertisement to be the only store in the town that didn't use advertisements. He prided himself on being the one exclusive house for gentlemen's and boys' clothing; the one known authority and supply for the local public school and private school uniforms. Only the best and most expensive came from Kirby's; a Kirby tab at the nape of your neck was a sure sign you were well dressed.

Further along, separated only by banks

and offices of solicitors, accountants, and one or two private firms who had nothing more to indicate their presence than a small, select brass plate, was a popular tea-shop (the town's eyesore), the Starlight Hall, which ran in competition for nightly dancing with the Falcon Hotel round the corner, and the top part of the King's Cinema, and beyond that again the Repertory Theatre.

The Repertory Theatre could just be seen from the window of the small vestibule on the first landing, where for no good reason there had been installed six book shelves without any books, a small wash-hand bowl too tiny to be of use, and whose taps were jammed and dry, and an old-fashioned hat stand. In here one day Delia found Paul Faversham.

The door was wide open and she glanced in, in passing, for a last view of the plane-tree outside. There was something fascinating in the gaunt black branches, and the pallor of the new leaves, furled into gigantic buds, against the pale turquoise of the early spring sky. The unexpected sight of a man standing there made her jump and exclaim: 'Oh, my goodness!'

He turned and grinned at her, doing his best to chase away the wistful expression that had been on his face.

'Why, Paul, what are you doing, dreaming out of the window? I thought that was my forte,' Delia smiled, preparing to go on down the stairs. It had been a concession, this going out for lunch at twelve o'clock, and to force home to her how great a concession it was, Sir Timothy always waited until she returned at one before going to his club for his two-hour lunch. 'Well, I must rush, or the only food worth eating will be snapped up.'

'Mind if I come with you?' Paul asked. She saw, for the first time, that his hat was in his other hand.

'No,' she said, hesitantly, and it was written all over her face that she thought he had been waiting for her.

'Don't look like that. I wasn't lying in wait, honestly. It's just that ... the Repertory Theatre...'

'It *is* ugly, isn't it?' she said, warmly, forgetting her first slight feeling of resentment. It was commonly accepted in the firm that Paul Faversham was 'after' her, and besides feeling nothing more than irritation for him, she felt it was undignified for the boss's secretary to encourage the attentions of one of the male clerks. 'I think it ought to be torn down. It's the worst looking building in the Square.'

'I didn't mean the architecture,' he said, quietly. 'I admit it's a fractionally ugly building, and just a theatre with no pretensions to beauty. But I was thinking of the stage itself. Have you ever thought of going on the stage?'

'Frankly, no,' Delia said, smiling in spite of herself.

'Well, I've always wanted it,' he confided, suddenly, with a slight embarrassment over the confession that she found rather engaging. 'It's just hell to be stuck here in a dead-end job working out accounts, within sight and smell of the greasepaint, almost within touching distance of theatres and theatre people, with a rep. of our own (and a good one at that) just across the Square, and getting no nearer to it.'

'Good gracious, I had no idea–' Delia began, then pulled up sharply. Of course she had no idea. She had never even bothered to say more than good-morning or good-night to him, or to ask him sharply why his accounts weren't ready for her, or why he hadn't returned her files to their proper places. How could she have known that he was stage-struck? How could she know anything about him?

'Look, Paul,' she said, using his Christian name in the easy familiarity of the firm, 'I've gone too far. I meant to go to the Blue Parrot. I'll have to go back. Goodbye.'

'Won't you come with me – I know a good place, far better than the Parrot,' he pleaded. 'Come on, give it a trial. I won't embarrass you by offering to pay for your lunch,' he added, neatly forestalling the objection she had been about to raise. 'That's if you've never been before to The Cellar Café.'

She hadn't. He led her to a street off the Square, a little old street called Seven Lamps Lane, where in a fine old house, narrowly sandwiched between two modern commercial buildings, the cellars had been turned into an intimate eating-place, with small tables on which were spotless cloths, and tiny lamps of wrought iron, with pink silk shades. It was peaceful, and not too 'old-world,' and Delia liked the feel of it from the first.

Three sisters, all well over fifty, kept the place, and knew their customers intimately. New people came by introduction rather than by accident, for there was nothing to indicate that it was a café. Miss Lou called out to him a cheery good-day, and Miss Bessie waddled over to take his order.

'This young lady is sceptical about The Cellar,' he told her, with that engaging smile of his, that had so enchanted Aunt Cora. 'Do your best with lunch – I leave it to you – but for the sweet...'

'Miss Ann's special,' she interpreted, a broad smile creasing her fat face up into regular curving folds. 'Right, Mr Faversham, we'll see what we can do.' With a smile at Delia, as if to say 'We'll show you!' she waddled back to the kitchen.

'It's nice,' Delia said, with wonderment in her voice. 'I get so tired of the fish-and-chip shops and the tea-shops. D'you know what I'd like to discover in this town? An old Georgian coffee-house – oh, not like Richenbor's, but the real thing. I'd like to go back a century, and eat as they ate then – when cooking *was* cooking!'

He nodded quietly, and with understanding.

She flushed. 'Does it sound silly? You didn't think Sir Timothy's secretary was a romantic at heart, did you?'

'You'd make a sensitive actress,' was all he said as Miss Bessie came up with two covered bowls of steaming soup.

'Will you come again?' he asked, after they had eaten rabbit en casserole and sauté potatoes, and Miss Ann's special, which was a delicious concoction of fruit set in milky jelly, finished by coffee with cream in it.

'I may come here sometimes when I'm not too rushed,' she said slowly, wondering if she could make it clear she wished to come alone if she came at all, without offending him. 'But usually I'm afraid I only have time to dash across to the Blue Parrot and snatch a hasty meal. I'll have to rush now, anyway.'

'I see,' he said, quietly.

He walked back with her, talking carefully about general things, and to her infinite relief discovered that he ought to slip into the bank and collect some forms before going back to the office. She escaped thankfully; thankfully because at the top of the stairs she ran into two of the youngest typists, who would have made a great deal of the secretary coming back with Paul Faversham, who was, by virtue of his youth and good looks, something of a hero to the typists' pool.

Miss Grayson was poring over a letter when she got home that night. 'It's from James, dear,' she said, taking off her reading glasses to peer at her niece. 'You look tired. Did you manage to get something decent for lunch today, Delia, or have you filled your long-suffering stomach with fish and chips as usual?'

'Oh, I got something good, for once,' Delia said, carelessly. 'What does my august cousin James have to say?'

'He wants us both to go down and stay a week or two with him. Spring in Cornwall – that would be very nice, don't you think, dear? What did you say you got for lunch?'

'It *would* be nice – spring in Cornwall!' Delia agreed, grimly. 'Doesn't that idiot *know* that I can't get off for a holiday just when I feel inclined, or does he think I'm the boss's little pet, kept for ornament only? I got rabbit en casserole – a new place.'

'Delia – that isn't a nice remark! "Boss's little pet," indeed! As if James doesn't *know*

33

perfectly well that your job is quite above board, but you ought to be pleased at his inviting you. After all, you might be able to take a week off your summer holidays, still leaving two for another visit later in the year! So you've found a decent lunch place at last! Where, may I ask?'

'It's called The Cellar,' Delia said, escaping from the room in search of a mythical handkerchief. 'Oh, lord, I hope Aunt Cora lets the subject drop,' she groaned to herself.

But Miss Grayson was on the scent. 'How did you find this Cellar place, dear?' she said, returning to the attack the minute Delia went back to the sitting-room.

Delia had to tell her, but made it sound so ordinary and everyday that Aunt Cora almost let the significance of it slip by her. But being Aunt Cora, she didn't quite.

'You know, Aunt Cora, I don't think I'd go to Cornwall this year, even if I could get time off from the office. I was uneasy on that last visit,' Delia said, slowly, after the subject of the lunch had been for the moment dropped.

Miss Grayson looked up shrewdly, but said nothing.

'It's not James, so much. He's a good old scout, but it struck me that Melita wasn't herself. Sort of strained, inclined to snap at us. Didn't you think so?'

'Oh, I don't know, dear. James is young, and men under the thirty mark are apt to be a bit intolerant. It's no fun being a doctor in a village miles from anywhere, and Melita isn't the wife to consent to be buried alive. Those are her own words, by the way. But, apart from that, they're happy enough together, and I think you'll find that if we accept their invitation, and go down there as if nothing had happened, it will blow over, whatever it is.'

'Then you *do* think there's something behind this invitation, Aunt Cora!'

'I never said I didn't,' Delia's aunt protested, mildly.

'It's a cover-up, isn't it? Getting us down there so that they don't actually come to blows? They sound as if they're on the verge of a break-up, to me!'

'No, Delia, I don't think it's as bad as that at all. I believe they're alone together too much and getting rather bored with themselves. A little company will do them good. I shall go, even if you can't get away, but before I go I'd like to see things a little more settled here.'

'What d'you mean, Aunt Cora?'

Miss Grayson looked straight at her niece. 'You know what I mean, my dear. I'd go away uncomfortable if I thought you were going to wear your heart on your sleeve, for that little minx of a Susaline to see and have

a good old game with. Won't you do something for me?'

'Well, that depends,' Delia said, slowly.
'When you put on that special winning air,
and look all wistful, it usually means you
want me to do something I wouldn't in the
ordinary way dream of doing. Let's hear
what it is first.'

Miss Grayson sighed, and turned her
attention to the eternal fair-isle knitting.
'Oh, well, I suppose it doesn't matter so
much. If you care to make a young fool of
yourself, why should I worry?'

'Stop that, Aunt Cora! You'll be saying
next that you're only an old woman whom
nobody cares about, and no one would
dream of acceding to a single wish of yours
and you're woefully misunderstood!'

Miss Grayson looked up with a guilty grin.
'All right, Delia. I'm an interfering old
busybody, but you're very dear to me. You
rank first, and James very definitely after!
You know that, don't you? And it grieves me
to see that you should be so fond of a man
who just regards you as a sister (a smack
below the belt, I know, but it was kinder to
do so than to let you dream improbable
things!), and the thing I wanted you to do
was to take up that young Paul Faversham.
Oh, only as a friend! Hold your horses,
young woman, while I explain! I'm not
asking for a hectic love affair – that would be

foolish. Besides, who knows if that's what the young man himself wants? After all, you deliberately make yourself look like a secretary all through, so you can't expect a young man to go into a flutter when you come in sight. Well, if you will hide your good points, it's no affair of mine. But he has shown signs of wanting friendship, and, if you were to reciprocate, you'd at least be able to hold your head up where that Susaline's concerned! It's undignified, to say the least, to let that little chit think you're after her man, or worse still, that she's been able to lift your man from you!'

There was a tiny silence, and Miss Grayson wondered for a miserable moment if she'd gone too far. She hoped she hadn't, but during the years that Delia had been in her care and guardianship she had often found that strong-arm methods were the best (and easiest) in the long run.

Delia broke the silence by a short, mirthless laugh. 'The things I take from you, Aunt Cora, lying down at that–! I must be a mutt! But you're a darling, and you take shameless advantage of that knowledge. All right, what d'you want me to do? Encourage the poor fellow by bringing him home to tea when Keith and Susaline are here next? Then tell him next morning I only did it to please my Aunt Cora!'

'Now you're being absurd. I merely mentioned it because while I'm in Cornwall no doubt Keith will want to bring Susaline home to tea again, and it occurred to me that if you were here alone you'd be rather miserable watching those two cooing at each other, but if you had a friend of your own here, well, it might not be so bad. Try it out, anyway. You may find his company rather pleasant. Paul Faversham was the one who took you to lunch, by the way, wasn't he?'

'How did you *know*, Aunt Cora! I didn't say so? And, anyway, he didn't *take* me to lunch – I paid for my own.'

'Um. The young man's got more sense than even I thought!'

'What do you mean?'

'Well, he must have been well aware you'd never have gone with him if he hadn't made it clear it wasn't an invitation. As to how I guessed it was Paul Faversham, the young man told me about his favourite restaurant, among other things, that day I was waiting for you at your office,' Aunt Cora said collectedly.

'Oh!' A little of the pleasure went out of the memory of that lunch, and Delia felt rather like a small child who has been nursing a tremendous secret, only to find that the adults knew of it all the time, and weren't a bit impressed.

When Aunt Cora went out to the kitchen

with the tea-things, Delia took the opportunity of a close scrutiny in the long mirror above the fireplace. A mirror was a thing to peer into, in order to see there wasn't a smut on your nose, or a hair out of place, before going into the boss's room. Delia rarely consulted one for any other reason, beyond a cursory powdering of the nose. Now the full force of Aunt Cora's argument struck her.

It was true. She looked like a secretary. An efficient secretary, smart as they went – with her neat tailored suit and expensively plain blouse. But where did it get you? It suddenly struck Delia Grayson with a good deal of force that beyond the dizzy heights of the commercial life, and the admiration of girl typists who had the ambitions of the very young, to step into your shoes one day, there was precious little in it.

'I'm twenty-six,' she murmured, in wonderment. 'Two years younger than Keith. Three years younger than Paul Faversham. Yet I look older – no, not older, but more mature, and yes, *wiser* – than either of them. I don't think I like that!'

She pushed her reddish-brown hair forward, but it merely looked untidy; with Aunt Cora's footsteps returning, Delia hurriedly resumed her chair, pulling her hair back with a guilty movement as she did so. It was no use. Better stick to the neat and efficient appearance she had always had. Evidently glamour wasn't in her line.

Half an hour later there was a peal at the bell. 'Are you expecting anyone, dear?' Miss Grayson asked, getting up to go. She liked to answer the bell herself, in case it was anyone after the rooms upstairs. Since the old professor and the school teacher had gone, they had been empty, and though Miss Grayson was not in actual need of the rent they brought, the loss of it made a difference.

Delia sat forward suddenly as she recognised Keith's voice. He seldom came in the middle of the week.

'Well, come in, Keith, and tell us all about it,' Miss Grayson was saying as she closed the front door behind him. 'You never used to apologise for dropping in whenever you wanted a chat!'

He didn't answer to that, and when he came in the room his eyes were raised immediately to Delia's. He looked tired, anxious, and all the idiotic happiness of the last time they saw him, when he brought Susaline to tea, had vanished. He was as he had always been before he met her, a young bank clerk, with no particular pleasures or joys, desperately bored with his job.

He slumped down into an armchair, and began right away. 'Remember I was going to chuck my job when I was here last? Well, I

40

meant it all right, though Susaline says I didn't. I meant to go to the manager next morning. But this new chap's such a fool. He doesn't catch on as to how things are outside his office door. He's absolutely overruled by the chief clerk. He just tells the manager what to do. Well, the next morning I noticed the chief clerk wasn't there. Odd, I thought, the chap's never late – don't tell me the impossible's happened! But no, he wasn't late. He was taken ill the night before, suddenly. And what happens? That fool of a new manager sends for me. He tells me, if you please, that I've been there next longest to the chief clerk, and I'd better hold his job down while he's away, and it's likely to be some time!'

'Oh, but that's marvellous, Keith, dear,' Miss Grayson said, flicking a glance in Delia's direction. 'I'm sure I wish that horrid chief clerk no harm, but in case he *weren't* able to return to his job, well, they might want you to step into his – well, into his space behind the counter, shall we say? You ought to be very pleased, my dear boy!'

'Well, I'm not!' Keith said, with a tone that was almost surly. 'It's the most confounded piece of bad luck. I cold hardly give my notice in after that, letting the chap down, and all that. Besides, it's more money, however temporary. But think I can get Susaline to see that? She's furious! Says it's messed

41

up the dancing and the plans we made, and everything!'

'Rather selfish, isn't it?' Delia said, unwisely.

Keith sprang immediately to Susaline's defence, and Aunt Cora shot at her niece a despairing glance.

'Not at all, Delia! After all, I did promise her I'd do it next morning, didn't I? But I was disappointed that she couldn't wait a bit before doing that!'

'Doing what, Keith?' Aunt Cora asked quietly.

'Well, we were supposed to be engaged. Now she says if I break my word once I'll do it again. Susaline's chucked me!'

CHAPTER 3

Life, that spring, took on a new meaning for Delia. It was a long time since Keith had been completely unattached, although it had been only recently that he had disclosed to Delia and Aunt Cora that he was serious about his new girl-friend and wished to bring her 'home' for their inspection. And now she had chucked him, and Keith was gloriously free again.

Freedom, for Keith Pemberley, meant so

many hours away from the bank, hours in which there was little or nothing to do. Since his parents died, and the house next door to the Graysons had been sold, and strangers come to live there, he had gone from bed-sitting-room to bed-sitting-room; sometimes in the country just outside the town, sometimes in the town itself, but always with the final dissatisfaction and removal. He had not settled down for years.

There was a time, when he was eighteen, and Delia a leggy sixteen, that he had found a cottage on the outskirts of Chiverstock, where a reasonably clean room and fair food had been offered him, but he had left that place because the landlady's daughter had made things difficult for him. She had evidently decided that she was going to marry one of her mother's lodgers, and tried to grab the first personable youth who appeared. That was when Miss Grayson knew that she would always have trouble with Delia over Keith, and started to pray fervently that the young man would reciprocate. At sixteen one might know to whom one is deeply attached, but the art of hiding one's feelings has not yet been achieved, or even thought of. Aunt Cora's alarmed look faded, as time when on, and things straightened out, but the fear lived on in her mind. With each new girl-friend Delia fumed and fretted, went moody or elated, as the young woman's success (or

Keith's waning interest) was more apparent, and only when the thing blew over did Aunt Cora breathe a sigh of relief and settle down to another brief spell of peace.

Keith was not flirtatious, but he had that appeal which caused every unattached young woman to be certain that here was a youth who needed petting and looking after and that she personally was the one to do it. It amazed him, the thought of the number of young women who were willing to be walked out in the evening along the tow-path or taken to the cinema on a Saturday, by him, and he never could understand how Keith Pemberley's alleged smart retorts to the current manager or the ever-present chief clerk could possibly interest these attractive young females. But Delia knew, and the wish to murder was often in her adolescent heart, and never got weeded out as she grew older.

Now Keith came back to her as he had always done. Not once a week, or twice, but every night, Saturdays and weekends, too. There were, in all, three blissful weeks of it, with the single exception that unlike those other affairs Keith didn't toss this one over-board and dance rare attendance on Delia herself, but kept the thought of Susaline so much to the fore that little by little even Delia realised that he was just spending all his spare time with her in order to tell her what he thought and felt about Susaline.

'Aunt Cora, when *are* you going to stay with James?' Delia asked, in exasperation, one Friday evening, as she prepared to look up trains and get her aunt packed and off. This was the third week-end that the impending visit had fizzled out, and it was getting to be rather in the nature of an anticlimax.

'I'm not,' Aunt Cora answered, composedly. 'I've made up my mind to write and tell him that I can't be spared just now, but that possibly I'll come down in the late summer.'

'Why?' Delia gasped.

'I want to stay and see what happens,' was the collected reply.

'See what happens? What on earth–' Delia began, but her aunt cut in briskly.

'My dear Delia, you've been in my care since you were quite a tiny tot, and I know just as much about you as your own mother could have done. In fact, I very much doubt if my dear sister-in-law would have bothered to read you as I do. Be that as it may, I have been painfully aware for years and years that you're quite inordinately in love with Keith Pemberley, and if something doesn't happen one way or the other *this* time he's free, I shall strangle the pair of you! For quite candidly I am getting too old to stand the stain.'

'Aunt Cora, how beastly of you,' Delia said, flushing. 'Even if you did see the way things were, you needn't have embarrassed me by mentioning the matter.'

'Nonsense, Delia! It's far and away the best thing to drag it out in the open, and get it off our chests. Besides, it's bad for you, at your age, to go on in this doormat fashion. Don't you feel, candidly, that you'd rather know one way or the other what it was going to be?'

Delia looked away. 'No,' she said, in a low voice. 'I'm content in a way to be there when he needs me. To be honest, it *is* getting a bit tedious this time having Susaline dished up for conversation at every turn. But some day – *some* day – he'll come to me, and want me only. I'm convinced of that. You can laugh if you like, Aunt Cora–'

'My dear,' the older woman said, earnestly, 'I'm *not* laughing, believe me! Smiling, perhaps, but sadly. You see, I've been through all this myself, and I had no one to help me! Oh, don't run away with the idea that I *wanted* anyone to help me – one doesn't, not at the time! But since then, all down the years, I've wondered if things might not have been very different if there'd been, shall we say, an old aunt or some such person to step back and take an unbiased view of both sides, and tell me. Because when you're one of the two (or three) parties concerned, you just can't see clearly!'

Delia was touched. 'No, I know that,' she agreed. 'But what happened, Aunt Cora? I never thought–'

'No,' the older woman said, briskly. 'I took good care that no one ever did. We all have our pride, you know! The case is very similar to yours in this respect, though. The young man and I grew up together.'

Delia was all attention. 'Yes?'

'I automatically decided I was going to marry him when I was old enough, but it didn't work out that way.'

'Was he in love with someone else, Aunt Cora?'

'No, not at first. The more important factor was that he didn't happen to be in love with me, either. Some Nosey Parker thought fit to acquaint him with how I felt, and I suppose that was my fault for wearing my heart on my sleeve. The young man was covered in embarrassment, and avoided me wherever possible. I took umbrage, and behaved in the most foolish manner possible – I decided to show him that that wasn't the case at all, and that he had been mis-informed, so to that end I flirted outrage-ously with anyone who happened along, became the talk of the town, and filled him (and others) with disgust. He found a nice, quiet girl and married her, and I was left to get over my idiocy and broken heart as best

I could. I never married anyone else, because to me no one else would do, and that also was foolish.'

'Was it?' Delia asked, sceptically.

'Yes,' Aunt Cora said, firmly. 'You see, my dear, it's this way. When a man and woman have grown up together, sometimes they do drift into marriage, but more often than not they don't. What usually happens is that whereas the woman decides automatically that the boy, now grown, is just naturally hers for life, the man has been so used to the girl's company that his reactions are merely brotherly. I don't say they never change: certain circumstances may bring about a complete change of feeling, and can but be tried. But I still maintain, on the whole it's best for the woman to clear off and meet someone else, someone quite fresh.'

'Why?' Delia persisted, mutinously.

'Because although she thinks she knows the man inside out, it is not as a future partner that she knows him, but *as* a brother. That's all the opportunity she's had for *getting* to know him, surely?'

Delia sat in silence, with very much the same scowl on her face as she had had as a child when she had wanted something badly, and fate had stepped in and prevented it. Aunt Cora smiled.

'Tell me I'm an interfering old woman, if you like! But I'm hoping that one day you'll profit by my words. Here, let me try this pullover up against you. It's my belief it never grows, no matter how much work I put into it.'

'Oh, damn the pullover! Sorry, Aunt Cora, but what did you mean about certain circumstances bringing about a complete change?'

Aunt Cora smiled, a little secret smile this time, as Delia obligingly rose to the bait.

'Well, that's what I was coming to, Delia, my dear! The surest way to manage our Keith is, unfortunately, a way in which you can be least likely relied on to carry off convincingly, and, of course, to bungle the job, and let the fellow see what you're up to, is, of course, worse than useless! You might just as well tell him your intentions in so many words!'

'That's an idea,' Delia said slowly.

'What is?' Aunt Cora's voice had a rare sharp quality in it, and was usually only evident when she was surprised – unpleasantly surprised.

'Well, why not go to Keith and tell him I love him?' Delia mused, seriously. 'Perhaps he's just never thought of it!'

Aunt Cora's incredulous expression became one of the purest, blankest astonishment. She clapped a hand to her forehead. 'On my soul, Delia, my girl, I wonder with all my heart how you scrape up sufficient intelligence to avoid getting kicked out of that highly efficient firm of yours, really I do! Of all the idiotic … the crassest pieces of lunacy … oh, my goodness, words fail me!'

'What's the matter?' Delia was genuine in her wonderment. 'I only said…'

'I know, I know. You're back in the era of fairy tales. The prince says, "I just never knew – if only you'd told me before, my princess," and drew her into his arms and they lived happily ever after. Really, Delia!'

Delia had the grace to blush. 'Well, Keith's different from other men. I thought…'

'You've been thinking on the wrong lines, my girl, for the past ten years!' Aunt Cora said, impatiently. 'Where you first went wrong was over Keith himself. I agree he *looks* different from other fellows – he always has! Haven't I found myself getting all sloppy and protective over him, in an aunt-like sort of way, of course – but in reality, Delia, he is *no* different. All men are alike in this respect – they don't like competition.'

'Competition?'

'Oh, my dear, don't keep repeating the last word of everything I say! You know as well as I do what competition is. If only you'd done what I started urging you to do, the day Susaline came to tea – cultivated that young Faversham! There's your answer, and your only answer.'

'Oh, how disgusting!' Delia got up to go to

her room.

'Well, before you throw the idea out of the window, just look at the possibilities,' her aunt invited.

Delia sat down again, with an outsize show of patience for the elderly and foolish. 'All right,' she agreed, wearily, 'let's.'

'You've made Keith feel that he's only got to come round here or telephone you, and you'll be ready to spend the entire evening listening to him on the subject of Susaline. Very well, the next time he phones you're oh, so sorry, Keith, but you're going out with a man you know. (Don't say whom, just say a man you know.)'

'And Keith sits down and cries his eyes out,' Delia said, sarcastically.

'No,' Aunt Cora, patiently explaining, and ignoring would be repartee, went on, 'but he does go away puzzled, hurt perhaps, because his ever-ready listener is not there on tap for him. He will probably loaf around during the evening, getting more worked up over the subject of how badly he's treated by women, and then it will occur to him to wonder who this other man is that you're out with. He might even call round here to see if it was just an excuse to avoid him (all men are egotists) or he may call to pump me for information. I shall, of course, not know a thing!'

'And he'll believe you!'

'Delia, if you're going to be obstructionist, I'm afraid I'm not willing to waste my time on you. This isn't for my pleasure, you know–'

'Oh! Oh, you old fraud, you know damned well you're thoroughly enjoying yourself!' Delia whooped joyously, getting hold of her aunt and pulling her out of the chair, to the detriment of the fair-isle knitting.

'Delia, be careful, do!'

'Can't be careful – I'm on the warpath which you so earnestly desire me to tread. Come on, you've been so decent, I'll take back all my spiteful little cracks, and try and do what you want. But where, in the name of wonder, do I begin?'

Aunt Delia looked incredulously at her niece. 'Do I even have to tell you that?' she asked, pityingly.

'Yes,' Delia grinned. 'You see, Auntie dear, what has escaped you is the fact that Paul Faversham, also, merely seems to want me for a willing and intelligent listener. He doesn't tell me about any Susaline. What he tells me all about is his own brand of "love" – his ambitions for the stage. He talks for hours; in fact, he sees me almost every day at lunch, and never once attempts to pay for mine. My fault, I expect, since I made it clear that first time ... nevertheless, he just never suggests that I ever see him other than at lunch-time. See?'

Aunt Cora bit her lip in chagrin, as she watched her niece swing out of the room to answer the front door. That would, of course, be Keith, come to take her walking through the quiet lamplit streets of the town, for another session of Susaline.

'Oh, well,' Aunt Cora thought as she watched them go out through the front gate, 'I'll just have to bide my time and see how she goes on. Funny about young Faversham, though. I could have sworn that day I was at the office…' She let her thoughts play around the subject of her niece for some time, and at last made up her mind where the trouble lay.

Delia looked tired when she came in at 10 o'clock. She flung off her plain felt hat and ran a hand over her forehead.

'Well, my dear, how did it go this evening?'

'Oh, it was hellish!' Delia burst out savagely. 'I'm sorry, Aunt Cora, I don't know what made me snap at you like that. But it's so odd. I haven't minded so much before, listening to his mushy talk about that nasty little blonde, but tonight he got to referring to her as an innocent babe, and told me all about her life in a smoky manufacturing town, with cruel stepfather flung in, and d'you know, my only reaction was to feel violently sick. I wanted to slap him. Keith, mind you! Fancy me feeling like that about Keith!'

She slumped into an armchair. 'Be a darling, and make me a hot drink, will you? I want something, and I don't know what!'

'You need a straight gin,' Aunt Cora said, surprisingly. 'I know the feeling, my girl – I told you I've been through it all before.'

The two women finally compromised with hot milk and biscuits, and sat talking until very late.

'Oh, it'll have to stop, of course,' Delia said. 'It's too dashed silly for words. There was I walking along with the most handsome fellow in town, with everyone looking envious – envious, I ask you!' She studied her sensible shoes, and the skirt of her rough spring tweed costume. 'I bet I looked a pretty good frump, beside Keith, too. He's so dapper, damn him!'

'That's better!' her aunt approved. 'That's more the spirit. *Now* I can get to work!'

'Oh, not Paul Faversham again – really, Aunt Cora, that's a mouldy idea. I'm tired of it.'

'No, not necessarily Paul Faversham,' Aunt Cora said, slowly. 'For the moment, my girl, I want to just make an alteration in your appearance.'

'All right, do as you like,' Delia said, tiredly.

'Would you say I was smart, or a frump?' her aunt thrust at her.

'Good heavens, no! You're too smart,

really, for your – well, I mean–' Delia floundered, reddening.

'Too smart for my age you were going to say! Well, well, perhaps I am. I may be allowed a little pleasure in my maiden existence, I believe. But that's by the way. What I wanted to know was whether you approved of the stuff my dressmaker turned out. For tomorrow morning, my girl, you're going to pay her a visit – with me.'

'Oh, no, I can't – I promised–'

'You didn't promise Keith tomorrow!' Her aunt sounded genuinely shocked.

'Well, I did before I got so fed-up with his line of talk,' Delia confessed.

'Well, that's one promise you're going to break, my girl. For first of all, we're going to the bank, and you're going to draw out some of that money you've been putting by for so long, for – well, shall we say, a rainy day?'

'No. We'll put it bluntly. For when I got married,' Delia said, with a trace of bitterness.

'Well, since we're calling a spade a spade,' Aunt Cora approved, 'we'll also go to the hairdresser's and do something about that hair style; we'll get you some shoes that belong to this year and not a decade ago, and we'll find a hat that will catch the masculine eye!'

'Steady on, Aunt Cora – I'm well known

in this town!'

'So much the better, and while we're about it, we'll get you some smart office clothes. My dear Delia, stop protesting – you don't have to go back to a past age in order to appear an efficient secretary!'

Delia let out a long breath. 'All right. Spend my money and have a good time, I don't care. In passing, which lingerie shop are you going to drag me in by the nose, to see transparent pieces of foolery?'

'I'm not,' Aunt Cora said, calmly, and with the pleased smile of a cat that has just finished off the cream. 'I'm going to take you by the nose to your room, to a certain chest which you keep locked, and dig out all those dreams of underwear you've been embroidering since heaven knows when for your trousseau! Don't burst a blood-vessel, Delia – you said we were putting it bluntly! Well, this is the blunt truth, my girl. Only in those particular pieces of underwear will you feel young and beautiful and important enough to have a man chasing you, for a change!'

CHAPTER 4

'I have to confess it,' Aunt Cora sighed bliss-
fully, during the following week, 'but I
haven't enjoyed myself so much for years.'

'I know,' Delia said, grimly. 'Just because
you had this idea, my boss has to do the
unexpected thing, and land me with a day
off, on Monday of all slack days! I just don't
have any luck at all!'

'Nonsense,' her aunt said, briskly. 'Monday was by far the best day to start in on my
campaign. Never did I think there was so
much scope in such apparently unpromising
material!'

'Thanks!' was Delia's dry rejoinder.

'Well, you must admit, my dear, not only I
was flabbergasted at the result of a day's
sitting in the beauty salon, but the beauty
wallahs themselves were purring with joy at
the transformation. Now, just take a look at
yourself again, just to keep your spirits up –
I never saw such a girl for neglecting the
uses of a good cheval mirror!'

'She always *was* modest, this aunt of
mine,' Delia grinned, allowing herself to be
planted in front of the glass and obligingly
looking. 'You're not pleased with me as a

57

person, but merely as a result of your own skill and persuasion!'

'Well, why not?' Miss Grayson looked with affection at the girl, and tried hard to make up her mind whether there was beauty there, or merely well-groomed fascination. She wanted to purr, too, in company with the folk at the beauty salon, her favourite dressmakers, the hat-shop and the shoe shop. All had expressed the greatest interest, which had become more marked as they realised what material they had to go on.

Delia wasn't one to stint money when she had to spend. She believed in buying good things. Now that she had caught something of her aunt's fever in what promised to be something of an adventure, she entered into the spirit of the thing as far as her purse was concerned, if not so far as enthusiasm could be measured, but Miss Grayson suspected that the girl was determined to give away nothing of the excitement that must be beneath the surface.

Delia, before the transformation, could only have been described by the kindest of people as short, dark, neatly dressed, and ordinary. It was, Miss Grayson decided, with the greatest of satisfaction, this quality of ordinariness that had helped the transformers so much. If her niece had had a prominent feature or anything at all unusual about her, it would have ruined their chances of doing anything for her. As it was, they all just happily went to work.

They discovered she had possibilities in colouring, too. The reddish-brown hair came up coppery and bright with one of their special rinses and the new hair style! Delia turned her nose up and moved away from the glass. Whether she didn't feel it was the thing for Sir Timothy's secretary to wear a curled-under fringe, and masses of high-piled curls at the back, or whether she was merely pretending, Miss Grayson couldn't tell. But she shrewdly suspected that her niece had come in for a good deal of attention and surmising at her firm during the days that had followed that highly interesting Monday off.

'Madame's eyes are a most helpful shade of dark brown,' gloated the facial expert. 'Pansy brown, and so helpful for matching the colour charts. A little mascara on the lashes…'

'No!' Delia had protested.

'Don't be a chump!' Miss Grayson, sitting near and watchful, had advised her niece. 'They're quite long really, but being light they don't show. Oh, don't worry, no one will think the worse of you for a bit of colour here and there.'

'How right Madame is!' the girl had purred, busily painting, rubbing, smoothing, pummelling, and creaming the protesting Delia, until even the critical Miss Grayson had to sit back admiring.

'The brows, too. Madame has quite nice brows when the straggling hairs are tidied up. And, of course, a little touch of colour on the brush...'

'Look here, how long's it going to take me to get all this muck put on every morning?' Delia had demanded.

'If Madame will allow me I will just run through a quick morning and night routine with her. It is *so* simple, and just a matter of getting used to it. Every scrap must come off at night before sleep, and nourishing cream patted in ... so...'

'I knew it!' Delia muttered. 'I was far better off as I was, just taking my hair down and brushing it, and having a good soap and water wash!'

The girl removed Delia's towels and pads, and delicately shuddered. 'Soap and water...!' It was heresy.

Miss Grayson grinned with pleasure at the thought. At the dress shop they discovered that Delia in her new guise could wear anything but mauve, and she didn't like that, anyway. Clear greens, clear blues, even a misty pink, all brought cries of ecstasy from the assistants.

'Is it a trousseau?' they wanted to know.

'Possibly, who knows?' Miss Grayson said quickly, with a suspicion of a wink, before

Delia could blunder in and spoil their enthusiasm. It was the same in the shoe shop, where Delia would have protested against high heels.

'Oh, don't be a ninny!' Miss Grayson warned her, in an undertone. 'I wear them – yes, at my age! – so why shouldn't you get used to them? You need them, anyway, to give you height!' And the vision of her nicely shaped foot in lizard-skin had won Delia over.

What Miss Grayson didn't know was how Paul Faversham took it all. He would have passed Delia by in the shadowed corridor outside Sir Timothy's room, if she hadn't wished him a prim good-morning.

He looked and came back, then jumped as if he had been stung. 'Good lord, whatever – what in the–?' then reddened painfully as he realised what he was saying. He stood there awkwardly; then, because she was waiting so obviously for his comments, he said, 'You look stunning, of course!' and made a hurried escape. He wasn't in The Cellar that day, but the three spinsters, after the first startled glance, all made some excuse to come to the table, one after the other, and speak to her, and their bright, curious glances had a lot of admiration and a flattering amount of surprise in them.

Delia thought, irritably, 'I suppose they think this is to catch Paul, and they're wondering why the deuce he isn't here today!' and her lunch was spoilt.

Sir Timothy's reaction was even more surprising than these, and the bright, inquisitive glances and whispered speculations of the typists in the pool and the male clerks in the counting-house. Sir Timothy was surprised, but frankly pleased.

'Bai Jove, Miss Grayson, it's good of you, I must say!' he said, with more enthusiasm in his voice than she had ever heard before. He was a big, florid man, with an eye for a pretty girl, as such; cosmetics, theatrical and otherwise, were his life's work, and all his staff (with the exception of Delia) had been chosen primarily for their decorative value, in the nature of advertisement. To have him prowling all round her now, taking in every point of her as if she were a stud specimen, or a wax model in a dress house, was so unusual that it almost unnerved her.

'Eh?' was all she could gasp.

He came round to the front and looked her full in the face. 'Really good of you! I've been delighted with your work, but it never occurred to me ... I wouldn't have dreamed of suggesting ... now really, you must have lunch with me! Speak to me on Friday about an increase; this is wonderful! I must work on this idea. I think you must attend the Association's dinner with me! Wonderful advertisement. No one else thought of it.

Bai Jove!'

He went and sat down at his desk, fiddling with a pencil, working rapidly on ideas. 'Yes, rather. And I think you must try out that new line we're putting on – by the way, you are using our stuff, aren't you?'

Delia flushed. 'Sir Timothy, I, that is, the beauty parlour–' she floundered, meaning to tell him the truth about her aunt taking her along, and feeling when it came to the point that it would sound so silly and undignified.

'Yes, yes, I know. Blighters never have anything in stock that you want. Where'd you go? Over the road? Bah, no good, no good at all. You must go to Maison Renée, use all our stuff. Look here, tell you what, though. Continue to go to your place, but take all the stuff you want out of stock. Get 'em in the habit of using ours. Then we'll nip in and get an order.'

It was useless to argue with him. He worked on his ideas all the morning, contacting various people, making appointments for them to come and see him, where he had been going to see them. 'We must let them have a good look at you. Bai Jove, what advertising!'

Later, he said, 'Look here, Miss Grayson, I can't let you go to all this expense yourself. Cost a fortune. You must have an expense account, and see that you use it as well as you've done already. I'm pleased!'

'You're lunching with Mrs Tankerdale today, sir,' she reminded him collectedly, and was conscious of a tiny thrill of pleasure at the shade of annoyance that passed over his face.

'Bless my soul, so I am! Well, tomorrow, then,' he said, but a glance at his diary showed that he was booked up for the next fortnight. Delia expressed considerable relief.

As the days went on she got used to people who knew her passing her by, then coming back and expressing surprise. In a smallish town like Chiverstock most people in town knew each other, and she was well known also on account of being the secretary of someone important. Like Sir Timothy, they were inclined to think that it was an advertisement stunt, though most people attributed it to him and not to Delia and her aunt. Delia didn't know whether to be pleased at their missing the rather more personal point, or annoyed to think that she was considered in the nature of a guinea-pig.

One day she ran Paul to earth in a far corner of The Cellar, a place he had never sat in before. It was quite by accident that she discovered him, so hidden was the little alcove with its solitary table. She drifted over to it and sat down, waiting for him to lower his newspaper.

His nose was twitching a little as he put down the paper and looked over at her.

'What's the matter, Paul? Don't you like my perfume?' she laughed. 'Hope you don't mind my sitting here. Say so if you do!'

'Of course I don't,' he said without conviction.

'I thought you wanted to lunch with me, a week or two back,' she thrust at him, with her usual direct methods.

'I did,' he admitted, struggling with a desire to be truthful and a desire to preserve some sort of good manners.

'Well? Don't you like me now I've stopped being a frump?'

'My position isn't easy now,' he said, slowly. 'You're Sir Timothy's now. He won't appreciate your being seen at lunch with me now he's done all this...' He broke off in acute embarrassment.

Delia was angry. 'What *are* you talking about?'

'Well, everyone knows it's a new advertisement stunt,' he said, mildly. 'They know about your expense account, too. Of course, they know you personally too well to think...' And again he broke off.

'How dare you!' Delia fumed. 'Oh, how dare you!'

Paul looked blank, then he got angry. 'Well, if you will do these things, putting yourself in such a questionable position...' And this time his trailing off said very plainly that he didn't care one way or the other what she did, but for heaven's sake leave him alone.

She cooled down. 'Yes, I suppose it does look odd, but I just never thought! You see, it wasn't like that at all. Oh, damn, you never can do right in this life – everything gets misconstrued!'

He politely raised his brows.

'You don't believe me, Paul, do you, and I don't know why I should bother to tell you the truth of the matter, except that I trust you to do the right thing and discourage other people from thinking wrong things about me! You see, it was nothing to do with Sir Timothy!'

Paul said nothing, but there was a spark of interest in his eyes.

'Honestly, he came into his room on Tuesday morning, after my day off when I got all this done (yes, I got it done myself), and he stared, walked all round me, looked pleased, and promptly decided I'd spent a heck of a lot of money for the good of the firm! The conceit of the man is beyond anything! He said it was a whale of an advertisement, and decided I should go to lunch with him and dinner with the Association, and heaven knows what else, just to show off our cosmetics! And the worst of it is that everyone else seems to think it's just a stunt on the firm's part! Oh, it's infuriating! Why shouldn't they think I'd done it myself –

what's so difficult to believe in that?'

'Well,' he said, slowly, taking refuge in the business of extracting meat from the bone of his chop, and managing refectory peas on his fork, 'it's the last thing anyone would expect you to do – I mean, getting yourself up like this! Why, you don't look like you any more – if you see what I mean!'

'But *why* shouldn't I want to improve myself – others do it?'

'If you can call it improving,' he murmured.

'You don't like it, do you, Paul?'

'Oh, it's no business of mine,' he said, hastily. 'You do as you please.' Then, because that sounded blunt and unfriendly, and probably because he had a good deal of curiosity about the whole thing, he said: 'If it's true you did it without any prompting from Sir Timothy, what *made* you? I liked you as you were, Delia.'

She hardly noticed his use of her Christian name. Angrily she stabbed at baked potatoes, and said, 'To be honest, it was no wish of mine. I was quite happy as I was. I just did it to please my aunt. You've met my aunt, haven't you?'

He nodded. 'A sweet woman,' he said, and sounded puzzled.

'But very smart, Paul, and she feels, I suppose, that it isn't right to have a niece who's so careless of her dress and hair. Makes

Aunt Cora feel over-dressed, I suppose.' She had no intention of giving away the real reason.

'Did you tell Sir Timothy that?' Paul enquired.

'No. How *could* I? Besides, it's no business of his. It would have sounded rather silly, too, wouldn't it?'

'It would have been honest,' Paul said. 'It would have forestalled gossip, too.'

'Well, you'll tell everyone for me, won't you?' Delia pleaded, and didn't realise that something of her outward appearance had penetrated to her inner self, via the looking-glass, and taken away a lot of her old direct-ness, substituting in its place a curious, provocative winsomeness that made her request difficult to refuse.

Paul watched her, but knowing her as she had been, he felt she was acting. 'No,' he said, 'I can't do that. For one thing, Sir Timothy'll get to hear of it, and that won't be so good for you. For another, I think it'll look just as foolish, now, at this stage. Many people think you care what they say, too. If it's the truth you've told me, why should you worry what is thought? It's your subse-quent actions that'll count now, you know!'

That was as much as she got out of him. People stared at them as they went back through the square to the office. They made a handsome couple, Paul was so tall and good-looking beside the new Delia. The high heels did something to her walk and carriage, too, that she hardly seemed aware of it, but Paul noticed it. He decided it was for Pemberley, in the firm's bank. Clerks going back to the bank after lunch saw the pair, and told Keith of the new development.

'Here, Pemberley, have a look over the top – you'll just catch a glimpse of them!'

'I don't know what you're talking about,' Keith protested, obligingly leaving his desk in what was for the bank a surprisingly quiet moment.

'See 'em? That *is* your cousin Delia, isn't it?'

''Course it's Delia Grayson,' someone else said. 'Old Sir Timothy's got his heart's desire now – a smashing advertisement and a smashing secretary, all rolled into one!'

'Know what they're saying all over town?' grinned another.

'*What* are they saying?' Keith demanded, getting down and looking ugly. 'Listen, Jones, she's not my cousin exactly, but we were brought up together, and I know her. You can just take that back!'

'All right, Pemberley, keep your shirt on! If you feel like that about her, better get hitched up to her before…'

'Before *what*?'

'Well, she'll be around a bit now, you

know. All the fellows are after her already, they say. Can't blame 'em, you know! Boy, she's a smasher now – didn't think she had it in her!'

'She hasn't,' Keith said. 'She's just a nice girl, gone a bit silly over clothes and things. Comes of working in a greasepaint factory. And don't give *me* advice, Jones. Delia's a sister to me, that's all – but I'll not have her talked about by little whelps like you!'

Miss Grayson was rather on edge when Delia got home that evening.

'Well, Delia, my dear, don't you think, after all my trouble, that I deserve to hear the result of my handiwork? It's almost a week, you know!'

'You shall hear!' Delia said, grimly, and told her aunt of the popular belief that it was Sir Timothy's idea. Miss Grayson was furious.

'Well, of all the– He's a thief, stealing my thunder! I've a good mind to go and tell him so!'

'I shouldn't, if I were you. Paul said the gossip will die down, and, anyway, what's it matter? Sir Timothy isn't the type to do any-thing more than take me around and show me off, in the interests of his wretched firm.'

'Oh, so Paul thinks that, does he? What else does he think?' Miss Grayson asked, with new interest.

'He thinks I look a fright, and he feels I

70

belong to the firm now, and he hasn't any right to be seen around with me. Noble, don't you think, Auntie darling?'

'Oh! Really, Delia, I do feel that if you'd–'

'I don't care about Paul, Aunt Cora,' Delia broke in. 'But I would like to know what Keith will think when he sees me!'

'Oh, yes, that young man hasn't been around this week, since you put him off last Saturday, has he? By the way, did you see Susaline in town today?'

'Um.' Delia wasn't much interested. 'Coming out of the Blue Parrot, after lunch. Why?'

'Did she see you?'

'Of course. Looked a bit staggered, I thought,' Delia grinned, thoughtfully powdering her nose from the outsize flapjack she had taken from the lizard-skin handbag that matched her new shoes.

'I see,' Miss Grayson commented. 'I thought that had happened.'

'Why?' Delia asked, idly.

'Because the inevitable's happened, my dear!' her aunt told her. 'Keith will be coming to tea to-morrow–'

Delia swung round, her face lighting up.

'He telephoned? Oh, why didn't you say, you old fraud!'

'Let me finish, Delia. He'll be coming to tea – with Susaline. Oh, don't stand there staring so blankly, Delia, my girl. Can't you

71

see what's happened? She saw you, in all your new finery, and did a bit of quick thinking. The engagement's all on again, Delia!'

CHAPTER 5

Paul Faversham lived on the other side of Chiverstock, with his mother, his brother and his brother's wife and two children. The Favershams were quiet people. Ian and Stella sat in the two armchairs night by night, Ian reading, Stella stitching clothes for the children – Bridget, the two-year-old and Lalage of twelve months – and old Mrs Faversham sat on the settee, surrounded by the family mending and any knitting she might be doing for the babies.

That was the nightly picture. If it differed at all it was on Wednesday evening of each week, when Ian took his wife to the pictures. For this reason Paul arranged to be home with his mother that night, but his other evenings were free.

Sometimes he sat by his mother on the settee, and discussed films and plays with Ian, or books with Stella, who was a prolific reader. Ian and Stella often took it in turns to read aloud, which old Mrs Faversham enjoyed. They read aloud to the children, too, before the mites were put to bed. At least, they read aloud to Bridget, but it was a family joke that Lalage had the more intelligent look on her face during the reading, as though she understood what was going on just as well as – if not better than – her sister.

Into this peaceful setting, one Friday night, came the discordant shrill of the telephone bell. Ian said: 'Just as I was going to start on *Great Expectations*. Hope it's no one wanting to barge in and talk a lot of nonsense like last week!'

He got up to answer it, and Stella chuckled. 'Poor old Ian, he gets so wild if anyone interrupts his reading of Dickens. It never seems to matter with any other author – have you noticed that, Mother?'

'I've noticed that he gets upset when poor Mr Griggson comes in for advice about his garden!' Mrs Faversham remarked with asperity. 'I'm sure he's a very nice old gentleman, and, after all, if no one in his family is garden-minded, I don't blame him for finding someone else to talk to about it!'

'Except that we don't know much about gardening ourselves,' Stella gurgled.

'Oh, I don't know!' Mrs Faversham said, stoutly. 'You and Ian have made a very nice little show in our garden, if you ask me! Oh, here's Ian back – who was it, dear?'

Ian sank into his chair. 'It was for Paul – a *girl!*'

'No!' Stella leaned forward. 'Do we know her?'

'Yes, we do,' Ian said, with a frown. He worked in the solicitor's office where the senior partner had charge of Delia's firm's legal matters. 'It happens to be Sir Timothy's secretary.'

'Delia Grayson!' Stella looked startled. 'That's odd, isn't it, after what you said, Ian?'

'What did Ian say? Why aren't I told about these things, heh?' Mrs Faversham demanded.

'Well, it's an odd thing that's happened, but it's all over town. You see, she was such a nice girl, a bit plain and utilitarian, and devilish efficient, and she's suddenly gone all film-starrish,' Ian said slowly. 'It's thought that it's one of Sir Timothy's stunts, but that seems a bit far-fetched to me.'

'What do *you* think, Ian?' his wife asked.

'I think (it's only a guess, mind you), but I think she did it herself. She's been setting her cap at Pemberley, you know, old girl – that good-looking, fair chap in the bank – the one I told you had taken over the chief clerk's job. Some say she's related to him. I don't know about that, but she's been seen around with him lately. Lord knows what's happened to the little blonde he had, but she seems to have fizzled out.'

'What a town this is for knowing everyone else's business!' Stella exclaimed, with mock disgust.

'Well, I must say!' her mother-in-law protested. 'Can you tell me what else there would be to make life worth living if we didn't know everyone else's business? What I say is, live an upright life, and it doesn't matter who knows your business, but it's very entertaining watching your fellow-townsfolk making fools of themselves!'

The other two burst out laughing.

'Is she going to ring up later, Ian?'

'Yes. I suppose that means *you* want to take the call?' her husband grinned at her.

'Ssh! Here comes Paul!'

They heard the key go in the front door, and to Stella's disappointment, the telephone shrilled while he was taking off his hat, and he answered it himself. They heard him say:

'Why, Delia! Is anything wrong?' and they all raised their brows at the tone in his voice.

'Um-um!' Stella commented, looking very knowing.

Her husband said, 'Stop listening in, you're getting as bad as Mother!' and started reading aloud, to the annoyance of the two women.

Delia, on the other end of the line, said, 'Paul, forgive me for ringing up at your home, but I want to take you up on a promise you made me a week or two ago.'

'What was that?' he asked, guardedly.

'You remember – you promised to take me along one night to the Dramatic Society – don't say you've forgotten!'

'Did I do that?' He sounded alarmed.

'Oh, well, if you want to back out now–'

'It isn't that, Delia. It's just that – well, I think you'll find it rather dull there. Weren't you dining with Sir Timothy tonight?'

'No, you know I'm not,' Delia said, rather crossly. Then, recovering herself, she said, 'I'd *like* to come to the Dramatic Society with you ... I've wanted to go for a long time, as a matter of fact, but I didn't like to try crashing in on my own. It needs courage, you know, to go barging in on new things by yourself.'

'I didn't think you were by yourself much,' Paul said, slowly.

'What d'you mean?'

'Well, that chap Pemberley in the Bank ... the one promoted to chief clerk ... I've seen you about with him, haven't I?'

Delia laughed lightly. 'Oh, Keith! He's almost a brother – we were brought up together. You'll never believe it, but I've merely been acting as big sister and trying to heal a broken heart for him, while his girl gave him the air. I believe she's back again, though, so my usefulness is over. Such is the function of a devoted sister!'

'Oh. Well, that's rather different.' Paul thought quickly. He didn't know what Delia was up to, but she certainly would be a sensation to take to the Dramatic Society tonight. Interesting, too, to see just how much she wanted to join that bunch of rather serious people with their play-reading and discussion. 'All right, I'll take you tonight, Delia, on the understanding that you tell me frankly if you're bored, because, you know, we're all pretty keen, and go into the subject thoroughly.'

He looked into the sitting-room, and Ian stopped reading. Stella raised bright, inquisitive blue eyes, but he studiously avoided them, and went over and kissed his mother.

Mrs Faversham blinked behind her black-rimmed glasses. 'A telephone call for you, dear! Who was it? Someone we know?'

'Curiosity killed the cat!' Paul said lightly, with a glance at the other two.

'We have been warned!' Stella chanted, with delight, but Ian merely frowned.

'Well, *they* can't expect to know all your business, dear, but you'll tell your mother, won't you?' Mrs Faversham said, with a bright, winning smile up at him.

'I'll think it over,' he laughed, smoothing her face, and adding quickly: 'My dinner in the oven as usual? Good, I'll have it quickly in the kitchen and be getting along. The class starts a bit earlier this week.'

They watched him go out. 'My, he's being close about something,' Mrs Faversham mused. 'Now I wonder–'

'Mother's started!' Stella laughed, but Ian, with a complete lack of interest, resumed his reading aloud.

Delia was waiting at the bus-stop when Paul arrived in King's Square. It was a fine, dry night; almost dark, and sweet-smelling. Spring was well advanced, and the trees almost covered. The square, with its tall lamp standards and gay posters outside cinema and rep. theatre, a place of near gaiety. Young people walked slowly through, and stream-lined cars nosed their way round the central garden, with its single statue of a forgotten benefactor of the town.

Delia wore a soft suit of dark yellow, trimmed with narrow brown fur. Her hat was minute and provocative, and had a large flower at each side, composed of curled brown feathers. Paul looked at her admiringly but with misgivings.

They were such serious people in the Dramatic Society. It was, after all, merely one room in the town's evening institute, but the twenty-odd people who called themselves a society had fought hard for the permission to start the venture, and worked hard to keep it going. He wondered whether they would not think Delia a rather frivolous element to be introduced into their midst.

These feelings were heightened when he took her down Turnstile Lane to where the Institute, a large white modern and extremely ugly building, had been erected right across the end. Lights shone welcomingly from almost every window, and in the great plaster-decorated entrance hall was a notice-board indicating the various classes being held, and the times at which they started.

Delia sniffed delicately. 'Um, like school again, isn't it?' she laughed softly, but Paul frowned. He didn't like to think the one thing he was keen on provoked amusement.

Delia noticed his silence, and thought of what Aunt Cora had said, when she left the house.

'Don't tread on the young man's toes, Delia! An evening institute may provoke mirth in this house, but I doubt if it does in his home!'

They walked sedately up two flights of stairs, other students behind and before them. Startled glances, inquisitive ones, and frankly disapproving stares were directed at her, and when the Principal of the Institute passed them and stopped to speak to Paul about the play they were doing, his expression was only too painfully obvious.

'Hurrump! A new member, Faversham?'

'Well, not exactly, sir. A friend of mine. She isn't sure if she'll like it well enough to join definitely, so I'm taking her along tonight as a visitor.'

'I see.' It sounded as if he meant that he didn't expect to see Delia there again, and wasn't altogether sorry.

'What's the matter with me?' she whispered, as they went on again.

'I think,' Paul said slowly, 'you'd have been very welcome if you'd looked – well, as you did a fortnight ago.'

'Oh!' Delia faced the rest of the evening with decided misgivings as to what sort of people would be there in that room at the end of the corridor, where already a small knot of people had gathered to chat before going in. She wondered, too, why she had suddenly decided to come.

'Panic, of course,' she told herself savagely. 'Just because Aunt Cora took me by surprise, about Keith and Susaline. Why didn't I think of that possibility? Of course that little wretch would try getting him back again, just to see how much hold she's got over him. But it won't last – she'll fall out with him again. And perhaps…'

With the exception of three very young men, earnest, bespectacled, and pimply, and a girl in her late twenties who looked already a candidate for spinsterhood, the Dramatic Society was elderly. Delia felt dashed.

The effect of their entrance was ludicrous. The faces of the women lit up on seeing Paul, and fell with startling suddenness when they saw Delia. Introductions were frosty as far as they were concerned, and timid and embarrassed as far as the men were concerned. They looked steadfastly at Paul all the time he was speaking, as if they were afraid of what would happen if they let their glances wander to Delia.

They were engaged on reading a play, which they hoped to produce towards the end of the term. They read it gently, Paul explained quietly to Delia, then left their seats to take separate parts out front (still reading), and when it was decided who was suitable for which part, and they all got the 'feel' of the piece, they took parts home to learn by heart, and began rehearsing.

Delia found towards the end of the evening that though Paul probably knew a great deal more about stagecraft (by inclination and private reading) he deferred comically to the fussy little man who took the class, and who deferred constantly to the elderly ladies with dramatic aspirations. It was, on the whole, a dull evening, apart from the fact that they discovered with reluctance that Delia had a good reading voice, and would make an excellent (and though unspoken, no doubt meant) a colourful heroine. She had youth and confidence to offer them, too, and Paul proposed that she be accepted as a member of the class.

'I don't think they like the idea at all, Paul,' she murmured, as they left the Institute, and stopped at a milk bar for ham sandwiches and hot coffee. 'I wish you hadn't suggested it. After all, you all know each other and have worked together since the beginning of the term. You can't expect them to like a newcomer gate-crashing.'

'You mean, you're sorry you're committed to come again!' he accused. 'Isn't that it, Delia?'

'No,' she said, slowly and without offence. 'As a matter of fact, I was rather keen on that play-reading. I found it interesting. Whether I shall be able to act is another matter, but seeing the others aren't much good at even the reading, well…! Yes, I think I'll come again, and damn the lot of 'em.'

She let him talk of plays and acting until he realised how he had been monopolising the conversation, and to make up he asked, contritely, 'Look, what are you doing to-morrow night? Let's go and see a film, by way of relaxation.'

'All right, I'll meet you at the King's.'

'Will you have tea with me, first, Delia? The Cellar is open until late on Saturday, you know.'

A sigh of relief escaped her. She had been quickly planning to leave Aunt Cora's after lunch, to avoid Keith and Susaline, and take a lonely tea in town, probably at the milk bar. 'I'd love to,' she said, sincerely, and didn't realise how much warmth she had infused in her voice.

Chiverstock stretched out in all directions, from its central square, into quiet roads which left the shops behind and gathered style and dignity the nearer they got to the outskirts. Aunt Cora's road lay on the outskirts of the park.

'It's a lovely night for walking, Delia, if your heels aren't too high,' Paul said.

'You're an awfully thoughtful person,' Delia mused, after telling him a mile wouldn't hurt – a statement which she regretted when they'd gone hardly halfway. 'Most fellows never think of things like that.'

'I've a sensible background,' he grinned, and told her something of his mother, his brother and wife, and the two small girls. 'In that atmosphere one learns how to be down-to-earth. Besides, before Ian married he and I used to take it in turns with the housework and cooking when my mother had a bout of bad health.'

'Um, so you're domesticated, too!'

'How quick you are to laugh at me!' he protested, flushing. 'Isn't Pemberley domesticated?'

'Why do you always bring Keith into the conversation?' Delia demanded, with irritation. 'Let me put him in clear perspective for you, once and for all, or else I'll never remember play parts for arguing with you over that poor lad. He's been part of my life since we were five – are you surprised that I've been about with him a lot, and possibly talk a lot about him? He even calls Aunt Cora "aunt," and I think she regards him as just as much of a nephew as I am her niece.'

'She's explaining him away too hard,' Paul thought, but said no more. Delia was limping by the time they reached her road, and he felt a pang of disappointment. Obviously she wasn't the sort of girl who'd walk for the fun of it, especially now she was all dolled up like this.

He said they would have to take a bus next time. Delia was furious. She hadn't taken into account that her new shoes wouldn't stand up to walking without punishing her. It seemed unjust to her, an inveterate walker, to be classed as a dressed-up doll who had to be considered, petted and taken on buses because her feet had to be remembered; and this was conflicting because not long ago she had found herself liking this new protective feeling on the part of her escort.

'I'm used to walking,' she said, sharply; 'I just forgot my shoes were new and needed breaking in. I'll come out in flat ones next time.'

'They won't go with the rest of the outfit, will they?' he asked, drily. 'Then: 'Oh, Delia, whatever made you start mucking yourself about like this?' There was real regret in his tone.

'I told you – it was to please Aunt Cora!'

'No, I don't believe it. No woman makes herself a fright to please another. I wouldn't mind betting Pemberley told you how much different you'd look! Or has that little blonde piece of his been giving you rotten advice?'

'Really, Paul, you haven't any right–! Besides, I thought you liked my new appearance,' she couldn't resist adding.

'I liked you best as you were,' he said, in a low voice. 'You were clean, wholesome, plain, and good – the sort of girl one could take home to meet one's mother.'

She gasped, but before she could think of anything to say he had rushed in with an apology.

'It was unpardonable of me, Delia! Please forgive me. Don't let it make any difference to tomorrow, will you?'

'He's jealous – jealous of Keith!' Delia thought, in wonderment, as she let herself in, and went straight into the sitting-room, where Aunt Cora was waiting with cups laid out and the cosy on the coffee-pot. 'What a funny thing to have happen to me – I wonder if Keith will get jealous of Paul?'

'Ah, Delia, I hope you liked your evening class!' Miss Grayson murmured, with a sly grin.

'Don't be catty, Aunt Cora! I like it! I'm joining it, in fact – they discovered I could read well, and I'm going to be an amateur actress.'

'Pah! Fiddlesticks! You couldn't act to save your life – if you could my headaches would all fade away!'

'*Now* what are you getting at?' Delia cried in exasperation.

'Keith's been on the phone again. There you go – getting all excited and worked up! It's nothing to be pleased about, miss, I assure you! He wants to know if his Susaline creature can bring along a man! Yes, you may well stare – I could slap that smug little face of hers. It seems she has a distant cousin come down from the north to work, and she's teamed up with him over this dancing tomfoolery in Keith's place. Ostensibly she wants to bring him to show off their new dance routine, but it's my belief it's nothing but an insulting way of offering you a partner to keep you off the grass where Keith is concerned. Well, what have you to say about it, Delia?'

'Don't get so worked up, Auntie, darling,' Delia purred as she flung off her new hat and poured herself some coffee. 'You'll just have to take the young man off Susaline's hands yourself tomorrow. You see, I'm going out after lunch, for the rest of the day. I'm dated up myself!'

CHAPTER 6

Aunt Cora's cooking was delicate, and, like her cooking, her methods were dainty. She used the latest gadgets, was surrounded by fresh-looking green and yellow striped kitchenware, and cutlery with handles to match. And, as Delia always said with comic dismay, Aunt Cora always looked presentable, no matter whether she was 'knocking up' a supper-time snack or had been caught mid-way through the preparations for a heavy dinner.

That Saturday she was not as methodical as usual, and, to her annoyance, burnt one of the items. 'Oh, I could fume!' she muttered to herself, going to the telephone for the fifth time, and answering yet another youthful male voice. 'Why did I encourage Delia to turn herself into a copper bombshell? – *that's* what's ruining my Saturday cooking!'

A warm spring breeze fluttered the dainty muslin curtains at the open window. The world outside looked a nice place, and it seemed a pity that Delia should have to be tied to the office until 1.30 just because she was Sir Timothy's secretary; the girls in the typists' pool had every other Saturday off, the pool carrying on with a skeleton staff.

Delia herself had never minded very much, except that it had been a nuisance where afternoon guests were concerned, for it seemed a strain to entertain after rushing about all the morning. This morning, however, was different. Sir Timothy dictated one letter only, then flung down his paper-knife and faced her. 'Delia Grayson,' he exploded, 'you're upsetting my life!'

'Really, Sir Timothy!' she had gasped, after a second's silence. 'What *do* you mean?'

He grinned a little. 'A bit extravagant for me, what? But damme, girl, look at yourself! Have you looked at yourself in the glass lately?'

'Three times this morning already, sir,' she told him, demurely. Already she was beginning to enjoy the sensation she was making in the firm.

'The counting-house is all upset, and the cashier tells me he can't get any sense out of the men. The typists are copying your hair-style, and getting dyed copper-gold, or whatever shade they can manage to get near that. Everything's upset, and I – Bai Jove, I'm worse off than anyone – I get ribbed on the telephone all day long by my fellow-manufacturers and others I have to be in business with, just because you've turned out to be a – a–'

'An ugly duckling?' Delia prompted mischievously. 'I thought you were pleased with my new appearance, sir.'

'So I was! Why, damme, the advertisement value was unthinkable – incalculable! Tremendous! But that's not it! And what's more, young woman, you know it!'

'Then what is it, Sir Timothy?'

'You! You yourself! You've changed. You used to be a nice, quiet, restful person who sat and effaced herself while I thought out what I wanted to dictate. Now–' He floundered, waving a hand irresolutely, as if by that hand he would express what his tongue couldn't find words for.

'And now?'

'Oh, damme, young woman, don't keep repeating my words for me! Find some more – tell me what it is I want to say, for I'm blest if I can think any more. It's like – Great Scott, it's like having a keg of gunpowder on the other side of me desk – here I am, nervously waiting for it to go off, and don't know when it's going to happen. I don't like it! D'ye hear!'

'Shall I go back to being a frump again, Sir Timothy?'

'No!' he shouted. 'No! Certainly not! You know I don't want that. But couldn't yer –

oh, damme, I don't know how I can put it into words. Look here, take dinner with me tonight, will you? Not doing anything, are you?'

How like him, Delia reflected, to ask her out first, then wonder afterwards if she had had any previous plans. He was annoyed, of course, when she told him she had a date, and commanded her to break it.

'I can hardly do that, sir, much as I'd like the evening with you. I don't believe in breaking one date for another – it isn't fair or honest.'

'Quite right! Quite right!' he approved. Then, with a sharp look at her, 'Who is the fellow, heh? Do I know him?'

'I don't suppose so,' she said, with a smile, thinking it hardly likely that Sir Timothy would know by sight a counting-house clerk, and feeling it hardly wise that she should name her evening's escort, that being the case.

'Huh! Not a regular, heh?'

'No, Sir Timothy, I'm not engaged or any-thing.'

That seemed to satisfy him, at least for the moment, and he let her go, but she was a little disconcerted when the florist's boy brought in a small cellulose box containing two gardenias and Sir Timothy's card. 'For a pleasant date, though I'm not permitted to be the lucky fellow!'

Delia panicked. 'Oh, lord, all I hoped was to smarten up Keith's ideas, and all I've done is to get a clerk jealous and the boss making a damned nuisance of himself. Why does it have to happen to me?'

Miss Grayson was fuming, too, when Delia got home. 'The telephone's been going for you all the morning!' she said, a trifle sharply, and a smell of burnt cake from the direction of the kitchen made Delia wary of her answer.

'All for me?' It was unnecessary. Aunt Cora had written their names down on the message pad.

'Yes,' she said, tartly. 'You seem to pick your escorts on the same principle as the milkman picks his horses. Three outsiders and a couple of also-rans.'

'Well, you've no call to be rude,' Delia said, reading quickly through the names. Aunt Delia, of course, knew them by sight, through business in the town. Impossible to live and work in Chiverstock without being known, unless you were a stranger, and then the chances were that you'd be even better known than the inhabitants, because strangers were rare enough to be of high interest to everyone. Mullins, the chemist; Richenbor's little boy, Peter; and young Kirby! Oh, and a couple of clerks from the bank. Well, if I must have admirers, what's wrong with that little bunch, as make-weight? The

91

favourites are your precious Paul Faversham and Sir Timothy!'

'What?' Aunt Cora looked alarmed, and paused for a minute, wooden spoon poised in mid-air.

'Aunt Cora, never have I seen you look such a sight over the kitchen stove before. I think I'll take myself out of your outraged sight as soon as lunch is over, and leave you in peace to your guests! By the way, think the new misty pink is all right for the cinema, with an intimate tea preceding it? Or shall we effect something more conservative?'

Miss Grayson walked back to the kitchen without a word, and Delia, chuckling, went into her room.

But Miss Grayson wasn't so angry; she was afraid. This, she recalled, had been the way she had acted herself, with the exception that she had not been transformed overnight into the most fascinating specimen in town by way of the local beauty parlour.

'Why did I do it?' she muttered, sorrowfully, to herself. 'What made me interfere?' But she knew the answer to that too well. It was heartbreaking to watch Delia heading for that familiar position, the unloved woman getting more hurt as each day went by.

Delia wore Sir Timothy's gardenias that afternoon. Paul spotted them immediately and flushed. 'You won't need this, then,' he said, and trust a small triangular package at her, which turned out to be a single, perfect, pale pink rose with a twist of silver paper round its stem.

Delia took it and held it to her nose. She was touched. It was easy for Sir Timothy to go to an expensive shop and splash money around, but this day was going to cost Paul something. Through the veneer of gaiety and thoughtlessness she was fast acquiring, her old kindness peeped through.

'Oh, Paul, how nice of you! Here, look,' and she unpinned the gardenias and stowed them into the vase on the tiny table between them. 'No one'll notice them, between the daffs and ferns,' and she pinned the rose in their place.

'Miss Lou'll spot them,' Paul said, gloomily.

'Then we'll say some other customer must have put them there,' she said, firmly. 'I like roses best, anyway.'

He did so much to make the day go well. He disclosed to her that she was the first girl-friend he had taken out. 'I've always worked too hard to be bothered with girls,' he said, with a touch of shyness.

'But your brother's married, and he must have found time—' she began.

'Ian married his typist. He couldn't get on without her,' Paul grinned. 'I spent most of my spare time in the public library, and with my scout troop. I like the open air.'

'You are a curious mixture. Now how do Boy Scouts fit in with the stage?'

'Easier than life in a greasepaint factory does,' he told her quietly.

She let him walk her home again after the cinema. Valiantly she kept up with him, in slightly easier shoes, and going at a slower pace. It was not that she particularly wanted the agony of walking in new shoes, but that a bus-ride would have got them home before the company went. She could hardly tell Paul that, so she did the next best thing.

'Let's walk through the posts and take the road above the park; it's such a lovely night, and I'd like to go over my lines for next week with you, Paul,' she said.

Since he had first taken her to lunch weeks ago, and had started telling her his ambitions, he had dreamed of her saying some such thing to him; dreamed of her wanting to be with him that extra amount of time, and dreamed of her being sufficiently interested in his passion for plays and the stage to want to linger, rather than escape from him. It meant that much to him that he missed the relief on her face as she let him pilot her to a roadside seat, where they went over the lines which he carried about with him, in the light of a nearby lamp. It was quite late when Delia decided to make a move.

'I didn't think you'd get so absorbed in it, Delia.' He sounded absurdly, pathetically grateful.

'I warn you, it's the play only that's absorbing me – not the rest of that bright gang in your Dramatic Society!' she laughed, lightly.

'Oh, I know, they are pretty dull, but good sorts, really, and terribly keen,' he defended them.

Abstractedly she said good-night to him, and let him make another date for early the following week. Now she was all feverish to get in and find out what happened during Keith's visit, and to collect Aunt Cora's impressions. But that lady was in no mood to talk very much.

'What's the matter, Aunt Cora? You look vexed!'

'I am vexed, Delia! I don't like that Susaline. I don't like her second or third cousin, or whatever he is – a Dago type, and slimy as they come! I don't like to see Keith looking all soppy over her, any more than I care about you looking all soppy over him! What's more, I don't like the way the whole thing's going, at all! I wish I'd gone to Cornwall, to stay with James, and washed my hands of the whole affair, indeed I do!'

'Here, let me get out of these glad-rags and into an overall and I'll help you clear away! Phew, what a mess! When did they go?'

'They've been gone twenty minutes, Delia, during which time I took a well-earned rest. I've only just started clearing away. I'm tired of hearing about dance-turns, dance-routines, the life of the dancing partner, and dance numbers. In fact, I'm very tired of Susaline.'

Delia came back from the bedroom. 'I heard all that – it's not like you to raise your voice! You must be put out!'

'Well, at least you look more your old self in that faded overall, with your hair all rumpled,' her aunt observed with some satisfaction. 'Here, you be getting the washing-up under way while I run the electric cleaner over this carpet. Sweet papers, cigarette ash, and *nut-shells!* Disgusting! I'm not going to have those people to tea in my flat any more, and if Keith asks me, I shall tell him so, and also tell him why! I think he's behaving like a great fool, and I never suspected he'd turn out like that!'

'I had a nice time,' Delia put in, mildly, hoping to take her aunt's mind off her anger for a minute, then steer her back to the subject when she was in a calmer frame of mind.

'Really! And which one out of the bunch I spoke to, may I ask, did you finish up with, Delia?'

'Don't be tiresome, darling; you know I went out with your precious Paul!'

Miss Grayson paused to pick up some of the larger pieces that the cleaner wouldn't take, and thanked her stars she had chosen a quiet machine when she had bought it. She was a good and considerate neighbour, and didn't like noises at any time of the day, least of all at night. Neither, however, did she like going to bed and leaving her sitting-room in a mess like this.

'Delia, what's Paul Faversham like? Really, I mean? He seemed a nice enough young man to me, but, of course, I only saw and spoke to him for a few minutes.'

Delia dragged her mind from Keith and Susaline, and the unknown cousin, to consider, and to be fair. 'He's kind,' she said, unwillingly. 'Considerate. And dull. At least, I suppose he's dull to me because, well, you know–'

'Yes, I *do* know!' her aunt agreed, grimly.

'But to a girl who was keen on him I think he'd be pretty wonderful! He's got old-fashioned manners, and you can see he respects women. You must admit that's as rare as the dodo these days! And, I suppose, if she were keen enough on him, a girl could forgive him being so taken up with the stage and play-reading, and all that. A man's got to have some sort of hobby, I suppose.'

Miss Grayson's face saddened. Delia had evidently struggled to be truthful, fair, but her struggle had answered her aunt's unspoken question. It was no use. The girl was so inevitably wrapped up in Keith Pemberley that she'd never have any use for any other man.

'What's Susaline's cousin like?' Delia asked, skilfully dragging her aunt back to the all-absorbing topic.

'Well, he *can* dance, I'll allow him that. But I just didn't like him. Susaline proposes to go in for dancing seriously with him, and being quite open about it before she fixes up with Keith. I think he's in need of his brains being examined, not to see what's coming. The idiot!'

'Fixes up with Keith?' Delia was puzzled.

Miss Grayson put the cleaner away, and took off her apron. There was an exasperated frown on her face, and her voice was more tart than Delia could remember its ever having been before.

'Look, Delia, we're talking about Keith and Susaline, remember? They're engaged again – I told you that yesterday, didn't I?'

'Yes, but they keep blowing hot and cold,' Delia murmured, putting away the last pile of plates and sitting down on the arm of a chair to regard her aunt with concentration.

'They don't *keep* doing anything of the sort,' Miss Grayson told her niece. 'They've done it once, through no wish of Keith's. Now Susaline has lost the urge to do it again, so it's very unlikely that they'll start throwing rings back at each other any more.'

She stared hard at Delia, but Delia only looked as if she was hearing an awful lot of nonsense that she couldn't find it possible to take in.

'Look, my dear,' her aunt said, more kindly. 'This is a small town. A town that isn't over-run with newcomers, or with new works or new houses or new anything. We're all in on ourselves. When a newcomer does turn up, like this cousin, he has only to say in a loud voice, "I'm new around here, who's going to put me wise?" and there are no end of people only too willing to make him *au fait*. That's what's happened with Susaline's cousin. While they were putting him *au fait* they told him about one Delia Grayson, who has left the chrysalis stage successfully behind, and is now what is termed as "a honey." Yes, my dear, that's how the young men are talking about you already! Oh, I know it's my fault, but I'm just trying to make you see–'

'It's all right,' Delia said. 'You don't have to apologise. A girl doesn't get swamped with dates, pleasant and otherwise, without catching on that she's changed a bit.'

'Well, dear, now work out the rest for yourself, if you can!'

'I can't. I'm tired, and it'd be easier if you told me,' Delia protested, lighting a cigarette and flopping back in the armchair to listen.

Miss Grayson sighed. 'I didn't want to have to tell you this in so many words, but come to think of it, I suppose it's kindest in the long run. What I'm trying to point out to you is, Susaline's heard her cousin talking, and she's seen you herself. She's reckoned up pretty quickly. She knows her power of attraction over Keith, but she's astute enough to know that you and I are the women in his life, so far as the background is concerned. He has no mother, no sisters. Only you and I. So she's wise enough to use her powers of fascination over him while she's sure of him. Well, Delia, don't sit there looking so dumb!'

'All right, then. They're still engaged. I don't see why you should be so angry about that!'

'They're not going to stay engaged long, my girl. Susaline's seeing to that. They've already set longing eyes on the furniture and carpets in the Arcade, and, what's more, they've fixed with the Registry to be married in three weeks' time!'

CHAPTER 7

'I didn't want it to be a shock to you, Delia!' Miss Grayson had said, as Delia sat slightly forward in the chair, a dazed look in her eyes, the colour slowly ebbing from her face beneath its skilful veneer of make-up. 'I wouldn't have done that for anything!'

And she had meant it. But even she hadn't quite realised what the news would mean to the girl. It is doubtful if Delia herself realised at the time. There was something so horribly final about settling on the date of a marriage and going so far as to fix it up with the Registry.

It was some days later before Delia could bring herself to speak of the matter. Then, and then only, did she demand more details. Up till then she had gone about in a sort of dream, a stunned silence. Twice she had seen Keith about town, though he had not seen her, and she had been grateful. But his air of gaiety, an expression of joy deep in his eyes, was enough. This was indeed final.

Final. The word drummed itself through her brain. Useless to tell herself that there was many a slip... People with that look on their faces were no good for anyone else if something happened to drive that look away. Yet the thought persisted: Keith is in love with Susaline, but one day he'll need me. He'll need me, and I'll be waiting for him.

She didn't say this to Aunt Cora. She didn't have to. Aunt Cora read her mind with ease and with sorrow. There was nothing she could do to help Delia, beyond carrying on as if there was nothing whatever wrong, and blandly accepting Delia's attitude as if it were the most natural and the most useful that any girl could offer, when an old friend or distant relation was getting married.

'What made them in such a hurry to decide that evening on the wedding and everything?' Delia asked first of all. It was nearly a week since she had first heard about it.

Aunt Cora felt a little easier. Now the girl could bring herself to talk about it, talk the subject out of her system, it might ease things all round, particularly for Delia herself.

'It was Keith's idea. He didn't want to wait,' she said.

'But,' protested Delia, puzzled, 'he surely isn't going to take Susaline to live with him in his bachelor room?'

'Oh, no,' Miss Grayson continued, casually. 'He asked if the rooms upstairs were still to let, and I had to admit they were. The idea seems to be that they take them as they are. If think it would be better if we turned it into a complete flat, and charged them accordingly.'

She watched Delia closely. Delia gripped the arms of her chair and closed her eyes. 'I don't think I could bear it,' she said, in a muffled voice, 'if they were to live in the same house with us.'

'They may not,' Miss Grayson said. 'I mean, they may live here, but it's doubtful if you will. I imagine you'll soon be married off to someone yourself and gone away.'

The idea, tossed so casually and yet so expertly, took root. Not perhaps in the way Miss Grayson expected, but it took root nevertheless.

'Yes,' Delia said. 'It's an idea. Not to marry – I think I'd loathe marriage with any of the men I know – but it's an idea to go and live somewhere else. I might take one of those maisonettes in that new block just out of town. You wouldn't mind my leaving you, would you, Aunt Cora?'

'Not at all,' said Miss Grayson briskly, but with a catch in her throat. She had had Delia with her so long that she would miss her badly now. 'In fact, I might give up this flat myself – let it off – and go and live in Cornwall with James and Melita. Well, that's an idea, anyway, though I daresay any place would be as interesting. I'm a little tired of this old house.'

They discussed the arrangements for altering the floor upstairs, in a desultory way at first; then, as Delia got used to talking about such a possibility, with more enthusiasm. It merely meant making over the two small rooms into bathroom and kitchen respectively, leaving the two large rooms for bedroom and sitting-room.

'And very nice, too, for a young couple starting out in married life!' Miss Grayson approved. 'A lick of paint here and there – the walls were papered not too far back – and I think it will be quite a nice bright little place.'

'We'll have to keep access to the attics ourselves,' Delia reminded her.

'Yes, well, we can keep the attic stairs door locked while our junk's up there, and make arrangements with Keith to go up and get anything we want. I don't think he'll mind.'

'What did Susaline think about living in this house?' was Delia's next question.

'Oddly enough, she jumped at the idea,' Miss Grayson mused.

'She would!' was Delia's only comment, but to herself she admitted that Susaline wanted that particular flat for the sheer pleasure of flinging her marriage, day after day, into Delia's face. Undoubtedly Susaline realised what it would be like, with the man you were in love with, living just above you in married state with a woman you heartily detested.

Keith was particularly obtuse over the whole business. He insisted on coming in two or three times a week to talk over furniture bargains, or ask Miss Grayson's advice about kitchen equipment, and sometimes Susaline came with him. It was always to ask for advice, but turned into an evening session of discussing their future life together, and the clothes Susaline would wear for the wedding. It always came back to that.

'You'll come to the wedding, of course, Delia?' she said.

Delia, about to refuse, was caught on the wrong foot by Keith. 'What a daft question, darling. Of *course* Delia will come – and Aunt Cora! It wouldn't be a wedding without they were there!'

There was no way out of it. Susaline added a poisonous touch by including in the invitation Delia's boy-friend ('that good-looker Faversham') as she called him. It seemed that everyone in town was interested in Delia's movements, and were betting heavily on Paul Faversham against Sir Timothy. Delia reddened angrily.

'I wish people would mind their own beastly business,' she burst out furiously.

'Of course,' Susaline went on, sweetly, 'Sir Timothy's likely to finish up with Mrs Tankerdale – she's so poised and soignée, don't you think? And, anyway, no one knew what she looked like before the beauty parlour got at her, and that *is* an asset, of course!'

'Little tease!' Keith said, fondly, pulling the lobe of Susaline's ear. Miss Grayson reflected that she, too, would have liked to pull that ear, and not so gently as Keith was performing the action.

'I thought we were discussing your wedding, Susaline,' she said, mildly. 'Somehow we seem to have got on to the subject of the next Lady Nodeleigh, and I'm sure that can't be of much interest to any of us here.'

'Except that I'd rather have Sir Timothy at my wedding than a clerk from a greasepaint factory!'

That stirred even Keith. 'Oh, come now, Susaline, that's not nice, darling! I like Faversham, personally. He often comes into the bank, and a nicer chap never breathed. We can't help the jobs we have to take, you know, and for all you know, you scamp, the greasepaint factory may pay him better money than the bank'll ever pay me!'

Susaline pouted, then turned on her amazingly beautiful smile, which melted Keith immediately. 'Oh!' she said, prettily. 'I didn't know the handsome Faversham was a friend of yours, too, darling – then, of course, we must have him to the wedding! That's settled!'

The subject of the reception was an irritating one. Susaline wanted a big one, at a hired hall in town. She wanted the publicity, in view of her future dancing career. She wanted the local newspapers, and the ones from the nearby cities. Small-town publicity on its own was of little use to Susaline. Keith, however, was all for a quiet wedding breakfast, which Miss Grayson had half suggested might take place in her sitting-room.

'But how can we pack seventy people in this little box – I mean, in this rather small room?' Susaline cried.

'Seventy people!' A concerted gasp from Keith and the two women. 'What in the world–'

'Well, I've a lot of relations, and they'll all be coming down from up north, you know. Then there's your friends – we counted ten, didn't we? And my new friends, the ones I've made at the Starlight Hall and other places here, that's another ten. Well, roughly seventy, anyway.'

'Darling, I'll be broke before you've done with me!'

'Well, if you can't afford the reception, I'll ask my stepfather to lend me the money for it,' Susaline snapped. 'But I'm going to have it. It's only right. After all, I'm not having a sumptuous white wedding in a church – I've given up that idea to save you the cost of morning suits for you and your friends. I think you might let me have something in return!'

The number for the reception was finally whittled down to fifty, and the big room upstairs in the Falcon Hotel was engaged. It was black-beamed and furnished in Tudor style. Many of the things were genuinely old, and the place was a favourite for large dinners and receptions. It wasn't cheap. Delia discovered that Miss Grayson had provided the hire of it, and the cost of the reception, as her wedding gift to Keith.

'Well, he has no parents of his own, and I've been as good as an aunt to him!' she said, defensively, to Delia, when her niece taxed her with it.

'Well, it's a terribly nice gesture on your part, Aunt Cora, considering—'

'Considering how I loathe that little blonde madam?' Miss Grayson said, grimly. 'I never gave her a thought – it was for Keith that I did it!'

Many surprising things happened in those three weeks. Paul meekly accepted the invitation to the wedding, and admitted to have been in the same form as Keith, at High School.

'I didn't know you knew Keith that well!' Delia said.

Paul shrugged. 'Oh, well, as well as any chap knows a form-mate, I suppose.'

'But you always referred to him as "the fair chap in the bank," as if he was a stranger you knew only by sight.'

'Why not? I hate his guts because you're so wrapped up with him!' Paul said, quietly.

Delia gave it up. Men were so funny. It didn't matter one way or the other to her that Paul was dying of jealousy or quite unmoved by other men friends she had; he was a very incidental part of her life, and his thoughts and moods affected her little. He was just tiresome at times.

Sir Timothy became more attentive, and actually cancelled a luncheon date with Mrs Tankerdale to take Delia to his club. The local paper printed a photo of them eating grapefruit, and Paul said it was in very bad taste, and didn't see Delia for two days.

A rival firm of cosmetics offered Delia what she considered was a crazily extravagant sum of money to use her picture on their hoarding advertisements, because of her superb colouring. Sir Timothy looked as if he were going to have a fit when she showed him the letter; she watched the purple veins in his forehead with interest.

'You know, Aunt Cora, he's rather good-looking – for an elderly man!' Delia said, that evening.

'Elderly? Oh, how old is he?'

'Oh, he must be a bit older than you, darling,' Delia said, carelessly.

'Thanks,' her aunt said, dryly. 'I happen to be forty-five. Could the decrepit Sir Timothy have touched fifty, do you suppose?'

Delia looked startled. 'Oh, sorry, darling, that was tactless of me. I never thought–'

'Because my hair is pure white doesn't mean I have one foot in the grave,' Miss Grayson said, severely. 'As a matter of fact, my life's secret is that it's bleached. I prefer a blueish tinge of white at the hands of my hairdresser than the streaky grey that would otherwise be my lot!'

'Oh!' Delia was, for a moment, speechless.

'Sir Timothy wouldn't have disclosed to you what his age really is, I suppose?' Miss Grayson probed.

'Well, I could find it, in one of the reference books, I suppose. But I took it for granted – I mean, with his silver-grey hair, and...'

'Yes, I know what he looks like. I've seen him,' her aunt said dryly. 'I myself should have described him as a tall, soldierly figure of a man, just under fifty, with a pinkish complexion, silvery hair, good teeth, healthy blue eyes, and a hale way of speaking and walking that many of the younger folk would do well to emulate. That, however, is probably merely my biased impression.'

'Well!' Delia gasped, with a smile. 'Did you get this – er – impression, the day you came to the office ostensibly to see me? The day you gave poor old Paul the once over? I must say you didn't waste much time!'

Delia, in self-defence, roped in Paul to tea

on the three Saturdays between then and the wedding. Surprisingly, he came. He spent a lot of time looking curiously at Delia, at her aunt, at her background, at the way she looked at Keith and Susaline, and he also did a fair amount of talking, to which Keith paid a nice lot of attention. On the whole, the two men were quite friendly, and to Delia's surprise Miss Grayson commented when the guests had gone, 'I never thought those two fellows could harbour such dislike for each other!'

'Oh, I don't think so, Aunt Cora. It was just that Susaline was so violently against spending their honeymoon in Cornwall. What made you suggest that they go to James and Melita?'

'Keith suggested it to me first,' Miss Grayson said. 'With a view to cheap lodgings primarily, I think, but also (to be fair) a wish to see James and Melita again. It's years since we all went together for that holiday, remember?'

Delia thought, with a stab at the heart, 'Do I remember! Aunt Cora can hurt as much as anyone else!' But in all justice to Aunt Cora, she thought almost immediately, it was, after all, better to look back on the past now without sentimentalising, because any promise which the past had held was now irrefutably wiped out by the finality of the present.

'So they decided, with Paul's help, on a smart hotel on the Broxmouth front; very wise, too. Plenty of dancing and tennis for Susaline, and nice stretches of open beach and country for Keith when he feels like going moody and getting away from it all,' Aunt Cora finished, briskly.

The day of the wedding was fine. That was, of course, inevitable for Susaline, Delia decided savagely, as she got into an (as yet) unworn outfit of sage green, trimmed with pale grey fur. It was almost Parisian in style, and gave her an almost exotic look. The hat was barbaric in style, and went up to a pointed shape which only the Delia of the beauty parlour could have worn. In fact, Miss Grayson decided, as her niece came slowly into the room pulling on new and expensive suede gloves, there was no one else that she knew who could have worn a hat like that – not even Susaline.

But Susaline could wear other things, and she did, with tremendous effect. It might be a Registry wedding, but Susaline wore white, and looked superb. A white outfit with elbow-length kid gloves, a white hat that was mostly tiny flowers and veiling, and managed to give a bridal effect without necessarily being a bridal outfit, and a dress that was tantalising in cut and cloth, and emphasised every curve of that lovely little figure. Susaline walked with a dancer's skill, and with her angelic smile turned on full blast she held the stage.

Someone had tipped off the Registrar that this wedding would have a fair amount of publicity, and luck was with Susaline in that a very wealthy wedding had taken place just before, and a magnificent array of flowers decorated the marriage room. The sun blazed through the bare windows; the Registrar told them severely that, although this was not a church, the wedding about to be performed would be just as holy and binding, and then Keith and Susaline were being made man and wife.

Delia looked on from her hard chair in the second row facing the long table at which the Registrar and his clerk sat. There was horror in her eyes, horror at the thing she was witnessing. Paul watched her and wondered. Keith couldn't be tying himself up for life with this girl, whose only passion was dancing, and whose smile – breath-catching and lovely as it was – could be turned on and off at will like a tap.

The Registrar ordered them to turn and face each other, and to produce the ring. Dozens of northern uncles, aunts, cousins, grandparents and other odd-looking people who had more or less obscure connections with Susaline's family, sighed ecstatically as they caught the first glimpse of the profiles of the bridal pair. This, they had told each other in loud braying voices, before silence had been ordered for the ceremony, was going to be a 'reet good do.'

They were all shown out afterwards into a large yard, where private and public photographers made good use of the trees in a neighbouring garden, as a background for the crowd and for the bridal pair. Then more press photographers (the small fellows, local evening and weekly) caught them once more as they left the front of the building, into the waiting cars, which would take them from this back street building, across the town to the Falcon Hotel, where again they would follow in the wake of an earlier reception, and get the full benefit of an outrolled red carpet and awning.

Delia went through a kind of horror-filled nightmare. Mechanically she lifted her glass and toasted when the others did; mechanically she smiled or clapped at the would-be wit of the northern cousins; mechanically she smiled and clapped when Keith said his graceful few words, because this didn't seem a real Keith or a real Delia; mechanically she made her good-bye, when it was time for them to go, in the car that had been prepared by boisterous relations, with a selection of old boots and 'just married' labels. Mechanically she threw confetti with the rest.

Then she and her aunt went back to the

quiet flat with Paul. There was peace here – peace to heal the mind, and if not to help disentangle the fury of riotous thoughts, at least to have the effect of pushing them down into temporary and rather restful oblivion.

Miss Grayson and Paul set out to be charming to each other, without very much effort. They liked each other. That was easy to see. Miss Grayson showed Paul the garden, and told him about the house in the old days, when she had occupied it all, and there had been other members of the family with them, when Delia was a little girl and Keith had been the boy next door.

Delia listened in a kind of wonder – wonder for her own calm and disinterested acceptance of the topic, and wonder at her aunt's wisdom in forcing it on her so soon after the wedding, so that she could, like a punch-drunk pugilist, make her comeback without losing her nerve. Paul helped. He seemed to understand, and his team-work with Miss Grayson was magnificent.

They inspected the flat upstairs. It was almost ready, and soon their furniture would arrive: one or two good pieces chosen by Keith, the rest of it obviously Susaline's choice – ornate modern chests, divans, cushioned furniture decorated by metal piping, everything that was vulgar and up-to-the-minute. Miss Grayson took a good deal of pleasure in describing it all in detail to

Paul, who wrinkled his nose in distaste.

It was, on the whole, a pleasant ending to an unpleasant day, and Delia felt, as she walked to the end of the street with Paul, before saying a calm, almost abstracted good-night to him, that this was just one of those curious before-dawn dreams, from which one wakes with an overwhelming sense of relief, because the dream wasn't so improbable after all.

She was hardly listening, therefore, when Paul dropped his little bombshell.

'I shan't be seeing you so much now, Delia.'

'Eh?' Her voice was blank, and she wondered for a minute whether she had missed a chunk – a relevant chunk – of the preceding conversation.

'It's just a month since – well, since we first saw the new Delia Grayson,' he said, smiling at her through the warm summer dusk.

'Yes, I know,' she said, rather impatiently. 'But what did you mean by–'

'I'm leaving the firm.'

'*What?*' It was incredible. He had been in Nodeleigh's since he had left High School. He was reckoned one of the candidates for the cashier's job when the old man retired in a year's time.

'Yes. And because I must have a job somewhere I've decided to have a shot at the rep.

company. I don't suppose I'm good enough, but the smallest part would be better than a clerk's job elsewhere.'

'Yes, but why did you leave if you haven't anything else to go to yet?' she asked, mystified.

'Because of one Delia Grayson,' he said, laughing shortly, 'my valuable services to Nodeleigh's are no longer required.'

CHAPTER 8

Delia went straight to bed when she got back home. It was perhaps, the first time she had not stopped up with Miss Grayson to have some sort of light supper, and a short chat, before both the women retired. Tonight, whatever had happened out there in the darkness, Miss Grayson ruminated, was a culminating point for her and her niece; she felt that things could never be the same again.

But then, in everyone's life, she reflected, there was a point, often approached quite quietly, unknowingly almost, and totally without drama, when things changed. Life had to be taken up again, and things would adjust themselves. But at the moment, she felt, as she answered Delia's too-brief good-night, and watched her niece go straight to her room, that she had not only lost a daughter, but a son, too. To her Keith and Delia had been just that: son and daughter. Better to her, in many ways, than some women's sons and daughters were. She had been prepared for Keith's departure. But Delia...

A short month ago they had been close friends, and life had gone smoothly for them, herself and Delia. Delia had her job, and her friendship with Keith. Miss Grayson had the confidence of both of them. They drifted in and out of the flat as if they enjoyed being there. Girl-friends came and went in Keith's life, but to the Grayson women he remained constant. Everything was so happy and so sure.

Now Keith had married the little chit of a dancer, and, although they would be living only one floor above her, Keith might well be millions of miles away, it would all be so different. While Delia, instead of being the girl with the safe job and the steady companion of Miss Grayson's middle years, was now a personality, by way of being a local beauty, courted by half the town, deep in an affair with either Paul Faversham and her employer or both, and already deciding that she should go away and live, because she couldn't bear to be in the same house with Keith and his new bride.

Miss Grayson sighed. It was her own fault

that the glamorising of Delia had been begun, but hardly her fault that it should gain such momentum. Like building a moderate sized snowball and watching it become a giant of its species, totally out of hand. How could she have altered Delia's going away? Only by refusing to let the floor upstairs to Keith and Susaline, and surely that wasn't reasonable? They both knew it was empty, but didn't she herself need the money? Not badly, it was true, but she had been telling herself only recently that that floor mustn't stay empty too long. Well, then! What was she moaning about?

She got up and mechanically tidied the sitting-room, and went to her own room. On the way she admitted to herself, with her usual honesty, that what was really troubling her was not the tide of the last four weeks, but merely the fact that for the first time in the girl's life Delia had not come to her voluntarily, and given her a confidence. Something had happened since she left the house with Paul; Miss Grayson would have dearly loved to know what it was that had occurred. Something had been said, or done, to make Delia look like that. But Miss Grayson knew that she couldn't force the girl's confidence, even if she had wanted to, and, heaven knew, Delia was no longer a girl: she was twenty-six.

Delia, lying flat on her back in her petticoat, with the eiderdown only half flung off the bed, also reflected that she was only four years off thirty, and wondered in a lethargic way whether those next four years would move as quickly as had the last four weeks.

She, too, remembered the old order of things, and for a fleeting moment something like nostalgia slid over her. It was a dullish sort of life, but secure. Now nothing was secure, and the worst of it was that everything that happened to or about her now needed something to be done about it. You could not just remain a looker-on; you had to adjust yourself to it, even do something about it. For everything that now happened was so relevant, so closely linked up with her personally.

Keith's broken engagement; his making it up again, and his sudden marriage. The improbable – he and Susaline taking the floor upstairs for a flat, necessitating her own moving out. The near future, without the comfortable presence of Aunt Cora. The odd sensation of being sought out by so many men, men that for the most part she didn't want, but whom she would undoubtedly cultivate, because there wouldn't be anything else left to do. Sir Timothy, and his rather tiresome (though at the same time flattering) attentions. And Paul...

It was so difficult to take in the stupendous fact that Paul had actually lost his job on account of herself. Paul went over the scene for her, in terse and clipped English, but she rebuilt it for herself from what she knew of the two men, and her version was probably nearer the mark.

Sir Timothy, Paul had told her, had sent for him and told him in rather brusque language that he was not going to tolerate clerks in his counting-house taking his secretary about.

'I never heard such unmitigated impudence, even though the chap *is* my boss!' Paul had said in a cold, angry voice that she had not heard before.

'And I suppose you were foolish enough to tell him so!' she had said, with amusement, not really believing at that point that he had been serious when he had said he no longer worked for Nodeleigh's.

'I reminded him that my women friends were my affair,' Paul said. Delia had a swift picture of the irascible Sir Timothy, his face reddening with quick anger, at being told something reasonable by a mere underling.

'And he didn't like it,' she hazarded.

'Oh, well, one thing led to another. He gave me to understand that he had prior claim, for some damn-fool reason, and I went a step too far and told him my intentions were honourable, and he didn't like that either. Finally, I suppose I did over-step the mark, and virtually he sacked me for being insolent!'

She was a little dazed. This was too much, coming on top of this tiresome and emotional day. She said nothing, and he shot her a quick glance.

'Delia, there's nothing in it, is there? What that damned fellow said? I mean, are you just fooling around with me while you're stringing along with him?'

How like Paul, so straight and honourable, so considerate at all times, and yet so tiresome at such a time as this – forcing a decision when she was least prepared to face up to it! She supposed that the best men were apt to do something like this just once in a while. She fought down a rising dislike for him, simply because she was tired and resentful of everyone. Like a weary child, she hated the universe and wanted bed. She wished she hadn't come out when he had suggested that it was a pity not to get a last breath of air, walking to the end of the road. All this fighting, she reflected, simply because I know I'm cornered and must make an answer now.

'I'm not stringing along with anyone, Paul,' she said slowly and with difficulty. 'I don't think it's in me. To be honest, life's suddenly become awfully difficult. Believe me, I'm not fooling around with you, Paul, but for the life of me I can't tell you just what I feel about you or Sir Timothy or anyone. I'm all

122

mixed up. I'm sorry you lost your job. I'm sorry Sir Timothy was so beastly; he shouldn't have been. I've given him no cause to act that way. But I can't say I shan't be seen about with him any more, if that's what you mean.'

She had tried to be honest, but it was an unsatisfactory speech. Paul, she could see, was far from satisfied. He looked angry and hurt, and she couldn't understand why he should.

'I see,' he said shortly. 'I used to think Pemberley was my most formidable rival, and that when he got married the way would be clear. Now I see I've got Sir Timothy to contend with, and he's got it all his own way, what with his money and his being with you all day long. I suppose if I eliminate him it'll be someone else. I wonder if the game's worth the candle, Delia?'

She said, 'I never asked you to...' but he cut her short.

'Don't take refuge in that old excuse,' and there was a rough edge to his voice. 'You rang me up and asked me to take you to the Dramatic Society, didn't you?'

'You started it, taking me to lunch that day!' she flashed back. Then the utter childishness of both of them was so apparent that the anger slid from their faces, and they stood regarding each other in the moonlight, like lost children.

'What will you do now, Paul, with no job?' she asked, in a small voice.

'The only thing that's left,' he said, and there was a dispirited note in his voice. 'A chap at the rep. said there's a small part going. I'll have a try for it. If I get in there will, at least, be a steady job. I might work up to bigger parts. Funny thing,' he said, with a short laugh. 'I've been mad to get on the rep. stage, and never dared throw up a safe job for it. Now I've got the chance – no job to speak of, and the need to get one fairly soon. But I'm not thrilled. Funny, isn't it?'

'Oh, Paul!' she said, because she couldn't think of anything else to say. The soft sweet smells of an early summer night were all around them. There was a seductive rustle in the leaves of trees that dotted these quiet out-of-town streets and one by one the lights of the little houses went out. It was getting late, yet neither was willing to terminate this uneasy meeting. To both it seemed vital that something definite should be come to, here and now; tonight. It was another of those tiresome milestones, milestones that gain such formidable distance overnight, if not surmounted at once.

He said, 'If I could only be sure...' and looked at her hungrily.

She forestalled him quickly. She didn't want to be pitch-forked into anything, not now; now, when she was so tired that, if pressed, she would agree to anything, just to be allowed to go home and rest. Bed, and the relinquishing of this tiresome façade of resistance, against odds that she couldn't see clearly.

'Paul, don't say anything, please! Just ... take that job at the rep. theatre, with all my good wishes, and see what comes of it. It's trite to say so, but it may be a blessing in disguise. It may be the chance that you would never have taken otherwise. Anyway, you weren't happy in the firm. And you can still see me each day at lunch if you want to.'

Anything, anything to take that look of aching misery from his face, that desperation from his voice.

'I hoped you would say that, Delia,' he said quietly, and his voice was warm and affectionate. 'I needed just that assurance, and you're the only one who can give it to me. I prayed you wouldn't withhold it.'

'Well, now you feel better about it, I think I'd better go home,' she began, with relief in her voice.

'I'll take you back to the gate.'

'No, no, that isn't necessary, Paul. It's so light, and it's just a step,' she said, quickly. She didn't think Aunt Cora would be looking out of the window, but you never knew. It might be accidental, but Delia felt suddenly reticent about all this. She found herself wanting to hide things from Aunt Cora, after this shattering day of guards down.

'Well, all right, then,' he said, reluctantly. 'Lunch every day together, then; that's a date?'

His tone was too urgent to refuse. She agreed it was a date, and although misgivings quickly crowded on her as to what would happen if she had to lunch with Sir Timothy at any time, she quickly thrust them to one side. Not, oh, not now, her tired brain cried.

He leaned forward suddenly and kissed her on the lips. It was a kiss of sweetness, gentle, beautifully done in its sincerity. There was nothing about it that she could possibly object to, and, before she could say a word, he said in a low voice, 'Good-night, Delia, my dear – and thank you.' Then he had turned and was swinging up the street.

Yet that kiss had done something to her. Something she hadn't been ready for. In her tired, almost overwrought state, she felt it was unfair, because Keith had never kissed her, and she had no comparison. What a kiss meant to a man like Paul also pressed down on her. Did he consider that she was almost engaged to him? What had he said to Sir Timothy? His intentions were honourable. How like Paul to use an old-fashioned expression like that, and yet she knew he would use it with terrific force, not in any way to arouse ridicule. Sir Timothy was probably writing her off even now as the sometime wife of one his ex-clerks. And that brought annoyance.

But with Monday and the start of a new week Delia saw that Sir Timothy was by no means changed in his manner with her. He said, casually, 'If Mrs Tankerdale comes through on the telephone, you talk to her. Tell her I'm out of Town.'

He did not interfere with her lunch plans, but as soon as she came back (after a wearisome hour with Paul, who had been frustrated in his attempts to see anyone so far at the rep.) Sir Timothy announced that he had booked a table at the club for dinner.

'Wear something special, Delia, because there's a fellow I specially want you to meet. On how you handle him depends our new factory at Clinkerton.'

Roughly once a week Sir Timothy managed to take her to dinner either at his club or at some big roadhouse or hotel, and showed her off to friends or business associates. He talked, meantime, of nothing more exciting than business, or current plays and books. Nothing personal, nothing she could object to, she thought bitterly, as she recalled that for this, for these quite neutral evenings, one man had thought fit to sack another.

'I should refuse to go out with him, refuse

to be nice to him, for Paul's sake, I suppose,' she told herself worriedly, yet that seemed stupid. It couldn't help Paul; it could only injure her own chances. Her salary had been raised three times. Everyone in the firm took it for granted that she was in some special way connected with Sir Timothy's private work, and treated her with a new respect. The old whispering over her appearance, the old bright looks of curiosity and speculation were gone. Life settled down at Nodeleigh's in a very pleasant fashion indeed.

No one mentioned Paul. Four weeks passed. He got his small part at the rep., lunched with Delia each day, told her about his new life in minute detail, and took her to the pictures every Saturday night. Delia got a maisonette, and with the added advantages of her new scale of pay furnished it quietly and tastefully and settled in. Every Wednesday, when Paul stayed home with his mother, Delia went home to see Aunt Cora. Usually Keith and Susaline were out that night. The end of summer approached, the little play was produced at the Dramatic Society, and Delia helped them out by staying faithfully in the cast, bad as it was, because Paul had had to leave when he joined the repertory company. With the end of term night school ended for them both.

And then, at the end of July, the even tenor of Delia's new life came to an abrupt halt. It happened on one of her Wednesday visits to Aunt Cora.

'Why, what's the matter, dear?' Delia asked, as she flung down her light top-coat, and dropped into the settee by the side of her aunt.

'I'm worried!' Miss Grayson exploded, and rumpled her usually immaculately set white hair. 'I've had a letter from James. Here, read it!'

She pushed a sheet of James's usual scrawl over to Delia, and sat drumming her fingers while the girl read.

'Oh!' Delia said, as she turned over and read the last few words, 'so the break's come at last. You'll go down there, of course?'

'Of course,' Miss Grayson agreed. 'But I must say I never thought Melita would leave him. I hope it's only temporary. I trust she'll come back soon. I don't like to see a happy marriage broken up.'

'Well, it's timely, this visit of yours to Cornwall; you need a holiday,' Delia said, briskly. 'What will you do? Close the flat up?'

'That's just it,' Miss Grayson said, looking distracted. 'I can't very well, as there isn't a separate front door for Keith's flat. And it would look so unfriendly to lock all my doors separately, especially as they go through the kitchen to the garden!'

'Well, good heavens, it won't hurt them to

use the side door to the garden for the short while you'll be away! Keith will understand.'

'That's just it, Delia. I'm not sure he will,' Miss Grayson answered. 'You know, I haven't said much about them on these weekly visits of yours. You seem to be settling down so nicely in your new life it seemed a shame to bring it all back again for you by dragging you back into this atmosphere. The fact is, Keith has changed a good deal since his marriage. Oh, I know it's only a few short weeks, but in married life a lot can happen in a shorter time than that.'

'What *has* happened?' Delia asked, in a strained voice.

'Well, he's got rather irritable, quick to suspect anything being said or suggested about Susaline, almost ready to pick a quarrel on her behalf. It seems it's all right if one lets Susaline go her own way and do as she pleases. That's all very fine, but she does take such liberties!'

'What sort of liberties?'

'Well, she'll come down while I'm out and borrow things. You know I don't mind lending if people ask me first, but I often find things are missing, and I know she's had them. She either doesn't return them, or can't because she's broken them. Even the best pieces. Look!'

Miss Grayson opened the cupboard door which contained the pale green china, now sadly depleted. Delia gasped.

'Well, you don't let her get away with that, do you?'

'How can I help it when she's so clever? She won't let me into her flat until it's when Keith is there, and he just shouts at the pair of us to shut up, because somehow Susaline turns the quietest question of mine into a quarrel. I can't think how she does it, but I'm getting so tired of it all. It's not only breakable things she takes, but towels and my linen, anything she fancies, and if I do manage to get anything back she practically throws it at me, and breaks into such a storm of weeping that Keith has to spend hours getting her calm again. You can imagine how a man likes that at night, after a day at the bank.'

'Well, the little–!' Delia exploded. 'Well, Aunt Cora, if that's the way things are, I don't see you need have any compunction in locking each of your doors when you go away.'

'What's the use? She gets in the windows – I've tried it. She's like a monkey for helping herself to things, and just as un-principled and difficult to argue with! I can't have the windows locked as well, the flat will be in a sad state by the time I get back!'

'What were you thinking of, then?' Delia asked quietly, knowing what her aunt was going to ask of her, and dreading it.

'I'd like you to close up your maisonette, Delia, and take the flat over. It'll only be for a week or two, I'm sure, but with someone here all the time, at least each night, and the weekends, it won't be quite so bad as leaving the flat completely unoccupied for a long period.'

Delia was silent. It was such a big thing to ask, and she knew that Miss Grayson knew that, and was needing her help so badly that she was still pressing the matter.

'It's something else, isn't it, Aunt Cora?'

Miss Grayson nodded. 'Yes, they're spoiling for a row, those two, on a big scale. Something's boiling up. It's to do with that cousin of Susaline's, and a dago friend of his, and, of course, all this dancing nonsense. Susaline's instituted rowdy parties in the flat. I have to call up sometimes in case bits of ceiling come down. And if I'm not here I'm afraid'

'You're afraid Susaline might take it into her head to use this flat for her parties, too,' Delia nodded. 'D'you really think Keith would allow her to do that?'

Miss Grayson tapped on the arm of the settee worriedly. 'Keith doesn't seem to have very much say in the matter,' she said, quietly.

CHAPTER 9

Miss Grayson left immediately for Cornwall. Delia closed her maisonette and took over the flat. It was nostalgia that first night back, sitting in the same sitting-room in the same armchair staring at Aunt Cora's fair-isle knitting she had forgotten to take with her and drinking tea from the familiar green china. It seemed as if Aunt Cora was only in the kitchen and would at any minute return and take up the conversation where she had left off.

But Aunt Cora was in Cornwall trying to straighten out the oddly balanced marriage of James and Melita and Delia was up here alone in a flat beneath the man she loved, who was at this minute quarrelling violently and, for him, with unexpected heat with his new wife.

Susaline had been unpleasant from the first.

'So you had to come back,' she sneered at Delia. 'You couldn't keep away.'

Delia tried to answer reasonably.

'Aunt Cora asked me to come.'

'Oh, so the old hag didn't trust me,' Susaline sneered.

Delia flicked a startled glance at Keith. Whether he hadn't heard or didn't want to hear she couldn't decide. Whichever the case he made no attempt to jump to Aunt Cora's defence, but stood looking out of the window with hunched shoulders and down-turned mouth and a new sour expression which Delia hadn't seen on his lean, sensitive face before and which she didn't like.

That expression 'old hag' when applied to Aunt Cora hurt unbelievably. It struck her that this was indeed a new Keith who could allow such things to be said and remain unmoved. As the scene progressed it got more unpleasant. Susaline wanted the flat downstairs to be used for a party and said so unblushingly. The flat was empty all day, she pointed out, even if Delia was going to be there at night. Why shouldn't she have the flat? Delia pointed out that they had a flat of their own upstairs. Susaline said it was too small. Delia told her that her suggestion was impudent and impossible. Susaline descended to insults, calling Delia the guardian of the fortress and wardress of the family cupboard. They kept on, Delia trying to be reasonable, Susaline frankly enjoying what was boiling up to be a quarrel until Keith could bear it no longer.

'For heaven's sake stop it, you two,' he snarled, and cast at Delia a look which might be interpreted as one of hatred. 'Why can't she borrow the flat while you are out? Think she'll spoil everything? You women make such a fuss. As for you, Sue, I've told you before that you'd do yourself more good if you didn't get so heated with people. Anyone would think we were having hordes of people coming instead of just a dozen.'

Delia said, 'Are you going to be there, Keith?'

'Naturally,' he said, coldly. 'The bank gives me a day off whenever I want it, and I always get one when my wife throws a party.'

'There's no need to be sarcastic,' Delia said. 'I asked because I thought if you were going to be there you'd see that it wasn't a rough party and you'd look after Aunt Cora's place for her. Now I'm not so sure. The answer is "No," Susaline.'

Delia prepared to walk out of the flat when Susaline darted in front of her.

'You're going to be awfully sorry,' she said with an ugly look. 'Sure you wouldn't like to alter your mind?'

'The answer's still "No,"' Delia said. And this time Susaline stepped aside and let her pass. But she was uneasy.

The party was for two days later. Before the day arrived Keith came down and saw her.

'Look here, Delia,' he began awkwardly, 'there's no sense in you two women quarrelling. Besides, experience has taught me that it's no good saying "no" to Susaline. What she's refused she takes – with a good deal more damage than if she'd been granted permission.'

There was a good deal of bitterness in his voice as he said it. Delia was profoundly sorry for him. Only she knew what it had cost him to say that.

'That may be, Keith,' she said. 'But you know as well as I do that Aunt Cora's put me in charge of this place and I can't in all honesty let Susaline overrun it with her friends just because she's holding out a threat. I'm warning you, Keith, and you don't know what it's costing me to do it. I shall take every precaution to keep Susaline out of this flat even if it means that I shall have to stay here myself and guard it.'

They faced each other angrily, mentally measuring up to each other. Two hostile forces, two people who knew how to keep their word, both being pushed in opposite directions by one person who had no conception of honesty and fair play.

'I'm so tired of women's quarrels,' Keith said. 'If only people would give in to Susaline life would be a good deal easier.'

'Probably,' Delia said, crisply. 'How nice for Susaline that would be. Aunt Cora's told me a little about it. You're only renting the upstairs flat, you know.'

Keith reddened angrily.

'And pretty steeply Aunt Cora's charging for it!' he snapped.

The interview was getting ugly. In the days to follow Delia found that every interview with Keith or Susaline got ugly. There was no common basis of discussion. The least thing that was said, however just it may be, they managed to turn into a quarrel and made her look in the wrong. They were both so skilful at it. That Susaline was quarrel-some Delia had suspected, but she was amazed at the alteration in Keith. He had been so easy-going, so pleasant to get on with. And now all that seemed to have gone. He was a different person – a person she didn't like very much. It saddened her, but for the moment there was the worrying question of the party to settle. She was so worried about it that she almost made up her mind to ask Sir Timothy for the day off, but as things turned out such a request would have been impossible. He had a meeting suddenly called, and that meant Delia must be there.

She saw Paul at lunch – a necessarily short lunch that day – and he asked her what was worrying her. Her drawn and whitened face shocked him. She half-played with the idea of telling him but decided against it. It would sound rather feeble. A feminine storm in a teacup and he couldn't do anything to help, anyway. He was working very hard, learning and rehearsing a fresh part each week, so she let the moment go and afterwards wished she hadn't.

'Delia, I'm all in,' Sir Timothy said at the end of the day. 'Get your hat on, girl, and we'll go out to a road-house for a quick dinner and a breath of fresh air. I brought the open tourer today.' He patted her shoulder approvingly. 'You're an amazing help to me. Know what my colleagues are saying? I've got the impossible – the perfect secretary with good looks.' He chuckled, pleased. 'Come on, Delia, hurry up.'

She turned agonised eyes on him.

'Oh, Sir Timothy, I'm so tired. I think I'd like to go home.' The thought of Susaline's party had nagged at her all day.

'Nonsense, m'dear!' he laughed. 'Get your things on and stop arguing. Best thing in the world for you.'

He looked at her sharply. 'Not otherwise engaged, of course.'

'Oh no,' she said, then wished she had thought quickly of another engagement. But it was too late now. Sir Timothy would take no further argument. She let him escort her to the car. Unprotesting, she went through the evening with him, but every minute was an agony, wondering, wondering–

She got no benefit from the carefully chosen meal or the choice wines, and the bathe in the road-house pool afterwards was

138

a matter of routine of which she remembered little. After a brisk rub down she collapsed rather than relaxed in one of the super-streamlined canvas chairs at the pool's edge, and merely waited, biding her time, until Sir Timothy should take her home.

But he was in no hurry. He was an excellent sportsman, particularly a swimmer, and stayed in long after Delia came out. He enjoyed the admiring glances which Delia so unconsciously collected from feminine as well as masculine eyes. She had a lovely body and looked well in the bright green swim suit, which was composed of abbreviated trunks and bra-top. Her feet had high, delicate arches, and he noticed with approval that she didn't varnish her toe-nails. They were pale pink and natural like little shells. And there was about her tonight a weariness which added to her already large stock of allure. Sir Timothy trod water and watched her and thought with satisfaction how well she would look in the gracious setting of his home. It was late when he returned her to Miss Grayson's flat. She bade him an abstracted good-night, and he was too mature and experienced to attempt to detain her at this stage.

He watched her go through the open gateway, foraging in her bag for a key, and could not know that she had already forgotten his existence. Her heart was beating a mad,

139

grateful tattoo because her aunt's flat was in darkness. The house was quiet, and the only light to be seen was in Keith's bedroom, where the shadow of Susaline brushing her hair played on the blind.

She let herself in and the relief, like a flood, which spread over her was overwhelming. She closed the door quietly behind her and stood leaning against it for a second, eyes shut, slightly dizzy. After a few moments she snapped on the light. The hall clock told her it was 11.30. All the doors were tightly closed as she had left them. She tried them one by one without quite knowing why and found them to be locked. What else should they be? But with Susaline you never knew what to expect.

She gratefully unlocked her bedroom and went in. The window was open a little at the top and the cool breeze blew the curtains slightly. She took a deep breath and prepared to fling off her clothes. She hated returning to stuffy, shut rooms. Then she stiffened and remembered. She hadn't left that window open. She looked round the room more closely. The usually immaculate dressing table had a liberal coating of face powder; her lipstick was opened; it had obviously been used; and cigarette ends with reddened tips were everywhere – on the dressing-table and stubbed out all over the floor. A close inspection of the bed revealed slight indents where clothes had been flung and people had sat on the edge. A cold fury shook her and fought with a slow puzzlement. She went out of the room and unlocked the other rooms one by one. All told the same story. The living-room was a heartbreaking mess; the kitchen a nightmare. There was broken china – not, thank heavens, the best – and someone had made inroads on the store-cupboard. Susaline had had her party after all.

Delia marched upstairs. Their bedroom light was out. She hammered on the door.

'Come downstairs, Keith, I want you,' she yelled.

After repeated knockings she got the door opened by Susaline – not Keith.

'I said I wanted Keith,' she said, 'not you!' And raising her voice above Susaline's ready vituperation she shouted, 'What's up, Keith? Haven't you the guts to come when I call you?'

He came then, sleepy-eyed and rather truculent.

'Well?' It was an uncompromising beginning.

She said: 'Come downstairs. I want to show you something.'

'Can't it wait till the morning, Delia?'

'No, it can't, Keith!'

Susaline butted in. 'I told you I was going to use the flat. Why all the fuss? Serves you

141

right for not letting me!'

'Are you coming down, Keith, or aren't you?'

He said, sullenly, 'I know what it looks like. I was there.'

Delia stared. 'So you were there. I suppose you picked the locks, and helped with the breakages!'

Susaline said, shrilly, 'We didn't pick any locks. We've got a key! If that mean ole cat hadn't stopped me borrowing things I wouldn't have borrowed her keys and got duplicates made! If you do anything nasty I shall tell everyone Miss Grayson left me the keys – I've got them and I can prove it!'

Delia ignored her. 'Keith, I give you fair warning. I'm going to seal up the flat, so that Aunt Cora can see what it looks like when she comes back. I can't take action – I don't own the flat! But, believe me, for this shabby trick I'll see you pay for it! If you can't keep this wife of yours from bothering Aunt Cora, who's been so good to you, I'll see you're made to suffer. I won't have her worried like it.'

Delia wasn't quite sure what she could do, but decided to speak to Paul about it next day. His brother, she knew, worked in a legal office, and might have some idea.

Paul was disgusted and rather prejudiced. 'What did you expect? I think, if I may say so, that your aunt was awfully foolish to have them in the place at all. She must have seen what that little blonde was going to be like.'

He promised to speak to his brother, but, as it happened, it wasn't necessary. When Delia got back to the flat that night to collect her things there was a different atmosphere. Puzzled, she unlocked the doors. All the rooms were as they had been when Aunt Cora left. Not a thing out of place, not a speck of dust anywhere, and – as investigation in the kitchen proved – every breakage had been replaced.

She stood looking, aghast. After a minute's startled silence she was aware of someone breathing behind her. She swung round. Keith stood there. There was a haunted, unhappy look in his face.

'Yes. I got it done. I got the bank's cleaner to oblige me. I think you'll find the breakages have all been replaced. If you find any damage I've missed, let me know. I'll settle it up.'

Delia moved closer to him, and spoke in a low angry voice.

'Keith, why did you do this? If I could have got a locksmith to change the locks in time I would have, but, as it was, I had to manage with the existing keys. I might have saved myself the trouble.'

'Were you so determined to upset Aunt Cora on her return?' he asked, mildly.

Delia snorted. 'She's going to be upset, anyway, and don't kid yourself – she expected something like this to happen. That's why she got me over here to stay. Unfortunately she didn't know her keys had been "borrowed" and duplicated.' Her voice was scathing and he flinched.

'I know,' he murmured, and sinking into an armchair, buried his head in his hands. 'Susaline's unprincipled, quarrelsome, mad for pleasure, but she's my wife.'

'Oh, Keith, why – why did you do it? Whatever was it about Susaline that got you? (Where is she now, by the way?)' Delia cried passionately, putting aside her anger in the utter tragedy of it.

'She's at the dance-hall, with her cousin and a bunch of Dagoes – as usual,' he said, without moving. Then, raising a haggard face, he said, 'Delia, don't pity me. She's just different to what I'm used to. She wants a bit of understanding, but I'll do it. One can do anything one wants to. And I want to.'

She listened in silence, stricken. He didn't know his words were like a knife going into her. It is doubtful if he would have cared if he had. She could see that his life was bounded (for the moment, anyway), by Susaline.

'She's very sweet,' he went on, a new tender note creeping into his voice. 'She can be so utterly lovely, and she can be hell. She has a sense of beauty that appeals to me, too, and that's why I don't stop her dancing. It's the only way she has of expressing that sense of beauty.'

Delia thought of Susaline as she had seen her last night when she had gone up and knocked at their door. Susaline had come to the door in a frowsy bath-robe and cheaply trimmed satin slippers – imitation ostrich feather borders, Delia recalled, with disgust – and everything the girl wore needed a good wash. Her nightdress was over-trimmed, and the lace slightly torn in places. Her face had been smeared with night-cream, and her blonde hair hung thick and flaky, fresh from being brushed. A sense of beauty? How men were tricked by Susaline's type of girl.

She let him ramble on. He got sickly sentimental at times, at others wistfully optimistic that Susaline would settle down. If only she would confine her dancing to the local hall, and give up this mad idea of a professional career, he mused. Perhaps he'd be able to persuade her. She was in love with him, in her heart, he was pathetically convinced.

'Can she cook?' Delia asked, in a sense of amazement that she herself didn't yet know.

'Not yet,' Keith grinned, half apologetically, 'but she's learning.'

'Who does the cooking, then?'

'Well, we muddle through, you know. I do

most of it. Or we go out to eat. Sometimes Aunt Cora…' And not until then did Delia realise how deeply Aunt Cora had got involved in the married life of this pair, and how she felt so responsible for them that she hadn't the heart to have adequate precautions taken for shutting her flat up when she went away. Delia saw, swiftly, that Aunt Cora's kind heart and old affection for Keith must have landed her in many things; probably, for all Delia knew, Aunt Cora was responsible for the running of that flat upstairs, the laundry and stores, the weekend cooking, everything. She wouldn't have been surprised if Aunt Cora hadn't included the shopping in her own. Did she expect Delia herself to carry on in that way? Or had she seized the opportunity of going away like this in order to give Keith and his wife a chance to stand on their own feet?

Delia didn't know, and was suddenly tired.

'Well, Keith, what's done is done,' she said, and determinedly began to lock up the place.

'You leaving?' he asked, with a queer, lost look in his eyes.

'I'll be back later to pick up my case. At least, I think so. Oh, I may stay here after all. I don't want any more parties or breakages. Better see that nothing else of that sort happens, Keith, or I may really lose my temper. It's not sufficient to clean up and replace things – it's the colossal cheek of using Aunt Cora's flat when she isn't here to see after things herself.'

He said he would see what he could do, but the tone of his voice didn't hold out much hope. He asked her again what she was going to do. 'Now, I mean? Are you going out to eat?'

'Yes, I think I will. A friend of mine invited me, but I said I wouldn't. I'll ring him up and tell him I've altered my mind, I think.'

'Oh.' He sounded crestfallen. 'I rather wondered … I thought perhaps you and I might … there isn't much grub in the house, and I don't suppose you want to cook…'

He looked straight at her, appealing. Delia wavered. A day or two ago she would have jumped at the chance of eating out with Keith. What did it matter, after all? Susaline was out with other men. She couldn't possibly object. And, anyway, Keith and Delia were almost brother and sister.

Keith watched her hesitation and broke in in an eager voice. 'There's such a lot I want to talk to you about. If you only knew Susaline as I do – I think, if I told you all about her, you'd understand her better, and like her. I do so want you to like her, Delia.'

That, of course, did it. Delia sickened. She realised that this proposed meal was simply to be a session of Susaline, with a bit of food flung in, and she revolted.

'No, Keith, I don't think I'll come and eat with you. It wouldn't be right, and, besides, you must give me time to get to know your wife in my own way. I'm one of those funny people who like to form my own opinions. I'm afraid you'd simply prejudice me. I think I'll make my phone call, if you'll excuse me.'

She went out to the hall, and had lifted the receiver, when a key rattled in the front door. Keith came out, puzzled. It was Susaline. She burst in, white of face, angry of eyes. It seemed she hardly saw Delia, or realised that they were there together. She glared at Keith and addressed her remarks to him.

'It's all your fault!' she started, and prepared for the usual storm. Keith went towards her, with the intention, Delia thought, of putting his hands on her shoulders to calm her, but Susaline roughly slapped him off.

'Don't you touch me! You're like all the men, only want a wife for one thing. I fainted when I was doing my exhibition number tonight. Right in the middle of the floor! Oh, I never felt so ashamed in all my life! Everyone knew why, and they laughed. I know they were laughing at me! And it's all your fault!'

Keith looked bewildered. Delia came forward.

'You look ill, Susaline. Don't you think you ought to see a doctor?'

'Mind your own business!' Susaline said savagely. To Keith she said, biting out the words, 'They called a doctor in. They would! It's all up with my dancing – I'm going to have a kid!'

CHAPTER 10

Miss Grayson came back from Cornwall unexpectedly the second week in August. It was a very hot August, a month that Delia had been spending in Sir Timothy's company mainly, for the sheer relief of cooling trips in his roadster in the evenings after work, and gay week-ends at his home by the sea. Sir Timothy's widowed sister, Gail, who kept house for him, comprised his sole family, and it was fast being accepted that Delia was by way of becoming the new Lady Nodeleigh. Delia herself said nothing, but was content to let the hot, enervating days slip by in this fashion, for Paul completely deserted her for his first big chance – that of second male of the company, to replace a dark, sinister-looking young man who had been offered a film contract.

'I'm terribly glad for you, Paul,' she had said, sincerely, when he had told her about it. 'But won't it mean that you'll have to work awfully hard?'

'That sounds as if you mean I shan't be able to manage the job,' he grumbled, looking hungrily at her. Nothing had been said of the night of Keith's wedding when Paul had kissed Delia good-night. But then Delia had given him no chance to reopen the subject, because for some remote reason best known to the firm July and August were the busiest periods of the year, and everyone, from Sir Timothy downwards, was so worn out at the end of the day that they were apt to shelve anything personal that could be shelved.

'I think you may find learning the bigger and more important parts a bit of a job at first,' Delia said, frankly, 'but knowing you, Paul, I bet you'll manage it, if it kills you!' She smiled at him, and after a second's hesitation got an answering smile.

They were at lunch, in their usual alcove. Each day they sat there, quietly eating, saying very little, and other customers, together with the three sisters who ran The Cellar, secretly speculated on whether the affair was serious or not. The customers held that Delia was playing the young man along in the most unfair manner, while she played for higher stakes, with Nodeleigh Manor in view. The three sisters, who had taken a liking to Delia that first day, were more romantic; they hazarded a guess that Paul would not marry her till he made good on the stage, and that she was meantime holding down a difficult job of her own by pacifying her employer, which to them merely meant acting as his best advertisement besides being a social secretary.

Delia knew nothing of all this. Gossip meant little to her these days. Her mind was taken up with the subject of Aunt Cora's empty flat (which she occasionally visited and sometimes stayed in) and that other subject, the coming child of Keith and Susaline.

It was because of this factor that she was chary of going back to her one-time home. Keith and Susaline were always quarrelling. The chief clerk had recovered and returned to his duties, and Keith had been put down again to his original job, which did nothing to please Susaline. Even his wage had been 'readjusted' as the bank kindly put it, and at a time when more money was needed this alone was inclined to ignite the ever-present tinder, and Susaline and Keith would be "at it" again. Neighbours began to talk. It wasn't possible not to know what was going on in that one-time quiet house. Delia knew of that much, at least, and in sheer embarrassment kept away as much as possible.

Aunt Cora's return was a relief. She brought Melita with her, and Delia broke a date with Sir Timothy, to go and see her aunt for the first time for nearly a month.

Melita Grayson was tall and languid, a pleasant enough young woman with an abundance of long dark hair which she dressed in the very latest styles copied from women's magazines. Her method of dress was extremely plain, with a provocative touch of trimming, and her choice of colour far too daring for that of the wife of a rural doctor. 'Unfortunate,' Aunt Cora had described James's choice of a wife when she first met Melita, but little by little the girl grew on her, and now Aunt Cora was as sorry for Melita's choice of a husband as she had once been for her beloved nephew.

'Now, Delia, Melita wants you to know everything,' Miss Grayson began, 'and I think I can cut a long story short by saying at once that neither of them is to blame.'

Delia and Melita exchanged grins, and settled down to listen to the older woman.

'Poor James is getting extremely dull, and harassed,' Miss Grayson went on, 'while this tiresome Melita here is growing more pretty and provocative each day. Added to this the advent of a gossip-monger of the first water, in their village, and a very attractive male who purports to paint Cornish scenery, and there you have the mixture. I decided at last to bring Melita away for a bit of healthy town atmosphere, which ought to make her yearn for Cornwall, and which ought to

152

make that wretched nephew of mine yearn for his wife. Ah, well, we'll see how it all works out.'

'Do you feel better for your holiday, Aunt Cora?'

'I suppose I do, Delia, though with all the hypocrisy of an old woman I'd like to be able to say I've returned to recuperate after my strenuous efforts to settle the affairs of these two young people.'

Melita laughed. 'Auntie, you're a positive pet.'

'Are you going to have any children, Melita?' Delia asked, bluntly.

Melita flushed. 'No. I wish I could,' she said, through tightened lips.

Aunt Cora frowned. 'That wasn't very tactful, Delia,' she remarked, puzzled.

'I didn't mean to be tactful,' Delia said. 'I was using shock tactics. Mean of me, I suppose, but I'm going to use some more. Ever thought of adopting one, Melita?'

'No!' Melita protested, in horror. 'I couldn't stand another woman's child!'

'Oh! Oh, well it was an idea. No offence?'

Melita managed a smile, but it had bitten deeply. She secretly pined for children of her own. The other two women saw as clearly as she did that James and she needed children to hold their marriage together. Miss Grayson cast a reproachful look at Delia.

'I merely mentioned the subject because we're going to have an infant around the place pretty soon that nobody wants,' Delia said calmly, and suddenly launched on the topic of Susaline's baby.

Miss Grayson was alarmed. 'I didn't know ... why, they've only been married a matter of ten weeks!'

'Well?' Delia smiled, and Melita relaxed sufficiently to softly guffaw, for Miss Grayson's face was a study.

'Oh, it's just that I didn't expect... How does Keith feel about it?'

'I believe he just dreads any new development in that marriage of his,' Delia said, slowly. 'Susaline, of course, was furious from the minute she first discovered it. She never lets up on an opportunity to point out that it was his fault, and that it's interrupting her dancing career, and will probably ruin her figure and her lissomeness for ever. She's probably right, but for the life of me I can't see what's so bad about that. Can you, Melita?'

'Can't say, never having seen her dance,' Melita answered, indifferently.

'Well, as a matter of fact, her dancing is a delight to watch,' Miss Grayson said, unexpectedly. 'I'd like to see that girl get on in the dancing profession – if she didn't happen to be Keith's wife. I'm really sorry for Keith.'

'And you thought it would be nice if I took the child off this cabaret girl's hands, eh?' Melita hazarded.

'Oh, it was just a mad idea,' Delia said. 'I get so wild when I see people like Susaline having a baby and not wanting it, while others are just aching for one and can't. I'd love to be married to some nice man and having lots of fat, chuckling brown babies. Hers will be a lovely child – bound to be! They always are when people don't fuss and die of anxiety over their coming. You know how it is!'

Melita's coming to town meant that Aunt Cora was no longer on her own so much, and Delia dropped out of visiting her aunt even on Wednesdays. It was in many ways a relief not to have to go to the house at all. Delia dreaded seeing Keith's haunted white face gloomily looking over the short net curtains of the upstairs windows, but, more than this, she dreaded hearing Susaline's now perpetually shrill voice carping over some small thing, as she stumped about the flat. Miss Grayson began to chafe over the footsteps – those too loud, and apparently unnecessary footsteps – constantly going back and forth above her head. It was getting tiresome, too, Susaline's eternal borrowing from the store cupboard, food items which she now seldom bothered to replace, unless it was Keith himself who made the gesture.

This, Miss Grayson confided to Delia, she liked least of all; she knew too well that Keith had gone without part of his lunch hour to go on a shopping expedition to replace the borrowed item, and that made Miss Grayson feel a brute.

So Delia had more time for Sir Timothy, and it was towards the end of September that he brought matters to a head.

'Bai Jove, Delia, I don't have to tell you how I feel about you!' he began, in his usual direct fashion. 'Come on, my girl, when's it going to be?'

She looked distressed. He had noticed once or twice before, when he had tried to pin her down to something definite, that that same distressed look had come into her face. His methods were always direct, and he didn't understand this at all. He said so, and it was at once impossible to go on any longer as she had been, putting off the evil day.

'I'm not in love with you,' she told him, in a voice that suggested that that was the one and only possible explanation.

He guffawed. 'I know!' he told her. 'And I'm not in love with you, so dammit, what're we worried about?'

'But you asked me to marry you!'

'And will you?'

'No, I don't think so.'

'But in heaven's name, girl, why not?

What's to stop you. You like me, don't you?'

'Oh, yes, but that's not enough. I wouldn't feel honest about such a marriage.'

He leaned back in his chair shaking his head. 'My dear Delia, at times you can be quite tiresome, 'pon my word! I don't love you! Does that make you feel better? Oh, I like you! I think you're a most pleasant woman. Besides, I want a wife, and it seems to me that you have everything a man in my position needs in a wife, and, in addition, you're young and strong, and a damned good-looking woman, too! Too good-looking to leave you around loose for some other fella to marry off! All excellent reasons, what? Now, my dear, what d'you say?'

'I'd ... like a little time,' Delia gasped. She felt choked with some unnamed emotion. She wanted to say to Sir Timothy, 'It wouldn't be fair for me to marry anyone while the only man I see is unhappy and already married to someone else!' But that, of course, would be disastrous, because had she not been going around with him for so long, and no doubt giving him the impression that she liked him most of all! Hadn't she told him there was no one else? No, she couldn't tell him about Keith. Besides, supposing he took it well, he might presume to give her advice, and that she couldn't stand. Keith was a taboo subject where outsiders were concerned. Even when Paul mentioned him – Paul, who had been at school with him and knew him well – she felt herself shrivelling up inside. It was rather like being undressed in public to discuss (or have discussed) this love of hers for someone else's husband.

Sir Timothy gave her a week to think it over. 'But let's not isolate ourselves from each other,' he begged. 'How about a show tonight, Delia?'

'Oh, no. I'd rather not. I don't want to see you while I'm seeing how I feel about you; it might prejudice me.'

'Nonsense, child. What drivel you do talk! I suppose what's happening is that you're paying a duty visit to that old aunt of yours? Eh?'

Delia eagerly seized the excuse. 'Well, she will be alone tonight. My cousin has left town, and gone back to Cornwall. She's been staying with Aunt Cora for quite a while. Auntie will be lonely.'

'Then I tell you what we'll do. Bring your aunt along, too, and I'll book three seats. No, wait – we'll take a box. Make it a gala evening. Damme, I must meet your relations, Delia. I've heard so much of this paragon among aunts that, bless me, I'm quite curious about her.'

Delia hedged and wriggled, but for once Sir Timothy was adamant, so in despair she went to the telephone and told Aunt Cora of the arrangement. Aunt Cora was delighted, it appeared, and had also been wanting to meet Sir Timothy socially. Delia, depressed, went back to her work and finished the afternoon.

'I think I'll wear my pink and grey striped taffeta,' Delia told her aunt, without much enthusiasm, as she got ready for the theatre that evening.

'With your new fur cape,' Miss Grayson nodded. 'Very nice dear. I've got a new dress I'm going to wear,' and she looked very pleased with herself. 'No you're not to come in and see it until I call you. I've treated myself since you phoned today. How do we get to Town? Have you arranged for a taxi?'

'No. Sir Timothy's calling for us in the car.'

'I see. What an eminently suitable man to have tow one around for the rest of one's life,' Miss Grayson said, irrelevantly.

Sir Timothy sat in the back of the car behind his impeccable chauffeur. Miss Grayson, peeping from behind the curtain, thought, 'He's superb, that man! Wonder why Delia doesn't show more enthusiasm? Paul Faversham was all right for a start, but...' And she let her thought slide away as she watched Sir Timothy make a leisured way from the car to the front door, a tall, graceful figure in tails and topper, with a box of flowers in his hand for Delia. 'Um,' the watching Miss Grayson commented to herself, 'attentive, too!'

Sir Timothy looked a little surprised when Delia introduced him to her aunt, but then Delia herself blinked a little. Her aunt wore a silver moiré gown, a lovely thing cut to show off the still good lines of her small figure, and which made her white hair, so beautifully, impeccably dressed, look positively regal. Miss Grayson was wearing, Delia noticed, the one piece of good jewellery she possessed: a relic from the old days, a very fine set of emeralds, which she usually kept in the bank.

'My! Aunt Cora's making a do of it,' she thought, in amazement, and saw, with further amazement, Sir Timothy's unfeigned interest. He helped Miss Grayson on with her silver squirrel coat, watched her pick up immaculate pale grey gloves and a tiny green kid evening purse, and followed them out. 'No one cares how I look,' Delia thought, in sudden amusement.

A quick look up at the first floor windows was irresistible. Susaline, her face stormy, was watching them go, and Keith hovered distractedly in the background. Delia knew what would happen now. Susaline couldn't bear to see anyone else in ankle-length dress these days without raising a storm about her absence from the dance floor and her deteriorating figure. The girl was so inordin-

160

ately proud of her lines that her clothes were usually cut skin-tight. One by one, Delia noticed on each visit, Susaline's favourite dresses were being discarded, and she had taken to wearing full-gathered skirts and floppy blouses – a style that neither suited nor pleased her, but did a lot to disguise her new condition.

'They'll quarrel now,' Delia thought, and resolutely pushed them out of her mind to enjoy what Sir Timothy had intended to be a most entertaining evening: a good play, in good box seats, and an amusing supper afterwards, at a new roadhouse Sir Timothy had discovered and was anxious to show off.

Delia noticed that her aunt was at her most entertaining, and no one could be more amusing than Aunt Cora when she set out to be. There was a winsome charm about Miss Grayson in this gay, evening-out mood, that took away that rather worried bothered look she had been acquiring lately, a look that had emphasised the coming years more than anything else. What was Aunt Cora, for heaven's sake? Forty-five. Oh, well, quite a bit younger than Sir Timothy, but near enough to his age to give them a lot in common, Delia supposed.

She let her thoughts slide forward. Soon, perilously soon, she would have to decide if this man was to become her husband. What would it be like to have a husband who was a good five years older than your own aunt, the woman who had brought you up and taken the place of your mother? A bit grim, Delia mused. But Sir Timothy was rich, amusing, tolerant, and had a great talent for getting the best out of life, whether in fun or work. He liked for ever discovering new things, too.

New things ... Delia realised, with startling suddenness, that she herself wasn't like that. An almost unformed picture suddenly began to take shape in her mind. A small house, with a garden, and small fat children waddling about, happily getting into mischief. A dog perhaps, and a cat with kittens. Household tasks, and getting ready at night for the man-of-the-house to come home. Bathing the children and putting them to bed, before she settled down with knitting and sewing. The sleepy animals before the fire, the wireless turned on – softly – to some good music, a play, or something amusing. Was that, after all, what she wanted? Where was this new glamourising of herself to fit in? Oh, well, she hadn't wanted it, anyway. It was Aunt Cora's idea. Besides, the man-of-the-house mightn't like it...

He was a blur in this fascinating picture. Try as she would, she couldn't get the imaginary man to turn into a fair, unhappy young bank clerk, and at last a tall, dark figure emerged, and Delia saw with disgust that Paul had intruded. She let him take shape, in the armchair facing her, and (as she knew would happen) the inevitable thick wad of paper bound into a play script appeared in his hand. He smoked his favourite short pipe and frowned anxiously at the typed red and black lines, the play to be learned for next week at the rep.

'Isn't it, Delia?' The voice cut in on her thoughts. Sir Timothy and Aunt Cora were getting up.

'Is it over?' she gasped in bewilderment.

'My dear child!' Sir Timothy said, slowly, and he sounded rather offended.

'Interval, Delia,' Aunt Cora hissed, 'and we're going to the bar for cocktails. Come along, do!'

She followed them, and was hardly aware of the admiring male glances as she went. There was a new problem gripping her mind.

In the space of one short week she would have to give Sir Timothy an answer. Already Paul was growing restive. How did Paul compare as a husband against Sir Timothy?

Keith, Keith, Keith! Her mind clamoured over the name, but her own common sense answered: He doesn't need me. Besides, it's undignified, hanging around waiting to see which way that little blonde is going to blow, and just now, with the baby coming, she's blowing hard in Keith's direction all the time. A new idea came, too. They might find that the baby – as babies sometimes did – would be the means of patching up their marriage.

'I'm not going to sit around and wait until that happens, not me!' Delia told herself, angrily, and set about matching Sir Timothy against Paul.

Paul won easily. He had no money or sense of fun, and he wasn't always wanting to chase around and show her off. But he had youth; youth and health and the same desire for a small home, and children, pets and his precious job on the stage. All of which she knew, understood, and yearned for and would be of use in, as his partner. That was just it. She would have a life-size job living up to what Sir Timothy required of her. A tiring job that would, she knew, become irksome when the glamour wore off. But the capacity in which she could serve Paul was easy.

But ... she didn't love Paul any more than she loved Sir Timothy. Could she honestly, and with success, become Paul's wife, while the image of Keith intruded for the rest of her life?

CHAPTER 11

Melita wrote from Cornwall, 'Darling Delia, be a pet and come and stay with us. Aunt Cora said you haven't had your holiday this year and late September here will enchant you. Besides ... I need someone to talk to.'

How like Melita, Delia thought, to write in that impulsive fashion. How did she know a holiday could be arranged as quickly as that? But, of course, Aunt Cora was all for the idea, though she looked a trifle queerly at Delia as she urged her to go.

'But I can't walk out on Sir Timothy like that,' Delia protested, then frowned. At the end of this week she'd have to make a decision regarding her future and his.

'I can't ... I can't marry Sir Timothy,' she told herself, passionately, in spite of an inner voice that cautioned her not to be a fool. She knew, all the while she was hedging and shelving the issue, that she was throwing away the chance of a lifetime as far as material benefits were concerned. Yet ... could she do it? Could she bring herself to do it without running the risk of regretting her action for ever after?

And so the doubt and indecision dogged her footsteps all through that week, until at last the day came when Sir Timothy rang for her and said at once, 'Well, Delia?'

She raised stricken eyes to his. 'Honestly, I still can't say one way or the other. I've thought and thought all round the subject...'

'Have you mentioned the matter to your aunt?' Sir Timothy asked, taking a turn round the room.

'No, no, of course not!' Delia sounded shocked. Fancy mentioning anything quite so private and personal to Aunt Cora! She shrank from the thought. Sir Timothy seemed relieved and inclined not to press the point.

'Let me have a little more time to think,' Delia pleaded. It wasn't fair to ask such a thing, yet she didn't want to give a definite refusal.

Sir Timothy was abstracted. He waved a hand at her. 'Yes, yes, of course,' but he appeared to be thinking of something else.

Delia frowned. Had she displeased him after all? It was difficult to assess where his thoughts were or what he was thinking, and that alone made her hesitate on the point of accepting him as a possible husband.

'You see,' she started to explain, and was unaware of the rather desperate note in her voice. 'Our relations in Cornwall have asked me to go down there – I wondered if I could

166

have some of my summer leave–'

He jumped at the idea.

'But, of course, Delia. You haven't had any summer leave at all yet! How forgetful of me! When d'you want to go?'

'I wondered if – next week–' She hesitated. It *was* rather short notice.

'Next week it shall be!' he declared. 'There's an easing off of work and, anyway, there's a typist in the pool who's been recommended – I'd like to give her a trial in your place. Take a month, my dear. You've worked very hard this year and I'm pleased with you.'

Delia blinked. From any other employer she would have thought this was preparatory to getting the sack. From Sir Timothy, however, it merely appeared to be belated amends for that forgetfulness of staff comforts that no one deplored more than he did.

'Think over what I've asked you while you're away,' he added, and then let the subject drop.

Delia told Paul about the coming holiday over lunch. 'I can do with a rest,' she admitted.

'So I shan't be seeing you for a month?' he mused, looking at her enviously. She showed no disappointment at leaving him nor had she expressed any desire to hear from him. He supposed that she was more obsessed with the thought of not seeing Pemberley for four weeks.

He ventured to put it to her. 'You won't mind if I write to you sometimes, about the rep. and all that?'

'I'd love you to write to me,' she said, warmly, and reflected that she'd never had a letter from him before. 'Make them long ones, and tell me your troubles, if any.'

'And you going for a *holiday!*' he laughed.

As they left The Cellar a shaft of golden sunshine touched her coppery hair and brought out a rich glow. A golden-brown leaf fluttered down from one of the plane trees that edged the square, and it rustled crisply along the gutter till it caught in the sink.

'Autumn!' Paul said, and there was a sad note in his voice. 'Delia, I can't bear to have you away for a whole month. It's like having you go out of my life altogether. Look, you may think it's an awful cheek on my part, but may I spend the week-ends with you? I can fix up at pubs. I'm getting a bit of leave myself, as a matter of fact – the next two plays haven't a part for me, but I'm to have the lead the week after–'

There was a desolate note in his voice. He was going to miss her, she thought, and it was a welcome contrast to Sir Timothy's casual manner.

Impulsively she said, 'Spend your two

weeks with me! Let me ask Melita to put you up–'

'No, Delia. I'd love two weeks in Cornwall with you, but it must be on the understanding that I find my own accommodation. Besides, I like the little inns down there–'

They wrangled good-naturedly about it for the last few minutes of the lunch hour, and when he was about to leave her she stopped arguing and gave in.

'Come and have a meal at my home tonight, Delia. I'd like my family to meet you,' Paul said, coming back after a second's hesitation.

'Well, I don't know, Paul.' Delia had misgivings about this family of his. He had told her enough about them at different times to make her feel they wouldn't like her much.

'I'd like you to come,' he urged.

'Just for this evening, then,' she compromised, though with misgivings. When Keith had first brought Susaline home they had assumed that the pair were to be engaged. Delia didn't want the Favershams jumping to any such conclusions. Neither did she want Aunt Cora to get any ideas in that direction.

'Going out tonight, dear?' Miss Grayson asked, coming into Delia's bedroom while she was changing.

'Yes. Can you suggest something in this preposterous new wardrobe you've chosen for me, Aunt Cora, that will be neat and quiet?'

'Oh, you're not spending the evening with Sir Timothy, then, dear?'

There was a note in Miss Grayson's voice that Delia couldn't quite place, and she watched her aunt thoughtfully as the older woman sorted through her wardrobe and turned out a navy skirt and bolero and a frilly white blouse.

'I'd wear the new navy bonnet with it if I were you, I think,' Miss Grayson advised.

'And the lizard bag and shoes?'

'No, plain navy, I think, Delia.'

As Delia stepped up to the Favershams' front door she wondered if Aunt Cora had guessed where she was going to spend the evening, for not even the Faversham family could find fault with her appearance tonight. She wore less make-up than usual, too, and she noticed that Paul opened the door for her he eyed her with approval.

'Mother,' he said, taking Delia into the sitting-room, 'I want you to meet a friend of mine, whom I think you'll come to like a good deal.'

Delia flushed with embarrassment and wished Paul's introduction had been a little more formal.

Mrs Faversham eyed her with a bright, bird-like glance and patted the settee beside her. 'We'll see, we'll see,' she said. 'Come and sit by me, my dear, and we'll have a little talk before the others come in.'

'I'll go and see if I can help Stella, Mother. Ian won't be long,' he said, and, nodding reassuringly at Delia, he went out.

Mrs Faversham smiled, a bright, disarming smile, and then turned on a stream of questions – questions which Delia told herself resentfully were quite impertinent, yet so guilelessly put that it was impossible not to answer them.

'Let me see, you're the sister of that nice young clerk in the bank, the fair boy; now what's his name, my dear?'

'No, I haven't any brothers. I think you mean Keith Pemberley.'

'Ah, yes, my dear. Well, then, he's related to you somehow, isn't he, as I understand he lives in your house? A cousin, perhaps?'

Delia said, with a nice mixture of patience and coolness, 'He doesn't exactly live in our house. He rents a flat in my aunt's home. I don't live there now.'

'Oh, you've moved! Nearer your job, I suppose, my dear?'

'Yes, Mrs Faversham.'

'Much nearer?'

Delia supplied her with the address.

'Oh! Oh, I see.' Faint disapproval appeared on the face of Paul's mother.

'*What* do you see, Mrs Faversham?'

'*Rather* expensive flats for a working girl to

live in, aren't they? Or perhaps I'm thinking of some other block of flats. Correct me if I'm wrong, my dear.'

Delia bit her lip. She didn't want to quarrel with Paul's mother, but without telling her every little private detail it was difficult.

'Well, you know, Mrs Faversham, it's relative, isn't it? I mean, what one girl can afford another can't. Besides, without knowing actual figures you can't judge either way, can you? I mean you don't know the rent of these flats, do you? And you don't know what I earn or whether I've private means or even if my aunt is helping me?' Delia smiled as she finished speaking, a nice, determined smile, which said that if Mrs Faversham wanted to remain on good terms with her she'd better stop being inquisitive.

'Now, Mrs Faversham, there's something I wanted to ask *you,*' Delia continued, carrying the war into the enemy's camp. 'Your elder son, Ian, isn't he in the solicitor's office, in town?'

'He is,' was the stiff reply.

'I *thought* that was Paul's brother,' Delia said, happily, knowing full well that the older woman knew Paul must have told her long ago. 'Aren't you *proud* of your two fine sons, especially now that Paul's on the stage?'

Mrs Faversham's lips folded tighter. 'I don't know that I altogether approve of the stage for a nice young man. Too many painted women to entrap and ensnare him. But then,' Paul's mother said, with a beautiful thrust, 'these hussies are to be found all over the place and not only in the theatre. Don't you agree, Miss Grayson?'

They smiled at each other, deceptively friendly smiles that would have fooled no one but Paul, who came in at that moment with Stella to be introduced to Delia.

It was not, on the whole, a happy evening. Delia sparred with them – Mrs Faversham, Stella, and the elder son Ian – the whole time. They seemed determined to trip her up into disclosing some detail, some incident, that would cause Paul to think twice over this friendship of his with her. That they disapproved of her was painfully obvious, though Stella looked a nice enough girl, and on the surface appeared to be friendly. It was that veiled hostility beneath the surface of all three of them which Delia could feel, and which she looked on as a sort of threesome campaign, planned beforehand, against her.

She didn't like that. She would far rather they had refused to have her come to the house, or said outright that they didn't care for her. But, then, either course would have been fatal for them as far as Paul was concerned. Looking at him now, over her cup of steaming cocoa (which Paul's mother sentimentally referred to as an old-fashioned nightcap), Delia was quite prepared to believe that if any of his family were foolish enough to criticise her, he would dig his heels in and be more friendly than ever.

'I hear you're going to Cornwall for a long vacation,' Stella said, with a bright, inquisitive glance.

'Yes,' Delia admitted.

'Soon?' Ian probed.

'Quite soon,' Delia smiled, volunteering no further information.

'It must be nice to just to able to fling up your work when you feel like it, and go away for a holiday,' Mrs Faversham said, not looking up from her work.

Paul was frowning. Delia said, innocently, 'It must, indeed. Do you know anyone who can do that, Mrs Faversham? If so, I wish you'd tell me where they work. I'd like a job like that.'

There was a little silence. Paul's mother looked up sharply. Ian and Stella exchanged glances.

'You see,' Delia said, 'I haven't had a holiday for two years. Last year my employer asked me not to take one until this spring, because of a muddle an old employee got everything into. After we'd ironed it out the winter was on us, and in the spring I somehow couldn't manage to get away. So, you see, I get a whole month, now, at the first opportunity I've had. I think I've earned it, don't you?'

Paul said, 'I've explained all that to my mother. You must have forgotten, dear,' but he sounded nettled.

Stella rushed in, 'Where are you staying, Miss Grayson? At one of those smart hotels on the coast?'

'I'm just going to visit a cousin of mine, and his wife. Purely a family reunion. Are you having a holiday this year?' she returned.

'We've had ours,' Stella smiled. 'But Paul's having a holiday at the same time as you, and by an odd coincidence he happens to be going to Cornwall. Do you think you'll be seeing him there?'

Delia looked in Paul's direction. He was red and angry, and doing his best to attract Stella's attention by staring at her. Obviously Paul's position tonight had not been the most enviable, and Delia would have given a lot to know what had happened after he had, with the utmost thought and duty for his mother, telephoned to ask her permission to have Delia to supper.

'I doubt it,' Delia answered Stella, in a cool little voice. 'You see, to those who don't know Cornwall, it's a surprisingly large place, with difficult connecting journeys and indifferent transport. Obviously you don't know the country well.' She got up. 'I must be going now. Thank you, Mrs Faversham, for a pleasant evening and for having me. Good-night, everybody,' and very firmly she looked at Paul.

He sprang to take her to the door. 'I'm walking with Delia to the bus-stop,' he told his mother, and his voice was stiff. His brother and sister-in-law watched him curiously.

Outside the house, he apologised. 'I can't think what was the matter with them all, Delia. They made me damned uncomfortable. Think you can forget it all?'

She smiled. 'Perhaps it might be as well if we didn't meet in Cornwall, Paul. They seem to think I'm some kind of contagious disease which you must on no account catch.'

He snorted, savagely. 'That's what comes of staying at home, an obliging bachelor, and making a baby of your mother. I had to look after her after dad died. Ian and Stella have not long taken to living at home with her, and that only because it suits them. But they'll find if they're going to behave like that I shan't find it suits me to stay there much longer.'

'Don't be angry, Paul. Your mother's right. I'm not really your type of girl, and you know it.'

'Oh, don't be so damned silly, Delia.'

She gasped. 'Well! It's hardly your way to talk like that, Paul.'

'No. I know it isn't. But I've just come to

176

a decision. That's all.'

'What sort of decision?'

'This. I'm spending the whole of the month with you – if you'll let me. I didn't tell you at first, it looked rather as if I were trying to be tiresome, but the fact is, I've no work to do for the next four weeks. There are one or two "bit" parts going, but I don't think they'll do me any good, and anyway there are plenty of players waiting to slip into them. I'll be taking the lead after this month, and I need a holiday, too. What do you say, Delia?'

She thought quickly, and realised for the first time that she hadn't been relishing the idea of that long journey on her own, and the first two weeks spent in the uneasy domesticity of James's house, while waiting for Paul to arrive. It would be nice to have him with her from the start of the holiday.

I'm being selfish, of course, she told herself. I only want him there as an excuse, so that James and Melita can't drag me too deeply into their family row, because of my companion always being around. But there was a little more than that to it, and for the moment she refused to peer too deeply into it. It was all closely tied up with running away from Sir Timothy, and the fact that Keith and Susaline were married and soon going to have a baby.

She sighed.

The answer's "no," isn't it, Delia?' Paul said, in a resigned voice.

'No, Paul, no. It isn't. It's "yes!"' she said, vehemently, and as her bus came whirling along and she took her leave from the elated young man she felt as though yet another page of her life had been hurriedly, yet significantly, turned over.

CHAPTER 12

Delia met Paul at the station to start their holiday, and he gasped in relief. 'Oh, my dear, you look—' he began, then without another word he took her arm and hurried her towards a compartment he had commandeered towards the end of the train. At this late time of the year the crowds had thinned out. So far they had the place to themselves.

'What d'you mean, Paul?' Delia asked, in amusement, knowing quite well what he meant. She had very little make-up on, her hair was again in one of the simple styles she had used at one time; though now it was cut shorter, it was not severe as it had once been. And she had discarded Aunt Cora's readymade glamour; she wore an old and favourite tweed travelling three-piece, and had a little bright green beret perched on the back of her bright hair.

'You look all set for a wonderful holiday,' he told her, soberly, and Delia experienced the delicious sensation of a man-friend's thoroughly appreciative glance.

'I'm glad you approve, sir,' she laughed, and wriggled happily in her corner seat facing him. 'Oh, I'm so *comfortable*, Paul. Flat shoes fit for walking and climbing, and stockings that won't ladder or tear. *And* I've packed odd skirts and sweaters only. I also happen to approve of that extremely well-worn and comfortable-looking tweed suit you've got on!'

It was wonderful weather, and Paul was quite unexpectedly a wonderful companion. He had a lot of interesting information to give her about the places they passed through, but he had more; he had a passion for the English countryside, particularly for the country for which they were bound.

'The West Country!' Delia murmured. 'Doesn't it sound exciting? You know, Paul, I've been there heaps of times before, mainly to see James and Melita, but never has it sounded so gloriously thrilling and romantic as it does this time. You know I'm *excited* about it! And I thought I'd never get excited about anything again.'

He smiled at her. 'I'm feeling rather like that, too,' he admitted. 'My previous trips have always been alone. Cornwall – seen through lonely eyes – is a grim, frightening place. But with a companion the beauty of the place is translated into something rich and vital. Still a little frightening,' he allowed, and Delia guessed he was thinking of places like Clodgy Point, with its hole in the rock through which the unwary could fall to the battering seas below, and the wild and lonely Zennor Moor, the treacherous path below the Lizard lighthouse, and the awfulness of St Michael's Mount on a windy day. 'But it's a haunting place.'

'Haunting is the word. Paul, I've been asked down here principally to help patch up my cousin's domestic affairs. I'm going to mutiny. This is my holiday – our holiday,' she told him, with shining eyes, and didn't know she was setting him on fire with the enthusiasm, the happiness of her. 'Let's make this a date to *see* Cornwall, as if we'd neither of us been there before. Let's!'

Melita met them at the station. They still had a four-mile journey, in the battered old car, to Haley's Gap, a stone house that had once been a farmhouse, roofed with old red tiles, windowed with tiny deep inlets in the stone walls, where diamond-shaped panes winked in the sunlight, and every fourth one was coloured. The house was approached through walls of solid rock and the road itself little more than a cart-track. It sloped sharply down towards the bay, and visiting motorists had a white notice-board in a prominent position specially for their benefit, informing them that this road should be negotiated only at their own risk. The doctor's house was the last in the village, and stood sharply above the cluster of fishermen's cottages in the tiny bay below.

Paul's eyes sparkled. 'Mrs Grayson, I'm almost tempted to admit my disappointment in not accepting your kindly offer to stay. No, I don't mean I'm going back on my word – I'm not. The inn is comfortable, and was recommended to me. But Mrs Grayson, to stay in a place like this!' He let out his breath in a slight hiss, and let his eyes rove around, at the pearly grey-blue sky of late September, at the deep mauvish-blue of the sea, at the greyish-brown of rocks and cliff-face, at the faded silver-cream of the sandy fringe round the foot of the cliffs, and at the incredible white of the old stone house. It's – very lovely,' he breathed.

Delia said, wonderingly, 'Yes. Yes, it is – very lovely. I suppose I've seen it so many times before that I'm used to it, but come to think of it, it's never been quite like this before.'

Melita flashed an interested glance at both of them in turn, and said lightly, 'Oh, that's because you've got a companion with you, and perhaps because you've come at a different time of the year. You've never been to Cornwall as late as this before, have you?'

They had tea in the long, narrow dining-room that had white-washed walls, black beams, and old black furniture. Melita had added brilliant touches of colour in the modern manner: red, yellow and green cushions, and curtains of cream linen with bands of braid in those three colours to match. James didn't like her modern taste in furnishings, and said so. James, Delia thought, was getting oldish and snappy, which was a pity; he had been good fun a matter of a year ago.

'Let's go down to the bay after tea, Paul. You've never seen this particular one, have you?' Delia said, quickly, after they had helped Melita to wash up.

Paul let her rush him off, although James showed signs of wanting to personally escort them, and Melita, Delia saw with a sinking heart, was already preparing to come with them.

Paul said, as they went out of the gateway that had no longer a gate, 'That wasn't very polite of you, was it, Delia? After all, you *are* their guest!'

'I've come down here, as I told you, to help patch up their silly domestic troubles, but that doesn't mean I'm going to have them hanging on my heels every minute of the time. Oh, Paul – Paul,' she burst out, in exasperation, 'what excuse have those two people for not getting on together, for not being happy? They've got everything – except...'

'Yes, except...' Paul nodded. Already Melita had said, rather bitterly, in his hearing, that there was no patter of tiny feet to make the place perfect.

'Oh, don't you take sides with them!' Delia burst out again. 'The whole thing makes me furious. Children are all right, but good heavens – if they wanted them that badly why don't they take one of those poor home-less mites and bring it up in these wonderful surroundings? Now that would be some-thing! Instead of sitting back, grousing and moaning, being bitter and making everyone else miserable! They've got everything else – a wonderful house in a wonderful county: beauty all around them – why, they've enough beauty to drown themselves in it, while we live in a stuffy town and are mighty thankful to get away for an occasional holiday.'

She paused to take indignant breath, while Paul watched her covertly with a new expression in his eyes. He said nothing, but let her run on again, while they swung down the winding, steep road to the sea.

'Just look at that gracious old house, and the garden! In high summer that garden's a riot of flowers, and there's a stream that runs through it at the back and widens out into a little pond, with a bridge over it. There are beautiful things to be seen out of every window, and even in mid-winter it isn't really cold here. They've got health, strength, and good looks and they've got each other. James's practice isn't bad, and what's more, it's interesting. He does every-thing in a very wide radius. They're well liked, too, and if Melita wanted to she could find heaps and heaps to do in the district, not only to help James, but more on the feminine side – committees, improvements, and things. The church here has only got one very hard-worked clergyman, and I've often envied the chance he holds out for someone energetic, like the doctor's wife, for instance, to step in and help. But Melita just sits back and moans about her childless state.'

The light was fading from the sky by the time they reached the bottom. There was the sharp tang of the sea, seaweed and lobster pots all mixed, and over and above it the tarry smell of the coils of rope on the edge of the tiny harbour, that harbour now unused because the fury of the sea had washed half of it away in the gales two years ago, and no one had had the energy or initiative to start a fund to repair it.

Paul and Delia stood on the edge looking at everything, then by mutual consent they started walking down the crazy steps to the beach. Hewn out of the rough rock, they had been worn, those steps, by countless feet down the ages. Delia looked back at them, and said, quite unaccountably:

'It felt then, Paul, as though other people were walking down those steps with us – people who walked down them ages before. Do spirits still tread over the same ground, d'you suppose?'

'Possibly. The spirits of people who've been happy, I think. Maybe ours will in years to come.'

'Why, Paul? Why specially ours?' She framed the question in a dreamy voice, as though it wasn't so specially information she was seeking, but that she was expressing a need to keep him talking. It pierced her senses that she liked his voice; that it was the sort of voice that fitted in so well with her own self that she had hardly noticed before that she did like it.

He tucked her hand under his arm as they turned and made their way round the little bay towards the spot where the rough rocks intruded into the sea's edge. Beyond this was a smaller bay, and another, and another, after the manner of the Cornish coast. Jutting up through the sea's surface were spiteful jags of black rocks like decayed teeth, rocks that had been the cause of many bygone shipwrecks. But it was evening, in a superb autumn, with the light fading rapidly

185

from the clear sky, and a full moon riding behind a provocative bit of cloud veiling, high above. Bygone sea terrors weren't in the picture.

'Because we're happy, Delia. And because, if we're not actually in love, we're moving steadily towards that state. Can't you feel it?'

'No. I can't feel anything, Paul. I'm drugged. Silly with happiness and Cornwall and freedom from town, and the good weather and–'

'And – what?' His voice was low and very tender.

She turned and raised a face full of sweet surprise to his. 'And, I think, because I've got you with me for a whole month!'

He lowered his head until his lips touched hers, and he pulled her gently but firmly into his arms. It was a long kiss, the sort of kiss she would expect from him; just possessive enough, without making her feel enchained. Infinitely tender. Roughness was foreign to his nature. It was a kiss to comfort and lull, rather than to excite, and conversely Delia felt disappointed. She wanted to be excited at this moment. There was a heady quality in the air, and she was aware that her heart was thumping madly.

Paul murmured, 'Let's walk through to the other bays,' and they strolled on again. Delia came down to earth, like a pricked balloon, and, like a pale ghost, the vision of Keith intruded.

She had not though of him all day. It was the first time that she had been with Paul for any stretch of hours at a time, and it struck her that though his personality appeared a quiet one it had a swamping quality that unobtrusively pushed out the memory of other people. She had been content and happy to be with him. Now she thought of Keith, and wondered what a kiss from him would be like. She tried, idiotically, like a mutinous child doing the wrong thing and knowing it, to imagine him taking her into his arms, and bending his fair curly head over hers as Paul had done. But if she were mutinous, so was her imagination, for the picture it produced was not of Keith bending over herself, but over Susaline – Susaline with that angelic smile, and that sweet way she moved her lips when talking to Keith. A burning wave of jealousy swept over Delia.

It frightened her. She had never experienced anything like it before. She felt sick. She wanted to leave Paul and run back up the beach, up those mysterious rock steps to the harbour, up the long, steep road to Haley's Gap and straight into the house to her room and into bed. Bed, where she could bury her face in the cooling pillow and fight out alone and undisturbed this new feeling that scared more than soured her. In spirit she made that journey to her bed, the little single bed with the patchwork quilt always occupied by her when she stayed with Melita. And in a sense it steadied her, even while she knew that she couldn't hope to make the journey on her own or with any speed, or with, indeed, any hope of getting to her room without encountering Melita and James, and the explanations that would inevitably follow.

Paul was silent. He had his own thoughts. In a way that kiss had disappointed him, too. Anger flooded him. Fool to let the night race away with him like that. He should have waited, waited until the month had almost worn away, and he had managed to win Delia's confidence by steady companionship and happy days. He understood that she hadn't been ready for that kiss, but he had not realised that if he had been less considerate and made it stronger, it would have had the effect of winning Delia over at once. As it was, he had sensed that she was wary from the first, and had not let her feel the strength of his love for her.

The peace of the evening gradually took possession of them both, and although they walked for an hour in silence they were almost in tune again by the time they regained the harbour steps, although not a word had passed between them.

'What's the programme for tomorrow, Delia?'

'Well, it does rather depend on the weather, doesn't it?'

He looked down at her, a grin creasing his dark face. She gave him an answering grin, and together they whooped in joyous laughter.

'All right, Paul, you win! Devil take the weather, we'll fix our plans regardless!'

'That's the girl,' he approved. 'I suggest a picnic trip to Kynance Cove. We'll take enough grub to last us most of the day, and we'll finish with a hot meal at an inn, somewhere or other. How's that suit you?'

'Oh, Kynance!' she crooned. 'Blue sea and great rocks with green caps on them, and yellow, yellow sands! What a lovely cove! Oh, Paul, what a wonderful idea for the first day's trip. You are a pet!'

'Do I get a reward?' he asked, lightly, and smiled tantalisingly to chase away that instant wary look in her face. 'Or must I wait until I've done duty as a guide for the day and been inspected and approved?'

A tiny breath of relief escaped her. 'You wait,' she told him, though she was smiling. 'Bring your camera – mine has a horrid trick of sticking, and I couldn't bear to lose any chances of good pictures at Kynance.'

He left her at the gateway of Haley's Gap, with last-minute instructions about the time

189

they would start next day, and she paused in the shadows to listen to his footsteps as he went through the cutting in the rocks to the village beyond. The inn at which he was staying looked very much like Melita's house: white stone, red-tiled, deep-pitted of windows, but with the added attraction of old, carved wood seats outside, and an ancient sign, carrying the arms of the district, in faded red and gold. Delia never discovered the correct name of the inn, but thought it might be known locally as 'Vickers's' since the people (and Paul himself) pronounced it 'Vickerziz.'

It was lonely out there in the shadows, after the last sounds had died away, and she turned, a little regretfully, wishing, as Paul had done earlier in the evening, that he had been staying in the same house with her.

There was a sudden rustle and a figure loomed up out of the darkness into the moonlit patch, where it resolved itself into a tall shape. Delia let out a little startled cry, but Melita's voice answered her, rather crossly it seemed:

'It's all right. It's only me. I got fed up with being in the house on my own, and went for a stroll round the garden. I might have saved myself the trouble. The moonlight gives me the creeps; makes the shadows even blacker.'

Delia agreed about that, and walked back into the house with her. It was as well, she considered, that she and Paul had not in-dulged in a tender farewell, with Melita within easy range and view.

'Where's James, then, Melita?'

Her cousin snorted disgustedly. 'Where he usually is when I think he's going to stay in with me for the evening. Delivering some woman of a child. They make a habit of having them in the evening when the doctor should be off duty – at least, it seems so to me!'

'Oh, well, they say you can't hurry Nature,' Delia soothed. 'You should be pleased to think your husband is doing such a useful job for humanity. I don't mean that to sound priggish, but honestly, Melita, just compare for a minute James and his important work with, say, those husbands who tinker with beaten brass, making useless little oddments to sell at stinking high prices for Christmas gifts, or those men who have the bad luck to sell all day little bits and lengths of stuff to bad-tempered dowagers, over a drapery counter. See what I mean?'

Melita didn't answer. She stood staring in at the kitchen door at a pile of clean-stacked dishes.

'Oh, come on,' Delia said, taking off her jacket and preparing to set out the table for supper. 'Let's knock up a snack. James'll be glad of something when he gets back.'

'I don't want anything,' Melita said, in a

despondent voice. 'Get yourself what you want, Delia.'

'I'll get something for both of us,' Delia answered firmly, 'and we're going to sit down and eat it together. What'll it be? Macaroni cheese? Finish up this bit of fruit and semolina afterwards? Right, and coffee? Or cocoa?'

She bustled about, brightly chatting, partly to forestall interested questions which Melita would surely put about herself and Paul, and partly to stop Melita confiding her own personal troubles. Delia felt she couldn't cope with that tonight.

They sat down together, and Melita approved of Delia's cooking. 'Where'd you learn?' she asked, with interest.

'Oh, from Aunt Cora, I suppose. She's a wizard cook.'

'Yes, I know. I'm not. I mess everything up. Wish we could afford a cook – there's a marvellous one in the village, and I know she'd love to come here. But what's the use? We just can't afford it, and if we could James wouldn't have one. He hates strangers about the place.'

'Oh, lord,' Delia thought, in dismay. 'Here it comes!' and sat back to listen to the torrent of grumbles that preceded a recital of their marital troubles.

After ten minutes of it Delia determinedly broke in: 'What's the case like, the one he's on at present?'

'Oh, the same as any other,' Melita said, indifferently.

'If he were my husband I'd want to go with him to help him, I think,' Delia mused. 'Has he got a nurse of his own?'

'No, he can't afford one,' Melita said, again with bitterness. 'He has some old woman in the village, whose services are buckshee.' She grinned suddenly. 'Oh, there's a professional nurse, quite a nice person, who skates about the place on a bike, with a posh-looking uniform, but you know the Cornishmen. If they can't have the doctor's own employee, they'd rather have their own old women. Daft, isn't it?'

'But typical,' Delia nodded. 'Wonder if it'll be a boy or a girl?'

'Probably won't matter which it is,' Melita said suddenly. 'The mother won't care, anyway. She told me last week she didn't want it, and didn't want to live, anyway.'

'Why?' Delia gasped.

'Oh,' Melita said, indifferently, helping herself to cold fruit and semolina, 'it's a long story. She was the daughter of the doctor who had this place. She married a fisherman, handsome young brute without a bean to his name. Her father was so wild he said he couldn't hold his head up in the place again, so he sold out to James. Let the practice go for a song, he was so anxious to get out, and that's how we happened to get it–'

'–being so hard-up,' Delia finished for her, with a grin. 'Seriously, though, it was a rotten thing for the old man to do, wasn't it?'

'Oh, I don't know. The girl was daft to do it. In a small place like this the doctor has some standing, after all. Besides, it was daft because the fellow was no good to her. He drank like a fish, up at Vickerziz, which isn't so good, being on the doorstep of this house, so to speak. Had to be carried home at night, and there was no money left in his pockets. I think he beat her, too, but I'm not sure. You know how people talk.'

'But what about the baby coming? How will they manage?'

'They? Her, you mean,' Melita said, calmly. 'He got drowned last time the boats went out. He was probably drunk, anyway. James thinks the upset brought the baby on – it's a month early. Why can people like that have children so easily, and I can't?' And Melita suddenly ducked her head on to her arm and was sobbing bitterly. All the old grievances came out between gasps. She had had a baby, it appeared, but it had died still-born. Not by James, but by her first husband. Aunt Cora and Delia had not known that. Melita had not told James about the baby before she married him. She hadn't known then that she couldn't have another, and James, she said, felt badly enough about her first husband, without mentioning a child. James, it appeared, had known Melita first, but she had fancied the second fellow, and married him, and he had died within a few months of her knowing about the child coming.

'Did you love him?' Delia asked, tenderly.

Melita shook her head. 'No, it was James – James all the time. I didn't realise it until after it was too late and I had married Gwynn. James was so solid, such an old stick-in-the-mud. Gwynn was good fun. But good fun's no good as a solid foundation for marriage,' she finished, angrily. 'But I was such a pig-headed fool, no one could tell me.'

'Did James ever find out about the baby?' Delia asked.

'Yes. What d'you think has made him so beastly lately? You know him almost as well as I do – you must have noticed the difference.'

'Yes. I had, and I wondered,' Delia admitted. 'Does Aunt Cora know?'

'Yes, of course.' Melita sounded surprised. 'Didn't she tell you?'

Delia lowered her eyes. 'I'm not living with her now, as you know, and I seldom see her for long enough to do into details. I expect Aunt Cora meant to tell me when she saw me next time. Was James very angry, Melita?'

'I think he was pretty wild. Oddly enough,

not because of the baby but because I hadn't told him at first. Men are funny like that.'

Delia sat talking to her until she was steady again. It was late and Delia felt tired. She wondered whether she might safely suggest going up to her room when James came in.

James was a short man, thin and sensitive of face, with pale thin lips and the eyes of a hurt animal. Tonight he looked more dispirited than Delia thought she had ever seen him before. It was midnight now and he had been called out at 6.30. He dropped his black bag and slumped into a chair. Melita said, 'You're back early. I didn't expect you until the morning.'

He said tiredly, 'They didn't call me until the baby was on the way.'

'What was it?' Melita asked, without much interest. 'A boy or a girl?' And, she thought resentfully, he hasn't even noticed I've been crying.

Delia decided privately that James had lost the baby and knew how he hated that. Melita ought not to have asked him that question.

As James didn't answer Melita looked up at him sharply. He was watching her with a curious, calculating look. He said, quietly, 'It's a boy.'

Melita thrust out her bottom lip. 'She

would have a boy. Was it a whopper or a little tiddler?'

He said, still with the curious look, 'Big enough. Eight pounds eleven ounces.'

'Phew!' she said. 'How marvellous to have a baby that size.'

James said, still looking at his wife, 'His mother didn't think so.'

'Oh, that woman,' Melita said, disgustedly. 'She was always moaning about something. I wish I had had the chance of a bouncing baby boy to bring up. Fancy eight pounds eleven ounces!'

'You may still have that chance,' James said.

Both women looked up at him sharply.

'What do you mean?' Melita gasped. James got up wearily and significantly looked up at the clock.

'I saved the baby but lost the mother.'

CHAPTER 13

Looking back over that month in Cornwall Delia often wondered why she couldn't see clearly then and to realise the way they were drifting, she and Paul – happily drifting amid the lovely, lazy autumn weather in the now deserted beauty of the West Country.

They were such lovely days, healing days, days calculated to wipe out all the memory of the past month in town when she had fretted and chafed over Keith and his affair and ultimate marriage with Susaline and the tiresome business of all the other men who had persisted in flocking round her after Aunt Cora's glamourising of her. It wiped out the memory of Sir Timothy, too, and of slights from such people as Paul's mother. Healing: that was what it was.

She did not realise that Paul was responsible for a lot of this feeling of easement and peace. He was such a wonderful companion, and since that first evening when he had kissed her he had made no move to go back to that mood or to suggest to her in any way that he felt for her in any other way than as a staunch companion and an understanding friend.

She felt she would have such wonderful memories to take back. There were highlights to be picked out. That first day at Kynance Cove when the whole world had seemed a symphony of blue; blue sky and sea, bluish tinge in grey rocks and a bluish tinge about the grass – for this, after all, was autumn and the foliage was failing. That was a day to be remembered; a day of warmth and sunshine, when they had bathed and extravagantly used separate caverns for their dressing rooms. Delia had rather foolishly tried to explore one and had got stuck where the cavern narrowed at the top. It had been an unnerving business being got out and she didn't notice Paul's strained white face so angry was she at being caught by her own childish prank. Then there had been the picnic on the rocks afterwards as they watched the sea come in and the great gulls settle and scream for food. And after that had been the incredible beauty of the wildest of wild sunsets where the rim of the horizon had appeared to burst into flame and had set them talking first on scientific marvels and then on spiritual things. As the sunset had grown wilder in its beauty Delia had experienced a pang of fear. Paul had seen it and understood and held her arm tighter.

'It's all right,' he had said. 'This isn't Italy where things explode or erupt, but it is a bit horrific, isn't it? Anyway, it's just a sign of wind and rain.' And she had felt comforted.

One morning they had gone in the doctor's old car at dawn (Paul driving) out to the last farm in England across the wild Zennor moor where great rocks pierced naked through the short turf; where the narrow road wound up and down and round about so that sometimes the sea was visible on the right hand and sometimes lay directly ahead.

Delia felt that whenever she found a bit of scenery she liked there always popped up to spoil it the stark and tragic stacks of disused tin-mine shafts and the lost, blind-eyed hovels of long deserted villages. Rabbits ran across the roadway, and Paul would brake suddenly with a queer, tender look and a muttered expression such as 'Poor little devil; let's let it get over.'

Once he had come out with a sudden confidence, a fleeting memory of his boyhood days. 'It was June,' he said, 'and my first visit here. They told me I was to look out for magpies, and when I saw one flying up from the hedge they told me to look quickly for some others because it was unlucky if you didn't see three.'

'And did you see three?' Delia asked, with a smile.

'I can't remember now,' he answered, 'but I know I had rotten luck that holiday. I fell when cliff-climbing and broke my leg.'

All these journeys had a curious intimacy. Perhaps because of the deserted time of the year, or because they undertook them early or late. There was the day at Coverack when they hired bikes and set out at dawn. They dropped their cameras in the sea and only one snap of that day – the worst one – came out, that of Paul leaning against the harbour rails smiling at her with an imbecilic grin with his legs missing from the knees downwards. Coverack … that miniature harbour with its tiny, rose-covered cottages above the cliffs and its steeply rising paths.

There was a wet patch the second week of their stay, and ever afterwards Delia thought of Mousehole and Lamorna as mist-grey places of drenching beauty and peace. They squelched through the silent streets of Mousehole together in gum-boots and heavy rain-coats, their food in waterproof satchels on their backs.

Delia said in a hushed voice, 'Mousehole is a secret village. The houses *know* something.'

Paul looked down quizzically at her. There was tenderness in his eyes.

'You know, Delia,' he said, 'I never thought you'd have such deep understanding. They may be dreaming of the fights when the last Spaniards landed here. Can you feel their ghosts? Cornwall is a land of spirits.'

'Yes,' she agreed. 'They seem to be talking to you. I can't quite put it into words, but somehow I'm more alive down here than in town. Town is so practical and prosaic but here it isn't a sin to be imaginative. They are all superstitious and fanciful. There's something almost of the wonder of the child – do you see what I mean? Great, tough he-men who aren't afraid of their imaginations.'

He took her arm with a closer sense of companionship. He, too, was to remember Cornwall place by place, as a land of stepping stones towards his heart's desire. This was Mousehole – that lovely little place

201

where their imaginations had reached out and touched. Two miles further on, in Lamorna, Delia showed her first complete trust in him. They had decided to climb up beyond the harbour. Rain fell, the fine rain that lasts all day. The path was slippery and at times showed signs of having fallen away. Delia hesitated and didn't want to go.

'I'm used to this,' he said. 'It's not really difficult if you put your feet where I tell you.'

It was an idiotic thing to do because he had noticed before that she had no head for heights and he should have left it at that. But she had roused the urge in him to force her to overcome this because she wouldn't admit her fear. Instead, she had a habit of making flimsy excuses. Her feet ached or her shoes were slippery underneath or she was tired and wanted to rest.

'Today,' he said, 'you must do it, Delia. You mustn't let Cornwall make you nervous. You'll miss half its beauties if you don't climb.'

He hadn't known what to expect from that. Certainly not the answer she gave him.

'You think I'm afraid, don't you, Paul? Well, I am. I'm a miserable coward. But that won't stop me doing it just the same because I'm with you.'

She put her hand out firmly and gripped his and with the gesture she put the onus on him. Literally she was putting her life into his hands.

He wished it wasn't a wet day. The path wound sharply upwards and round; a mass of slippery stones and slippery soil. In places the earth had washed away so that a glance down revealed only the boiling sea below. Delia kept on solidly without protest, putting her feet where he told her, trustingly hanging on, doing what she set out to do and not enjoying it a bit. At last he stopped.

'This is no good. It's sheer torture for you, my dear. You'll finish up hating Cornwall and you mustn't do that.'

Relief flooded her face though she said nothing.

He said, 'We'll go down again.'

Terror, blind terror, chased over her face.

'Not *down,*' she whispered.

He said quickly, 'There's no other way, but it's not so bad as you think.'

A frozen look came over her face. 'All right, Paul,' she said, and edged to one side to let him pass and take the lead going down.

Neither of them could recall clearly what happened next. One minute she was securely on the path; the next, there was a tearing of soil and stones and she was gone.

His heart lurched, and he was down flat, leaning over the edge. Somehow her hands were in his, and both were straining to hold on, straining with every ounce of their separate beings. Inch by inch he got her up again on to the path. Her face was wet with rain, and chalk-white with terror. They huddled together in a sitting position on the narrow edge. Delia pressing back against the cliff-face, with her eyes closed.

It was some time before he could get her to move and make the painful journey down, a journey that was punctuated by coaxing and threats, so frightened was she that it would happen again. When they reached the bottom she was near collapse, and let him take her unprotestingly into his arms, murmuring endearments to her, partly to soothe her, partly because he was so beside himself that he forgot all his previous resolutions to withhold his emotions until the end of the holiday.

Then it came to him that she was past understanding what he was saying. She slumped inert against him, conscious only that they were down, and once again on soil that was flat or as near flat as was possible on this coast.

He said, curtly, 'Pull yourself together, Delia. We've got to get to the inn somehow, to get you some brandy. Come to think of it, I could do with a strong drink myself.'

His tone lashed her into action, and she was soon striding along beside him, white of face still, but no longer a shaking mass of frightened female. And Paul being Paul, he made her repeat the experiment the next day (the rain having stopped), and the next and the next, in small doses at first, then attacking steeper climbs. 'You mustn't lose your nerve,' he told her, with conviction, and, like a child, she obeyed him, so long as he was by her side all the time helping her.

Things, Delia noticed, were far less strained at Haley's Gap as the month wore on. Melita moaned less, and was inclined to be more cheerful. One day Paul, in a thoughtful mood, suggested to Delia that they invite James and his wife to accompany them on a day trip somewhere.

'Where d'you think they'd like to go?' he wanted to know.

'Newquay,' Delia said, with a grin. 'Or somewhere similar. Without deck-chairs, restaurants, and a cinema and shops to alleviate the sight of too much sea and rock, poor old Melita won't be up to much by the time the day's over.'

'Newquay's a nice place,' Paul said, staunchly, then, catching Delia's eye, burst out laughing.

But Melita herself chose Truro, and it turned out to be a happy day for all. James wanted again to visit the cathedral, and Melita went round the shops. For Delia and Paul there were enchanting walks up the creeks to choose from.

James, Delia and Paul got back to the car at the proposed time for tea, but Melita was missing.

'Shall we go and find her?' Delia wanted to know.

'All the grub will be gone,' Paul said, grinning.

'Oh, you're just thinking of all those cream cakes we've been looking at, in that tea-shop over the way,' Delia laughed. 'I think men go crazier over sweet things than women do, despite their masculine protests.'

James sat looking ahead, a queer concentrated look on his face, but for once he didn't get angry because Melita was allowing the shops to claim her full attention and keep him waiting.

'What's she gone for, anyway?' Delia asked, curiously. 'I thought it was only to look round.'

'Oh, she was looking for something or other special,' James said, carelessly, but there was a tiny hint of suppressed excitement about him that for the moment puzzled Delia.

When Melita did come back she looked flushed and happy. Delia thought in amazement what a long time it was since she had looked quite like this. Melita was laden with parcels, soft parcels, wrapped in brown bags on which were drapers' and wool-shop advertisements. Delia frowned.

Melita said to James, 'I had a wonderful

time, darling. Got everything I planned to!' and dumped the parcels in the back of the car. 'Come on, you two, I'm starving! Where's this marvellous tea-shop you profess to have discovered?' she cried gaily.

And the mood of gaiety persisted throughout the meal, and all the way home. Melita, for some reason best known to herself, was happy. Shopping did wonders for her, Delia recalled, but she had a feeling that it was something more than mere shopping that had achieved the miracle this time. James was subtly different, too, but on reflection Delia admitted to herself that James had become steadily more human for some days now.

That night, after supper, Delia went to her room to wash her hair and set it, and when she had almost finished Melita knocked softly on the door and poked her head round.

'Delia! May I come in? If I don't talk soon I shall burst!' and without waiting for further invitation she sidled in, her arms full of the parcels she had brought home that day from Truro.

'You seem to be in,' Delia laughed. 'I'm afraid I'll only be able to give you my divided attention until I get these pins all fixed. Oh, Melita, you don't know how lucky you are to have naturally wavy hair – these perms need so much attention unless one doesn't mind looking windswept. Sleek and bandbox being my style, I have to work hard for it!'

'I'll help you,' Melita offered, not so much from a love of doing other people's hair, or indeed of helping them, but because she wanted to get the job over quickly, and grab Delia as an undivided audience.

When it was finished, she said, 'Come over and look at these things I bought today!'

They went and sat on the bed, while Melita feverishly ripped open the parcels, one by one, and laid the contents out all over the bed.

'Baby clothes!' Delia gasped, thoroughly taken by surprise. 'Melita, aren't they utterly lovely?' and she fingered the tiny matinee coats, the wee dresses, vests and pilches with gentle fingers. Most were white, but there were some palest blue garments; some of the white ones had blue ribbon threads through. 'Blue for a boy,' Delia mused.

'Of course,' Melita said, happily. 'Can't you guess? James has got it all fixed up – we're to adopt the wee mite whose mother died the first day you were here!'

CHAPTER 14

Letters came to Delia from Aunt Cora roughly once a week, and in this last week of their holiday it struck Delia that while Aunt Cora had said a lot about Keith and Susaline, and the unfortunate way their marriage was turning out, she had had very little to say about herself. In the past the doings of Aunt Cora had been well to the fore in Miss Grayson's correspondence, not so much because she was self-centred, but because she was so enthusiastic about everything she did, and managed to make the telling of it all quite amusing reading.

Delia wrote back, 'But what have *you* been doing all these weeks? You haven't said a word about that – I do hope you haven't been up to any mischief!'

This invoked an unnaturally prompt reply (as though Miss Grayson had merely been waiting for an opening) and six long pages of close, small handwriting, going into elaborate (often too elaborate) detail. Delia read it through, then read it all again, unbelievingly. Finally she put it down, and felt as if she had sustained a severe blow between the eyes.

The weather was breaking. Delia felt she wouldn't be sorry to get back to town. The smiling, sunshiny face of Cornwall in autumn garb was turning decidedly grey, and although it could hardly be said that it was cold, yet there was enough chill and damp in the air to make it miserable to be out all day long. And she had no wish to be staying in too much at Haley's Gap; James and Melita seemed to have discovered that rather special brand of happiness that precludes even the closest of relatives and friends. It simply wasn't made for sharing. The baby had not yet arrived; legal procedure was still in the balance, and in the meantime the child was being cared for by the old midwife, who was of the opinion that the doctor's flighty young wife was no fitting person to take over too soon a young baby. Melita wasn't altogether sorry. Her idea of a baby was when it had reached the interesting stage; the first month, when it was mainly asleep or demanding food and attention, was the most tiresome time.

Sometimes Delia spent a whole evening with Paul in the cheery warmth of the inn parlour, before a crackling log fire, but after receiving Aunt Cora's letter she had an abstraction about her that Paul was quick to notice.

'Getting tired of being with me so much, Delia?'

'No. No, of course not, Paul! Why do you ask?'

'What is it, then? Cornwall beginning to pall on you?'

'No-o. Not exactly. It is a bit chilly at times, though, and the sea is – menacing I think is the word I want. Don't you feel it?'

'Town-brat!' he teased, laughing. 'Yes, as a matter of fact I do. But don't forget we may still have a few good days in this last week of ours. It's still only October – not really late in the year for this part of the world.'

'Oh, Paul, I'm beginning to ache for town. We've seen everything here, haven't we?'

His face fell. 'Have we, indeed! We haven't been to Polperro yet–'

'Oh, no, I forgot, Paul! Oh, I do so want to see Polperro – I've never been!'

'Or Land's End–'

'Oh, everyone sees Land's End!'

'I know, Delia, but it isn't only the actual Land's End I want you to see. I ought to have taken you there first, when we had that wonderful weather. On really clear days you can see right across to the Scilly Isles. I've only seen those once myself, from England. Have you been there?'

'No. You can only get there in an awful old tub, or a cranky old crate that looks as if the wings'll fall off at any minute.'

He grinned. 'All right. If that's the way you feel, then we rule out the Scillies. But

Land's End is a definite date, my lass, even if we have to go on a misty day and not have any good visibility. And you're going to Polperro if I have to dot you on the head and drag you there!'

But even his banter could not draw forth more than a very fleeting smile, and he wondered again whatever could be the matter. She had been drawing closer and closer to him by degrees, so much so that he had almost made up his mind about what he was going to do towards the end of this, their last week.

'Delia, won't you tell me what's wrong?' he asked, gently, pushing another glass of cider over to her.

She shrugged. 'Oh, it's sort of lonesome at Haley's Gap. James and Melita talking babies, thinking babies, planning babies. The cot arrived today, and Melita's been poring over catalogues from the stores up in Town. Why does everyone seem convinced that you must send to London for really good value? I should have thought Truro would have had quite decent cots and prams! The perambulator she's picked out, by the way, is the biggest, the most stream-lined, the most vulgarly light colour, the most ostentatious pram I've ever seen!'

Paul laughed quietly. 'Jealous? Delia, I'm surprised at *you!* After all, Melita can't have children of her own – this is rather an event in her life, and if she's got any sense she can see it's had the effect of bringing back her husband to her.'

'Yes, but they're always shouting poverty–'

'My dear, when the one and only baby bursts into life isn't that the time to make a bit of a financial splash? Well, that's the way I'd feel about it, anyway, and if old James feels the same, good luck to him!'

'But I keep thinking of the poor mother in that miserable little grave on the edge of the churchyard. And that quiet, unattended funeral.' Delia shivered a little. 'Who cared that she'd died? No one in this village – she was an alien, marrying one of the fishermen. A foreigner the villagers called her. No one among her own people – they considered it unmitigated bad taste to marry the wastrel of the village (and probably they were right), but, after all, the fellow must have had something to attract her. She must have cared for him to want to die when he had died.'

'Oh, I think perhaps she was rather fed-up with her position here, and the fact that her father disowned her. Bitter old cuss he must have been, and James gave me to understand she had always been a poor thing, not much spirit to stand up to people. He didn't seem surprised that she'd caved in and not cared a damn.' He sat staring into the fire. 'But I agree with you it wanted a bit of doing for her father not even to attend the funeral.'

'Yes,' Delia said, in a low, furious voice. 'Fancy telling James to fix everything, and to send him the bills. Oh, that was beastly, beastly!'

'Have they decided what they're going to call the baby, yet?' Paul wanted to know.

'Um. Melita wants it to be Jimmy, after James. James has decided to give it its mother's maiden name as one of its Christian names, and to arrange for it to legally take over his surname. Young Jimmy Grayson'll be lucky, with the background he'll get. It wouldn't have been so good if that drunken clod of a father had lived.'

'I suppose being the grandson of the previous doctor made a difference to your cousins adopting it,' Paul hazarded.

Delia shrugged. 'Well, of course ... they do know what sort of family is behind it. Not like a stranger's baby.'

'But you're not going to tell me that's all that's bothering you,' Paul persisted. 'Is it Sir Timothy? Have you heard from him? He isn't still pestering you to marry him, is he?'

'How did you know–?' Delia began.

'My dear, do you think that it has escaped anyone's notice the attentions he's been paying you? Chiverstock's been watching you both with a lively interest for some time, you know.'

Delia flushed a deep red and looked away. Paul misconstrued, and thought she was merely embarrassed at his mentioning the matter.

'I'm sorry, Delia, but, you see, I know you and they don't. I know you won't marry the fellow, because you're not in love with him, and you've too much integrity to marry just for money and position. Besides, I know, too, that you wouldn't show *me* such deep friendship as you have this last few weeks if you'd been meaning to marry Sir Timothy.'

'No. You're right,' she said, in a weary little voice.

'Has he been bothering you?' Paul persisted.

'No. I haven't heard from him. I don't think I shall, either,' Delia said.

'Oh, why?'

'I told him before I came away that I didn't think I could marry him. It wasn't definite, but I think he's pretty sure I don't care for him. He's proud, and he wouldn't make a nuisance of himself.'

Paul let it go at that, but he felt she was holding something back from him. He didn't ask if she'd heard from her aunt. It wouldn't have made any difference to him if she had, because her aunt was the only person who did write to her, and he was well aware that they always mentioned Pemberley and his wife. But he hardly thought Delia was still bothered about them.

'I'm tired, Paul. I think I'll turn in early,'

Delia said, suddenly, and without question he took her back to James's house, and left her. He was puzzled, and a little hurt that she didn't confide in him, but he wouldn't dream of pressing her any further.

She escaped Melita and James after the briefest cup of cocoa, and hurried to her room, where she again took out Miss Grayson's letter.

'I hardly know how to tell you this, my dearest Delia, for fear of hurting you; you see, you seem to have grown away from me just lately, and the confidences we used to enjoy have vanished. I have no way, therefore, of knowing how you felt about Sir Timothy, or whether you will mind if I tell you he had become interested in someone else.'

Behind the carefully worded phrases Aunt Cora's face appeared anxious, distressed. A few months ago tears would have pricked Delia's eyes at the thought of her aunt being so bothered on her own account, but now ... after this letter Delia felt numb. There was nothing left. No feeling of tenderness, or, indeed, of resentment. It was true she hadn't confided in her aunt of late. Not because she no longer loved her as the mother she had always been, but because she had been growing away, in a process of growing up.

'I ought to have left Aunt Cora long before,' she told herself, irritably, as she again took up

216

the letter. 'It would have made it that much less hard for her to bear the breaking away. Funny thing, parents and guardians never believe one ever grows away from them, and becomes an individual!'

She rustled the closely written sheets impatiently, and read once more:

'Sir Timothy telephoned me one afternoon, to have a chat about you. It seemed to strike him as strange that you should be so ready to go away for a whole month if you still cared for him enough to marry him, yet he felt from the way you answered his proposal that you were not intending to say yes.'

At that point, in the first reading, Delia had been furious at the thought of her employer and her aunt discussing her at length, over the telephone, but in the light of what followed the whole thing took on quite a different complexion.

'He seemed to want to talk about it at greater length, and asked me to dine with him.'

A flicker of a smile crossed Delia's face. Aunt Cora being Aunt Cora, she would probably have gone carefully through her wardrobe for something to suit the situation. She would probably have chosen her purple velvet dinner gown, as her idea of what a guardian should wear on the occasion of discussing her niece's probable future with a desirable male such as Sir Timothy. She would be aware, too, that the depth of the purple made her pale hair gleam almost white. Yes, Aunt Cora certainly looked fine in that dinner gown.

'I'm afraid we got on to other subjects, and found we had many mutual friends and interests. He asked me to dine with him again, and – to tell you the truth – we've seen quite a lot of each other during this month.'

The whole tone of Miss Grayson's letter was rather apologetic, as though the thought of her niece's employer getting very friendly with her was somehow *infra dig*. Yet for Delia, reading between the lines, the letter conjured up a series of very clear pictures.

Aunt Cora, looking regal in sweeping black lace, at the theatre; in correct mist-blue tweed at the races; in her one rather lovely fur coat on that chilly day when he had insisted on taking her to a very dull exhibition of paintings, and then on to his home to meet his sister, with whom she had got on very well. Aunt Cora was an asset to any man, Delia had to admit. She had poise, breeding, a fund of the right remarks to make with rare charm in the right places, and a delicacy and wit which made handling people child's play to her, and play that she enjoyed very much.

'And so, my dear, when Sir Timothy asked me if I would care to share his life with him,

I admitted that I would. I did not feel that I was robbing you of anything, because if you had wanted him truly you would have said so before you went away.'

'Oh, for heaven's sake,' Delia muttered to herself. 'Did she have to rub that bit in so much?'

It appeared that in the midst of their enjoyment of each other's company, and their sober yet none the less happy plans for their future, Sir Timothy and Aunt Cora had realised what a difficult position it would be for Delia, who was still, of course, Sir Timothy's secretary, and had no income of her own to enable her to give up that post to ease the general position. Besides, she was still keeping on a rather expensive flat from her salary, although she had been living in Aunt Cora's flat while Miss Grayson had been in Cornwall. That maisonette was still being paid for, week by week, while she was away, and Delia could see how Miss Grayson was nervously totting up the bill, knowing that Delia had dipped well into her savings to pay for her glamourising.

'Thank goodness she didn't know how much I really did spend on all those new clothes,' Delia chuckled, 'though I've still got the main part of it untouched. (Thank heavens!) But I'd have loved to be there when they were both discussing me and my miserable future.

'Sir Timothy and I feel we want to see you settled as his niece-by-marriage should be settled. There'll be an important social life for you now, my dear, and we both hope that you'll enter it with us, just to please us. You're quite beautiful now, you know,' Aunt Cora had written, conservatively, obviously afraid of her praise going to Delia's head, yet determined to face the obvious truth. 'And there'll be some splendid matrimonial chances for you in this new life, if you will allow Sir Timothy and I to launch you. Of course, we wouldn't expect you to live in the same house as us, but we would like you to accept an adequate allowance, so that you could keep on your flat, and dress according to your new position.'

For the tenth time of reading this paragraph Delia's face flamed. What did they think she was, she who could have been Lady Nodeleigh herself such a short while ago, if she'd wanted to? Now they wanted to kick her out of her job, pay her a good allowance to make her presentable, and marry her off to a suitable young man, out of harm's way! Oh, it was outrageous and just like Sir Timothy.

She allowed herself again to fume over it, until reason once more asserted itself. Aunt Cora would have told Sir Timothy about Keith and Susaline. Sir Timothy could hardly be expected to see Keith as she herself saw him; as the boy next door with whom she had grown up, who had foolishly married a girl like Susaline, and now in his misery turned to Delia for spiritual comfort, and that Delia found she couldn't get him out of her system. That was all, she told herself crossly. Yet she knew very well how Sir Timothy was regarding Delia Grayson. As his one-time prospective bride, now making a nuisance of herself over someone else's husband! And that, Delia admitted with fairness, was exactly how the rest of Chiverstock would look at it.

Wild thoughts chased through her head. She would leave the town. Go and find another job in some other place. Cut herself off from relatives and friends. Live a separate life where they couldn't single her out for their beastly charity.

Then these thoughts passed, and she went back to the letter. 'We do so hope you will do this, just to please us, my dear, and we want you to attend the wedding, too, of course.'

The final insult, Delia raged. But, of course, she would have to attend the wedding. It would look so bad otherwise.

What a rotten end to a perfectly lovely holiday, she told herself. Why hadn't she seen this coming? Of course, Sir Timothy already showed signs of interest in Aunt Cora the first night he took them both out together. It was, she supposed, inevitable that he should find a gracious woman of Aunt Cora's years (forty-five, wasn't she?) more acceptable to filling the place of his wife than someone young and fun-loving like herself. In all honesty she would have found it deadly dull, entertaining the sort of people whom Sir Timothy liked, and Sir Timothy himself was somehow not capable of putting the tremendous life into his pleasure that Paul, for instance, did. It was odd the way quiet old Paul compared with Sir Timothy. That very quietness of Paul's was, when you thought about it, filled with life and virility. There was strength in it, and ... youth.

Delia sighed. Life was so beastly difficult. Always something cropped up that jolted you out of your complacent rut. Why couldn't it all stay put for just a little while? Why did that silly Keith have to go and marry Susaline? They could have been so happy together, Keith and herself. They had known each other all their lives, and were used to each other. Surely that was the ideal basis for marriage?

At that point she heard Melita coming upstairs, and she wondered if she could put out her light and pretend to be asleep. But it wasn't Delia's way to descend to subterfuge, so she waited, feeling that she needed nothing less than Melita's bright chatter at this moment. She hastily folded up Aunt Cora's letter and put it away, as Melita poked her head round the door.

'Oh, not asleep, Delia? Thought you were tired! Why, you haven't even undressed!'

'No, I just slumped into the first chair, and sat,' Delia said, with truth. 'I didn't know I could be so tired.'

'Oh!' Melita hesitated. 'Well, you won't want me here if that's the way you feel, but I saw your light through the curtains, and thought I'd come up. There's something I wanted to say to you.'

She still waited, so Delia smiled and patted the edge of the bed near her.

'All right. Come on in, if it's a chin-wag you want!'

'Oh no. It isn't that at all,' Melita protested. 'It was just – well, to tell you the truth, James and I were just talking about you. We're so happy together, with the baby soon coming and all, and we feel we want everyone else to be happy, too. Well, we got to talking about you, and this being your last week's holiday here, and everything and ... Delia, has Paul proposed to you?' she suddenly burst out breathlessly.

'Eh?' Delia looked blank.

'Well, hasn't he?' Melita was disappointed. 'If he hasn't yet, he's going to – isn't he? Don't say I've read all the signs wrong. I must be slipping.'

Delia had a queer feeling go over her. Paul.

In her feverish thinking about Sir Timothy and Keith, the two men who loomed largest in her life, she hadn't taken into consideration the man who had been by her side for nearly a month. So easily and naturally had Paul slipped into the rôle of the companion-perfect, that she just hadn't seen him in any other rôle. With all the things that had happened this last three or four weeks she had forgotten how tender and near to love-making he had been that first night.

'Oh! I hadn't thought,' she said, in a low voice.

'Well, you *are* a nitwit,' Melita said, frankly. 'I've been waiting for it hourly. You can see a mile off the fellow's crazy about you. Wonder why he's held off so long?'

Delia said, in a kind of wonderment, 'You mean he's in love with me?'

''Course, fathead! You're not in love with him, are you?'

'No.' Delia's answer was definite. 'But I'm awfully fond of him.'

She hardly heard Melita's chatter flowing on, so stricken was she with the thought of how good and kind and gentle and forbearing Paul had been all this time, when all the while he had been aching with love for her, and not daring to say it for fear she flew at him, or took it into her head to go off back to Chiverstock. Poor Paul.

'I'm not presuming to give you advice,'

Melita's voice jerked her back to attention. 'But remember, won't you, that I married the man I thought I was crazy about, when poor old James stuck around in that faithful way of his, and I couldn't see he'd make the best husband. I was lucky, I soon got free to marry James after all, and he still wanted me. But everyone isn't that lucky.'

'What's that in aid of?' Delia asked, smiling, but guiltily aware that Melita was thinking about her feelings for Keith.

'I'm not going to pry,' Melita said, getting up to go. 'You know best what you're up to. But it stuck out a mile, when I was staying with Aunt Cora, that the handsome blond upstairs interests you more than somewhat. But he's well and truly booked for life, duckie, and if you don't mind my saying so, he doesn't look like the type who'd go heavily for divorce, even if wifie did take it into her head to clear off with some dancing bloke. I know the type.'

Melita wasn't clever, but she had the good fortune to know when she'd said enough. She got up then, and said good-night. Into the silent room, after she had quietly closed the door behind her, Delia felt a breath of fresh air creep. Melita's words had done her good. Melita might be frivolous, discontented at times, kicking against the grain, and wishing for the moon. But having discovered her own mistake, she was too good-natured to keep it to herself. She wanted Delia to have the benefit of it, and had had the courage to come out with it, where her husband would have been inclined not to interfere.

'Well,' he said, when Melita went downstairs to him; 'did you get thrown out for your pains?'

'No, I didn't, James, and, to tell you the truth, I'm rather glad I didn't do as you wanted me to. I think we'd have been wrong to say nothing. That ass Delia wasn't even aware that her nice man-friend was aching to marry her. I've given her something to think about, I can tell you!'

James grunted. He didn't like to feel he was in the wrong. Moreover, he firmly believed that no one had the right to interfere in someone else's love affair, particularly with someone as complex as Delia.

'I hope our meddling won't have a disastrous result, that's all!' he said, gloomily.

But he needn't have worried. There were other factors for Delia to consider, after Melita had left her. She had to keep up her end, in view of her embarrassing position where Sir Timothy was concerned. She had to rescue herself from the invidious situation in which she had put herself, regarding Keith, for it seemed (after what Melita had said) that she had most shamelessly worn her heart on her sleeve and that at most everyone was aware of it, and in a small town like Chiverstock that wasn't wise or comfortable. There remained for her the alternatives of letting Sir Timothy and Aunt Cora marry her off (a course from which she shrank) and that of going around with the local boys who had shown such an interest in her since she had acquired a new exterior via the beauty parlour. She shuddered.

If Melita had spoken the truth there remained Paul.

Delia thought all round the situation. The main thought that kept recurring was that it wouldn't be fair to Paul to say yes if he asked her, since he was in love with her, and she had nothing so deep to offer him in return. But Melita had hinted that a happy marriage need not necessarily be founded upon mutual love. Was that true? Or were James and Melita an exceptional couple? Finally, she weakly gave in, because she was tired, and because the swamping effect of all these problems was too much.

She told herself, as she slowly and tiredly got undressed, that if Paul still wanted her to marry him after she had made it clear to him that she was not in love with him, she would let the onus rest on him.

Paul left it to the last day. That much he had managed, because he had promised himself not to worry her before, but it had been a hard struggle.

They had been to Polperro. Delia looked flushed and happy when at last, after walking round the quaint, narrow old streets, looking at the tiny stream that ran between the two main rows of houses and hotels, and examining the contents of the antique shops, she found what she wanted: a quaint old urn carved out of stone.

'I think Aunt Cora will love that, don't you, Paul?'

'Yes. It's just her taste. Keep it till we call for it, will you?' he asked the dealer. 'We don't want to lug that all round for the rest of the day.'

Delia made to leave the shop.

'What's this made of?' she heard Paul ask the dealer, and found him examining a strange trinket, on a thin gold chain.

'It's an anchor, isn't it?' she asked.

'It's ivory,' the dealer told them.

'D'you like it, Delia?' Paul asked.

'An anchor,' she repeated, without answering him. 'That's it,' she said, looking up at him with a new light dawning in her eyes.

'What is, my dear?'

She laughed, a little shakily. 'Oh, nothing. Just a silly idea of mine. Yes, it's a beautiful piece of work, and a very unusual trinket,' but she put it down and sauntered to the shop door.

Paul nodded to the dealer, who wrapped it

up, and after settling the bill he hurried after Delia. She had left the shop and was staring thoughtfully down into the deep inlet that formed such a wonderful natural harbour. He stood behind her, taking it all in: the tiers of quaint old stone houses, one upon the other, in a half-circle above the inlet, and the green of the shoulder of the cliffs, high up behind.

'I want to remember this day for ever,' Delia said. 'I wonder if I'll ever come here again? D'you know, Paul, I don't think I want to. This day's been so perfect it could never be like it twice. No, this'll have to last me a lifetime. Polperro only happens once.'

'The day isn't over yet,' he reminded her, and together they made their way towards the sea, up through the winding rock steps to the place where the green cliff-tops began, and up and over the high bluffs till the little village was hidden, and only short green turf high above the incredible blue of the Channel was to be seen.

They sat down on one of the wooden benches which dotted the cliff paths, and Delia sighed in contentment.

'I'm happy, Paul,' she said, and smiled into his eyes.

'With Cornwall? Or ... with me?'

'Both,' she said, with scrupulous regard for the truth, but added, to his delight, 'Cornwall couldn't do it on its own, though.'

He got out the trinket. 'You liked it, didn't you, Delia?'

She took it in gentle hands. 'Oh, Paul, I didn't mean you to ... it's such an expensive thing...'

'If I give it to you, will you tell me what you meant in the shop?'

She wrinkled her brows. 'I'll try. It's a feeling I have about you. It isn't exactly that I want to lean on you, because I'm hardly the leaning type. With a job like I've got' – she hesitated, recalling suddenly that she no longer had the job, at least not for very long – 'with a job like Sir Timothy's secretary has to hold down,' she amended, 'one loses the urge to lean. But with you I feel sort of ... safe. You reminded me of something, and I couldn't place it till I saw the anchor. You *are* an anchor, Paul.'

He slipped the chain round her neck. 'Could you do with an anchor for the rest of your life, Delia?'

It wasn't exactly the way she thought he'd frame the question. She had reckoned on his asking her if she loved him, so that she could explain her feelings. Now, it was difficult to attempt to do that, since he had expressed no wish to know how she felt. He merely asked if she could do with an anchor, and for the moment she asked for nothing more.

'Yes, Paul,' she said, sincerely. 'That's just what I could do with.'

CHAPTER 15

Miss Grayson and Sir Timothy were married in London by special licence, and went off straight away to the South of France for a four-week honeymoon. It was the middle of November and Sir Timothy wanted to be back well before Christmas, because of the pressing needs of business. To that end he had extracted a promise from Delia to stay on and train the new girl, the one he had picked himself from the typing pool, to take over the job of secretary, and Delia was to leave on his return.

Cornwall seemed far away, Delia thought, as she stood at the window of his room one day towards the end of that grey, dismal month looking at the square, and the people hurrying about huddled into topcoats, and the leaden sky that threatened snow. It had been such lovely weather down there, on the whole, and the return to Chiverstock coinciding with the break in the Indian summer had seemed to her merely a precipitating of herself and Paul from a semi-tropical climate into the bleakness of the north so sharp had been the contrast.

It had not been easy coming back in this

fashion. It had been something of an ordeal to face the battery of curious eyes, not only on the score of her leaving her job, but because everyone had seemed so confidently to expect that she would be Sir Timothy's new wife. No one knew exactly what had happened to bring about the change of arrangements, although there were many wild rumours. From Delia herself they could, of course, get nothing by way of confirmation. She was sternly businesslike, though pleasant, but the combination was tedious to keep up. Remarks like:

'I bet you've got a smashing job to go to, to give up this one, Miss Grayson,' from daring typists, merely brought from her a lift of the eyebrows, a vague smile, or a 'Do you?'

Older members of the staff, such as the elderly cashier, who put on a persuasive front, and ventured, 'You know, my dear, I've known you since you first entered the firm, and it grieves me to hear all these rumours about you. Wouldn't it be better to just tell everyone the truth, and put a stop to all this wild surmising?' almost startled the truth out of her.

With her careful reply, 'There's no need for people to listen to rumours – after all, it's my business, not theirs, what I do, isn't it?' he subsided, dissatisfied, and he left her with a greater feeling of tenseness. She must be on her guard all the time, she told herself fiercely, *all* the time.

She told Paul about it, with reluctance. There was a thoughtful look in his eyes, as he asked the inevitable question: 'When did you first hear about your aunt and her wedding, Delia?'

She had to admit, 'In Cornwall, but I couldn't tell you then, Paul. It would somehow have spoilt the holiday.'

That was before the wedding. Aunt Cora had thoughtfully asked him to attend with Delia, although she had only a hint of what was going to happen. Delia had insisted on Paul's giving her a month, before tying her down to an official engagement. Engagements in Chiverstock meant an announcement in the local paper, and she was not quite ready for that yet. Something – she couldn't say what – held her back from that. She was not quite ready. Paul seemed happy enough in having an understanding with her, and waiting the full month, but there was a slight, almost imperceptible change in his manner. A wariness, as if he were not quite sure of her, and was puzzled.

'I would have been happier, Delia, if you could have told Sir Timothy you were going to marry me.'

'I know, Paul. I'd have liked that, too, except ... he's such a stickler for the conventional. He'd have wanted me to announce it right away, and have publicity and all that – you know what he's like. Aunt Cora's like it, too. Those two are a pair.'

'And you? Why don't you want the whole world to know? Not ashamed of the poor match you're making, are you?'

She flushed. 'That's unkind. But merited, I suppose. Honestly, Paul, it wasn't that at all. To tell you the truth, after that holiday in Cornwall, with its lovely intimacy, I didn't want prying eyes staring at us both. I didn't want people saying, "Oh, a holiday romance." You know the way they do talk! I wanted to keep it to ourselves, for the time being, anyway.'

'Sure it isn't Pemberley still in your system?' he asked, and there was almost a harsh note in his voice.

'You've no right to say that!' she flashed, in sudden anger.

'Haven't I?'

'All right, then, Paul, perhaps you have. If you must know, it is Keith. Oh, Paul, be thankful I'm the sort who wants to face her marriage with an absolutely clear mind. That's all it is, honestly! I want to know, for sure, once and for all, that I'm not feeling the old way for him any more. Remember, I've known him all my life. It's hard to weed out someone you've cared for over a period of so many years. I don't want to marry you with a dread of coming face to face with him in the street, and Chiverstock's such a small place.'

'We might not live here when we married.'

'Well, that's worse still, Paul. It would seem like running away from something I couldn't face, and if we ever had to come back – as we should, you know, if only to go through the town on the way to visiting Aunt Cora – I'd have the old dread. You wouldn't like that, would you?'

'I'd like to feel I took first place in my wife's thought so that no other fellow could ever intrude,' Paul said, stiffly. 'Are you trying to tell me that this is the reason you've decided to live in your aunt's flat while she's away?'

'No. No, you know that isn't true. Aunt Cora asked me to, to give an eye to the place. They didn't want to stop and settle the sale of the house before they were married. And there are so many things of Aunt Cora's there that she'll want to take with her, and she can't trust Susaline. Who could?'

'I don't see why she couldn't change the locks, and leave the place sealed up,' Paul said, reasonably.

'Well,' Delia reluctantly admitted, 'I haven't seen Keith for so long. Seeing him every day *now*, in his quarrelsome moods, might have the effect of putting me off him for ever.'

'It's a dangerous experiment, Delia,' Paul

said, and she could see he didn't like it.

That was when she had first taken on the flat, two weeks ago. There were two more weeks to go, and she could see that she was no nearer her clearing up of her own doubts.

It was true that she now had a greater opportunity of seeing Keith at all odd times, and could see how he had changed from the pleasant boy that she and her aunt had once known. But then she also had an opportunity of seeing Susaline at the same time, and so far she felt that her sympathies were going all out to Keith.

Susaline had just reached the ungainly stage of her time. She had, to her grief and rage, lost that perfect little figure she had had, and was of necessity wearing loose clothing, and flat, comfortable shoes. Each time she saw Delia (who had since her return to Town resumed her up-to-the-minute wardrobe) it was like fresh fuel to the flames.

'Go on – look at her! She's just going out in some new finery!' Delia once heard Susaline scream at Keith, and, unable to resist the temptation of looking back, she saw his white face at the window. She knew she was good to look at, but she also knew that if a man really loved his wife he should feel that in her condition she was the more important subject in his eyes.

'I won't marry Paul if that's the way men feel about their wives when the figure's gone!' Delia told herself fiercely, but she knew that it wasn't only that factor that was making Keith unwilling to show the same affection to Susaline. It was Susaline's constant complaining, nagging, picking quarrels all the time.

'I want to go out – I never go out now, not even to the flicks! Why don't you take me out, Keith Pemberley? Ashamed to be seen with me now?' Delia would hear Susaline scream at her unfortunate husband.

What Keith said in reply was often indistinct, but sounded as if it might be propitiating. Sometimes he would snap at her, 'Oh, for heaven's sake get ready, then, and let's go out!' but Susaline would reply to that, that if that was the way he felt about it she wouldn't trouble him, she was sure, and then the inevitable quarrel would flare up and continue far too long. Afterwards, Keith would slam down the stairs and out of the house, and Delia would watch him with an ache in her heart as he slouched, with hunched shoulders, and hat pulled down, a tragic caricature of his former self, up the street and away for hours.

'I want to go dancing!'

'Susaline, be sensible, you can't go dancing, in your condition.'

'My condition! My condition! Who got me into this condition, Keith Pemberley? Tell me that! I bet it was because you didn't want me to go dancing any more! A fine way to keep me home, a rotten way, just like you *would* choose! Oh, I should have known, from the first, what marriage with you would be like. I was a fool. A damned fool.'

'Why *did* you marry me, Susaline?'

'I thought you'd be good fun. You could dance better than anyone I knew, and when you married me you stopped going dancing. You cheated, you cheated!'

Tears would follow, and Keith would be exhausted in his efforts to calm her down.

'Think of the child, Susaline – you'll do it an injury, and possibly yourself.'

'I don't care! I don't want it – think I want to spend my days pushing a pram and washing nappies! Oh, I hate you, Keith Pemberley, I hate you!'

All the quarrels went on those lines. Delia knew their separate replies by heart. She was tired of hearing it all. Tired of making inroads in her larder to save Susaline going out, because she couldn't bear to see Keith going out, ashamed, with a bedraggled shopping bag on his arm and a list in his hand. Tired of shutting the windows on fine days so that neighbours wouldn't hear more of it all than was absolutely necessary. Tired of banging about on the days when the windows were closed yet Susaline's abuse was still clear enough to be heard up the street; banging about in the hope that she would at least make indistinct the things those two upstairs were shouting at each other in a futile attempt to wound and inflame. Yet Delia couldn't bring herself to close the flat and go back to her own place before Aunt Cora returned from her honeymoon.

Last night had been the worst so far. Susaline had caught sight of Delia in her new winter coat, a lovely swinging thing of deep emerald green, trimmed with soft bands of dark brown fur, with a tiny fur hat and muff to match. She had been going to see Paul at the rep. He was gay and happy. He had been given the part for the lead, the one promised him before he went away to Cornwall. He was making the grade, by leaps and bounds, and Delia had felt a glow of pride as she had watched him at his work. But for Susaline, from the upper window, there had been no admiration, only bitterness, and the memory of her bitter young face had haunted Delia all through that happy evening.

She had heard the girl say to Keith, 'I'm not standing for it any more. I'm going out in smart clothes. I don't care, I'm going out in high-heeled shoes, and I'm going out in my smart things I had just before – you try and stop me and see!'

The cry of a cheated child, Delia thought, as she moved away from the window of Sir Timothy's room and returned to the filing.

Susaline, of course, would not be so foolish. Or would she? Who would tell how that curious mind of hers would work, all the hours she was left alone in the top flat of Miss Grayson's house, while Keith was at the bank? All those hours when other women were busy over gas-stove or sink, or with essential sewing or knitting, preparing... Susaline had refused to prepare a thing.

'I don't want the baby – let it come, with nothing to wear! Buy some things if you want to see it look nice!' she had yelled at Keith one evening.

Delia felt depressed. She resolutely attacked the filing, but through her head rang thoughts that threatened to put her work into confusion. For a woman like Susaline, with nothing but resentful thoughts and little to do, it was a dangerous thing to do, sitting up there at that window, with the quiet street below, and not a soul to see or speak to.

Might Susaline carry out her threat? If she did, what harm could it do?

Delia angrily pushed Susaline out of her thoughts, and Keith went with her. 'I won't let them worry me like this,' she told herself, and determinedly got out Aunt Cora's last letter, a letter which spoke of brilliant sunshine and a gay life. New clothes, new people, new kinds of entertainment, and a rippling tone of happiness which even in

Aunt Cora's equable temperament was something new and to be taken note of. Suddenly Delia was glad that Aunt Cora had married Sir Timothy, despite the awkwardness of the situation for herself.

'Yes, I truly *am* glad,' she found herself thinking. 'Aunt Cora's taken care of herself, preserved her appearance and figure, kept up her interest in clothes and people and happenings. She deserves something like this!'

That, at least, made a brighter turn to this dismal day. Delia had never liked filing, and had always made a point of attacking the job with a brightness of manner which suggested she loved it, and no one but herself knew her true feelings about it.

Miss Turner, the new secretary, came in at that moment.

'Oh, you've finished it, Miss Grayson!' she said. 'I've only just got through the letters, or I'd have come before.'

'Never mind, there was a biggish batch,' Delia said. 'I think you've a fair idea of the filing system now, anyway, and I wanted something to do.'

'You like filing, don't you?' Miss Turner said, wandering over to the window cabinet with an empty basket.

'It's an important thing, and one that grows on you,' Delia said, evasively, and hoped she didn't sound priggish.

241

'Funny the way in most firms the job's given to juniors,' Miss Turner commented. 'I think the secretary *should* do it, don't you?'

She stopped to look out of the window before coming back to the table where Delia stood. Delia looked speculatively at her neat back, her smoothly brushed dark hair, and her impeccable though unspectacular appearance, and wondered if Sir Timothy would suggest the girl getting beauty treatment as Delia herself had done.

The thought was chased from her mind by a gasp from Miss Turner. 'Oh – she's over! What a smack – I bet she's hurt herself.'

'Someone fallen down?' Delia asked, walking quickly to the window.

'Miss Grayson, look!' the other girl said, a startled note in her voice. 'It's Mrs Pemberley, isn't it? She's going to have a baby, too. She can't get up!'

Delia stared at the small, blonde figure on the opposite pavement, spread-eagled and still, her handbag a few yards away, and a small crowd rapidly collecting.

'Susaline! Heavens, she's done it now!' Delia heard herself mutter, in horror.

'Here, Miss Turner, hang on here – I've got to go down to the bank and tell her husband. No, wait – the bank'll be closed now. You telephone the bank, let him know what's happened. He may not have been near the windows at the time. I'll go down to her, maybe see about the ambulance...'

All the time she was speaking Delia was struggling into her coat, grabbing her handbag and gloves, and finally dashed out of the room leaving the last sentence in mid-air, unfinished. Miss Turner watched her thoughtfully.

Keith had been told by one of the other clerks who had been near the bank windows at the time. He came out without his coat on, and ran by Delia's side without recognising her.

'Go back and get your coat, Keith!' she shouted. 'I'll go on. You'll probably have to go with her, you know!'

He did as she said, without a word, and joined her in a minute or two. Snow began to fall. Someone had fetched an ambulance in those few minutes. The hospital was a short distance away, just outside the town. Susaline had been carried into a nearby shop and was being supported in a chair. She had strained her ankle and was in pain, but whether from the ankle or other causes or both it was difficult to say. Her eyes were closed, and there was a bluish tinge round her mouth. She moaned incessantly.

Delia pushed her way to the front. 'Susaline, it's all right. It's Delia. Keith's coming. Don't worry.'

Susaline's eyes opened, and she stared

glassily. 'Go away,' she muttered. 'Hate you! Hate you!'

'What's she say?' someone asked.

They all hazarded different translations of the slurred murmur that came from Susaline's lips, but it was Delia only who heard. She straightened up and stood by Susaline's side, silent and tight-lipped, until Keith came over.

He said, 'Thanks, Delia. I've got the rest of the day off. Told the manager what had happened. She'll be all right, won't she?'

Someone said, 'Here comes the ambulance.'

The two attendants pushed their way through before Delia had time to answer, and she was glad. Keith's pathetic question hung lifeless in mid-air. There was no reassuring answer to be made to it. No one in the crowd, least of all Delia, was hopeful about Susaline's being all right.

CHAPTER 16

Delia went in the ambulance with Keith and Susaline. There was no nurse there. The man who had had the forethought to telephone for the ambulance had not mentioned that it was a maternity case. It was possible that he thought it was an ordinary road accident. He looked a little busybody of a man, the sort who would rush off and telephone for an ambulance without bothering to ask helpful questions first.

'Will she die?' Keith asked, looking at Susaline's drawn face and purple lips.

'Oh, I don't think so,' Delia lied. 'I wish I knew what to give her. I've got a small flask of brandy in my bag, but I'm not sure...'

Keith said, 'Smelling salts might help?' but Delia shook her head.

At intervals he asked nervous questions. His voice had lost some of its strength, and showed signs of breaking.

'Will the baby be hurt, Delia?'

'Delia, do you think she'll have another child later?'

'Oh, it won't stop her dancing, will it, Delia?'

To all of them Delia made the stock answer in varying forms. 'We don't know, Keith. You mustn't think the worst. We can only hope and pray.'

'Pray?' He looked bewildered at her, and it came to her then that he never attended church, although she and Aunt Cora had often asked him to go with them. Paul and she had slipped into an easy habit of church-going together in Cornwall, and he had the unembarrassed air of a man who is not unused to attending church services.

She shrugged away the memory. No time for thinking about Paul now. She had to give her full attention to Keith.

It was a curious feeling she experienced towards him in that ambulance. It was a short journey, yet it seemed to her to hold them suspended throughout the ages. She was seeing a new Keith, a Keith rather like a small boy who desperately needed help but was just growing up enough to feel that he was too old to ask for it.

Would Susaline die? She asked herself the question unemotionally, and followed it with that other question: what would Keith do then? How serious was it to fall over like that? She couldn't say, because she hadn't seen it happen, but Miss Turner, she recalled, had sounded horrified.

Delia glanced down at Susaline's feet protruding from beneath the thick red blanket.

'So that was it,' she murmured. 'She did put on those ridiculous shoes after all.'

'Her high heels,' Keith said, brokenly. 'She loved them so. No one could blame her, could they?'

'For endangering her child's life and possibly her own?' Delia asked, through stiff lips. 'Well, I don't know. I know this: I wouldn't do it.'

'Susaline didn't want this baby,' he whispered.

'Did you, Keith?' she asked, curiously.

He hesitated. Then, 'Every man yearns for a son.'

'What if it's a daughter?'

He dropped his head in his hands. 'I don't know. Oh, I don't know.'

She realised he was crying. She didn't like that. Men did cry sometimes, she knew, but this hardly seemed the time. Paul, she felt, would not go to pieces at a time like this, but would be a tower of strength. She could imagine him sitting grasping her hand tightly, infusing strength through the cloak of semi-consciousness, so that wherever she had drifted, she would feel he was near and it would help her.

Keith, she felt, as she looked over at his bent, fair head and shaking shoulders, would be precious little help to any woman.

Inevitably she felt a traitor. She had no business to be thinking that way about Keith. All men couldn't be of iron like Paul. A wave of pity for Keith flooded over her. He had had a rotten life. No home background. Only Aunt Cora to guide him, and a crusty and ancient male guardian who didn't want the bother of the boy and was no help at all. Paul, on the other hand, had had parents (until recently, when his father had died) and a brother; a secure home background, too.

In that frame of mind she stepped from the ambulance and laid a hand on Keith's arm to steady him while they watched Susaline's stretcher being slid out and carried into the hospital. Through the waiting hours she stayed by Keith, holding tightly to him, giving him what comfort she could by way of reassurances. But it wasn't easy.

It was a general hospital. They sat on benches in a long corridor, waiting. Accident cases were wheeled through. A man sitting bolt upright in a wheel-chair, looking almost at death's door, was pushed past them. It was warm in the corridor, warm with the dry heat from hot pipes. Outside, snow fell intermittently. Nurses, looking too cheerful and healthy to be in such a place, hurried by in ones and twos. All was busy life, life tending the sick and the injured. Was it possible that Susaline and her baby would not be all right?

A nurse came and suggested that they go out and get a hot meal and come back again. Nothing could be said as to the patient's condition yet.

'Is she in a ward?' Keith asked, piteously.

'Oh no, in the operating theatre,' the nurse said, with a reassuring tone in her voice. 'She'll be all right, but it takes time.'

They went out and made a pretence of eating. Delia had been conscious, in the hospital, of curious eyes on her, and wondered if her scarlet coat and black astrakhan accessories were too bright and out of place here. The thought made her smile, and Keith looked at her reproachfully.

'The baby won't live,' he said, and his voice had an accusing ring, almost as if he considered her smile would make it bad for his wife and child.

'It may be premature,' Delia said. 'I've heard of rare cases where five months' babies...'

'No!' Keith said, violently. 'It couldn't live!'

Delia was doubtful of that herself, privately. She also felt it highly doubtful that Susaline would come through, either. That nurse had been too non-committal, too hearty.

'Why aren't I upset about Susaline?' Delia asked herself, amazed. But the answer was that Susaline was too wilful to have the good luck to have a baby, and too truculent towards her to command much sympathy.

After the meal they went back to the hospital and waited until nearly midnight. Then they were told that Susaline had been put in a ward. Comfortable, they said, but not yet out of the anæsthetic. It was not possible to see her. Come back tomorrow.

'But the baby?' Keith kept saying in that pathetic little-boy voice.

'The child was still-born.'

'I wonder they don't sound more sorry,' Delia found herself thinking as she walked beside Keith in silence. 'But, then, I suppose so many cases die it wouldn't do for them to let anything but the most practical sentiments creep in.'

She hailed a cruising cab and they got in. Keith slumped back into the corner. Delia lit a cigarette and stuck it between his lips, but he let it go out. She smoked herself, hard, one cigarette after another. It had been a beastly day. She recalled with a sense of shock that she had been going to spend the evening with Paul. What was it they had been going to do? Oh, yes, supper at The Cellar after the performance. She hoped he wasn't angry. She could have telephoned if she'd remembered. Oh, well, Paul would understand. She was too tired to bother about that now.

When they let themselves in to Aunt Cora's house, she said at once, 'Keith, I think bed is the best place for you, as well as for me. I'm all in. I'll say good-night right away.' That was a precaution, because he suddenly had that yearning look that she had come to associate with the need for a long session of talk about Susaline. She didn't want to hear him talking about Susaline tonight.

He said dispiritedly, 'All right, I suppose you are tired. Good-night.'

He went upstairs, with that old sulky look on his face, leaving her there. No word of thanks for being with him all those hours at the hospital. No expressed hope that she hadn't broken a date to go in the ambulance with her. Just sulkiness because she didn't want to listen.

She shrugged. 'More damn fool you, Delia Grayson, to let yourself in for it!' she told herself, and went to bed.

In Chiverstock, when an accident happened, it was news. Even a small incident such as a woman expecting a child, tumbling, and being taken off in ambulance to hospital, deserved a paragraph in the local press. So Paul, as it happened, knew about the incident as soon as Delia had the opportunity to tell him. In any case there were plenty of verbal versions of it flying around, which came to his ears, especially as the glamorous Delia Grayson had been seen to go in the ambulance with Keith and Susaline.

The minute Delia saw him, sitting in the corner alcove of The Cellar, she knew that he had heard. It wasn't that he looked sulky or bad-tempered. It was just an awareness about him, a guardedness, which told her that he was going to let her do the talking.

She gave him a brief account of the incident.

'I couldn't do anything else, Paul, could I.'

'No,' he allowed.

'And I am truly sorry, Paul, about our date last night. I ought to have remembered and telephoned a message at the theatre.'

'It would have helped,' he agreed.

'Did you wait long?' she asked him.

'I waited for you,' he said, quietly. 'Let's leave it at that, shall we, Delia?'

She didn't know how to cope with him in this mood. She supposed it was his jealousy of Keith which was making him behave so distantly. What she didn't appreciate was that from Paul's angle this was merely a pointer to the way things would always be. If Pemberley called for help she would go unthinkingly and, for the moment at least, she would forget Paul's existence. That, at any rate, was Paul's conviction at this moment.

But he didn't say so. It might have helped if he had. Instead he did his best to make the lunch go smoothly as always and Delia pulled her weight, too, but both felt that it was a shocking fiasco and were glad when it was over.

'Paul, I won't be coming to lunch tomorrow.'

'Oh, going to the hospital with Pemberley, I suppose?'

She looked up in surprise. 'How did you know, Paul?'

'It isn't difficult to work that out. I happen to know it's the hospital visiting day. I also happen to know that you wouldn't miss a chance of going anywhere with Pemberley.'

'That's unkind. He's asked me to go with

him. It's only natural. Don't forget we were brought up together.'

'How easily you make me look in the wrong, Delia,' he said.

'Well, aren't you?'

'No, I don't think so. After all we are un-officially engaged, aren't we? That being the case, how about if I came along, too?'

Delia had a swift vision of Keith last night going all to pieces. She didn't know what they were going to hear today. Supposing the news weren't good? Of what use would she be to Keith if Paul were with her?

'Oh no, Paul, I don't think that would do at all. After all, you don't know Susaline as well as I do. Anyway, only two are allowed by the bed at the same time.'

'So you don't want me. I thought so. Good-bye, Delia,' he said, quietly. And started to walk away.

Delia hurried after him.

'Paul,' she said, blankly, 'you can't go like this. When am I going to see you again?'

He smiled a little twisted smile.

'That's for you to say, Delia. I expect you'll have a use for me when Pemberley's wife comes out of hospital.'

'Oh!' Delia gasped in exasperation and hurried back to her office.

When she and Keith reached the hospital she stood frozen in the grip of apprehension. Ever since leaving Paul the day before she had been thinking over his words, wondering whether she did make use of him – whether she was being fair over this misunderstanding. So obsessed had she been over her relations with Paul that she had hardly stopped to think what news would greet them when they reached the hospital. It was true that Keith had telephoned last night for news and had been told there was no change. That might or might not mean anything. She did not know what he was thinking. Twice she had tried to get out of coming, but each time he had begged her to go with him.

She said, 'Don't you want to see Susaline alone, Keith?'

'No,' he muttered, through stiff lips. 'Ill people always frighten me.'

So Delia had bought some hot-house roses for Keith to take and a bunch of black grapes for herself and had gone with him.

It was only when they waited with those other people queueing until the visiting hour should strike did she realise the possibility that there might not be anyone to visit.

The minutes dragged by, and at last they were allowed to go up. 'Maternity,' Delia told a porter. And it was not until she nodded hard at Keith that he seemed to come awake sufficiently to mutter in a thick voice unlike his own, 'Mrs Pemberley.'

Delia waited with bated breath while the

porter made the enquiry. And it was only when he came back with the information 'St Anthony's Ward' that Delia let out a sharp breath. Susaline, then, was still alive.

She glanced at Keith. His expression was wooden. Impossible to tell what he was thinking.

They followed the porter in silence. When they reached the door of the ward, a small room with three beds and half-glass partition, Delia hung back.

'Go in alone, Keith, first,' she said. 'Susaline won't want to see me yet. Here, take these things with you.'

The nurse came along at that moment and whisked the roses away from him. 'Oh, for little Mrs Pemberley,' she cooed. 'I'll put them in water.'

Delia watched her take them away and gave Keith a little push. He was still clutching the grapes. She watched him go across the small ward to the third bed in the far corner. Susaline looked pale and unfamiliar without her thick coating of make-up. Her wavy, blonde hair hung loosely over her shoulders and made her look rather young and childish. She had on an ugly white cotton night-dress with a high Russian collar provided by the hospital, and this again made her look very strange.

The occupants of the other two beds had visitors round them and were taking little

255

notice. Delia saw Keith hesitate, then bend stiffly over and give Susaline a perfunctory kiss. Susaline turned her head away sharply. He thrust the grapes at her and she brightened. They looked nice, Delia thought, in their fancy white box with the cellophane top. Susaline seemed pleased. Keith's lips moved, presumably telling Susaline who brought them. That much Delia deduced from the sudden stormy expression on Susaline's face and the sight of the box of grapes whirling across the ward to hit, with a thud, the far wall. The other patients and their visitors looked up startled. Keith glanced round and reddened. Delia smiled a little ruefully. She had no need to worry; Susaline would soon be well again. She left a message with the nurse returning with the roses in a glass jar.

'Please tell Mr Pemberley that I decided not to wait.'

CHAPTER 17

The early days of December fled by and soon it was time for Delia to relinquish her one-time job. Aunt Cora and Sir Timothy came back from the South of France. Susaline was discharged from hospital. Paul became a frequent visitor at the house, and it seemed to Delia that from all directions came a sudden clamour about Christmas.

It was, of course, Paul who made the first overtures to heal the breach in their friendship despite the finality of his last remark to her. He telephoned to her one night. She was sitting in Aunt Cora's armchair thinking over the events of the past year and trying to assess what the future would be like when the telephone bell suddenly rang.

Paul's voice cut across her thoughts.

'Delia?'

'Yes. Is that you, Paul?'

Whether it was the absence of hostility in her voice or perhaps the rather pathetic tired note she did not know. Whatever it was, Paul's voice had softened when he spoke again.

'Delia, don't let's go on like this. It's so childish. Besides, I'm lonely for you.'

She hadn't the will to argue with him, and when he suggested going to the pictures that evening she fell in with the idea willingly. That was the first of many such evenings again and she was very glad. For with Susaline's return from hospital the old quarrels began again. They were subdued in tone, it was true, but nevertheless Susaline had come back home in a disgruntled mood. It was true they didn't shout at each other any longer, for which Delia was very glad. But there were long silences, and Keith still went out with hunched shoulders and banged the door.

Susaline seemed to have taken a dislike to Delia since the accident. She never mentioned the grapes, and, although Keith must have told her how Delia went to the hospital with him she never bothered to say thank you. Usually she passed Delia in silence with averted head.

Aunt Cora came home full of gay spirits. Delia had rather dreaded that meeting with them both, but Sir Timothy could be very charming when he chose and made the first meeting since his marriage on the neutral ground of an expensive restaurant. There, in an atmosphere of thick pile carpets, soft-footed waitresses and a delightful tea, Sir Timothy formally accepted his former secretary and intended bride as his niece. It was all so easily done. He said, 'We've talked it over. Your aunt and I feel that it would be better for us to be Cora and Timothy to you rather than "aunt" and "uncle."'

He said it with a puckish grin.

'To tell you the truth, Delia, the thought of having you call me "uncle" fills me with horror. I'm much too young for any such title, am I not?'

Delia, watching them both, felt a pang of happiness. They were so gay and so much in tune: so settled with each other. Their future was obviously assured. Sir Timothy, appreciating this, was undoubtedly determined to have no hitch. He explained smoothly and in well-thought-out sentences what he intended to do now. He touched lightly on his visit to the office to go through the work with Delia before she left. He mentioned a dinner party he and Aunt Cora had planned at his home in the country presumably for the purpose of introducing Delia neatly into his family circle in her new relationship. It was all so skilfully arranged. He told her what they meant to do about Aunt Cora's house. His solicitor had found a purchaser who would allow Keith and Susaline to keep on their flat. Someone had been found to take over Aunt Cora's flat furnished after she had removed her treasures. Finally, the vexed question of Christmas.

'We do so want you to spend it with us, Delia darling,' Aunt Cora urged. 'We've planned a really old-fashioned Christmas. You know the sort of thing – holly and greenery, log fires and red candles, seasonable food, games and music, and some really pleasant guests.'

'That means some nice young men to be dazzled by our lovely Delia,' Sir Timothy said, facetiously.

Delia panicked. How they had it all cut and dried, she thought. She could even guess what was coming next. A wonderful party dress and jewels from Sir Timothy. She shrank from the thought of it all.

'You're darlings both of you and it all sounds so heavenly, but much as I'd love to spend Christmas with you, I can't.'

'Oh, Delia, you're not fixed up already?' Aunt Cora wailed.

Delia nodded.

'After all, darling,' Delia pointed out gently, 'it's only a week or two to Christmas, and somebody asked me early on.'

She had difficulty in suppressing their eagerness to find out who the someone was. She had the feeling that if she said Paul, Sir Timothy might be high-handed about her turning down his invitation in favour of his ex-clerk. She didn't want to spoil things for Aunt Cora, who already seemed to be getting the complex that her husband was right and everyone else was wrong. She also didn't want things spoiled for herself by any belittling of Paul by either Sir Timothy or her aunt. So she gaily insisted that her Christmas invitation was a secret and firmly stuck to her point.

It was true that Paul had suggested that they should spend Christmas Day together and possibly Boxing Day. But even if he hadn't Delia felt that Christmas in her own flat alone would have been better than accepting Sir Timothy's invitation.

On returning to Aunt Cora's house Delia

was met by Keith at the foot of the stairs. He said, 'May I talk to you for a moment?'

She said, unwillingly, 'Well, all right, but where's Susaline?'

'Oh, she was fed up and went to town to do a bit of Christmas shopping.'

'Is she well enough to go out on her own yet?'

'She seems all right,' said Keith. 'In any case you know Susaline. I can't keep her in if she wants to go out.'

Delia led the way into the sitting-room and threw her coat and muff over a chair. Keith said, 'It's this letter I've had from some solicitor fellow. Did you know that Aunt Cora was selling the house over my head? She might have told me!'

Delia stared at him. 'Why should she?' she asked, reasonably. 'It's her house. She can do as she likes with it. She doesn't have to explain to us.'

'Didn't you know about it, then?'

'Not until this afternoon,' Delia said, shaking her head. 'I've been to tea with Aunt Cora and Sir Timothy. They told me what they'd been planning for both of us. I must say I think they've been pretty decent.'

'Possibly – for you!' Keith retorted.

'Well, what have you got to grumble about?' Delia asked, trying to follow his thoughts. 'After all, you're staying put. If Aunt Cora had wanted a higher price for the house she could have turned you out, you know. It's no fun selling a house with one floor let – and at such a low rent, too. You and Susaline ought to be jolly grateful.'

'How do we know the new landlord won't put the rent up?'

'Well, if he does, you still can't grumble. You've had the flat all this time for little or nothing!' Delia said, sharply, fast losing patience. 'Is that all you wanted me for, Keith?'

'No. As a matter of fact it isn't. I wondered if you could help me about Susaline.'

'Oh, my dear, I think that's something you should work out for yourself,' Delia said, wearily. She was conscious that she was very tired of the sound of Keith's wife's name.

He looked injured. 'I only meant, as regards a Christmas present. She won't say what she wants, and – well, I thought, being another woman, you might know of something.'

She looked at his woebegone face, and had hard work to suppress a smile. He was at once the truculent young husband and the injured little boy, and try as she would, she couldn't chase away the feeling that it was an extremely endearing mixture and it drew her every time.

'Well, now, let me think. But for heaven's sake don't make the error you did over the grapes and let her know I had any hand in it!'

He promised eagerly that he would be careful not to repeat the mistake, and Delia obligingly thought.

'Has she got a nightdress case like a doll or a cuddly toy?'

It appeared that Susaline had. Her cousin, the dancer, had given her one for her last birthday.

'Well, what about one to match, to stand on the dressing-table and hide all her bottles and pots of make-up underneath?'

Keith was doubtful. Delia wondered if he privately thought Susaline would never bother to be so tidy, and that as the dressing-table was at present, there simply wasn't room to stand such a doll.

'Well, then, I tell you what. Give her one of those gift boxes with three or four different bottles of perfume in. All different scents, in sweet little bottles, and not too expensive. If you wanted to splash out, you could give her a gift token to go with it, so that she could match up some new make-up like the perfume. Women like to buy their own make-up because of the colour shades and textures.'

Keith brightened. 'I say, Delia, that's marvellous! I never thought of that.' His face fell almost immediately. 'Oh, where do I get that sort of thing?'

'Oh, Keith, Keith, and the girls in town think you're a lady-killer!' Delia cried, and burst out laughing, despite his hurt expression. 'Any good chemist or store, you nit-wit, or a beauty-parlour. Haven't you see such things in the windows?'

He admitted he hadn't, and added that he was always too worried about his job to bother about looking in shop windows.

'You should do!' Delia told him firmly. 'It would do you good, and keep you *au fait* with the way Susaline's mind works.'

She got rid of him at last, and began making lists for her own Christmas shopping. Paul rang her up and demanded that she met him earlier next day so that he could take her to choose a gift from himself.

'I know better than to ask you what you'd like, Delia. What I will do, though, is to march you round the shops, and the minute I see your face go animated, I shall pounce on the article that caused it.'

She laughed. 'Paul, you're a genius! Just the sort of man I like!'

'D'you mean it, Delia?' Pathetically anxious, and yet struggling to preserve its dignity, that voice of his.

'Yes, I do mean it,' she assured him solemnly.

A sigh escaped him. She heard it distinctly over the wire.

'Happy now, Paul?' she murmured, laughing a little.

'Happy enough to take courage in both hands and ask you something else. Will you spend Christmas with us at my home, Delia?'

It took her by surprise, and she didn't answer for a minute. There had been some talk of going out with him on both days, but she hadn't thought that it was likely she would be asked to go to his home after the last unfortunate visit. She wondered if it was his mother's idea of keeping him in the house over Christmas. She was a possessive woman. Or whether they thought it would sicken her, Delia, after two days of their nastiness and innuendoes. She couldn't decide.

Paul misinterpreted her silence. 'Oh, it's not my invitation entirely. It's mother's. And it's all above board. She's writing to formally invite you, but I thought I'd just mention it first to sound you – see if you'd take to the idea sort of thing.'

'Am I so difficult to please?'

'Well, I gathered from your manner that you didn't care overmuch for that last visit home.'

'Your mother wasn't exactly nice to me, was she, Paul?'

'A little touchy, perhaps,' he said, after a slight hesitation. 'After all, she took a little time to get used to Stella when she was new to the family.'

He didn't realise it, but just that last sentence swayed her. If, as he said, it had been the same with Stella, and that Mrs Faversham was merely possessive over her sons just at first then that wasn't so bad. Delia accepted.

'Oh, Delia, you don't know how I feel about that, my dear!' he said, and it puzzled her a little as to why it should mean so much to him. For her, it was a blessed way out of an awkward situation. She didn't want to lie to Aunt Cora, and now she could say in truth that she was spending Christmas in someone else's house.

'I'm going to guard my face,' she told Paul the next day when she met him for their shopping expedition. 'You shan't have such an easy time leaping on the thing I like!'

He squeezed her arm. 'I know you pretty well, Delia. I shall be able to spot the thing that takes your eye, don't worry. And in record time, too.'

He was right. She gave herself away by crying out in pleasure over a small travelling set of petit point brushes and mirror in a streamlined leather case with a zipper all round. The leather was powder blue. Paul stood staring at it as the assistant made out the bill.

'Have you got one of those little manicure sets, Delia?'

'Um. Pretty ancient, but you remember it – we spilled the contents the day we went to Lamorna.'

'Is there one in powder blue to match this thing?' he asked the assistant. 'Good, I'll have that, too.'

'Oh, no, Paul!' she protested.

'Quiet, woman,' he admonished her with a grin. 'Christmas comes but once, and this is my first since knowing you!'

'It'll be the last if you go on like this,' she threatened. 'Ugh! Snowing again. Means it, I think, this time.'

'Don't you like a white Christmas, Delia?' he said, looking up at her thick, coppery fringe. 'There's snow in your hair and a bit on your lashes. You look good enough to eat.'

She laughed, a comfortable, throaty little laugh.

'Happy, Delia?'

'Terribly. Paul, would it disorganise your family very much if we went to midnight Mass on Christmas Eve?'

His eyes glowed with pleasure. 'I'd been tossing up whether I'd ask you to go with me, but I wasn't sure if you'd care for it.' He whistled a few bars of a carol as he steered her across the road towards The Cellar for lunch. The parcels he carried were in Christmas wrappings, gay, holly bedecked. His dark, pull-down felt was peppered with white, and his dark face was creased and smiling. 'I don't think it'll upset the family. Stella's usually up pretty late doing last-minute things to the iced cake, and Ian likes to leave the decorations to the last minute. Delia, let's be officially engaged!'

She hesitated.

'Oh, come on – there's a jeweller's simply inviting us. I've seen a stone I bet you'd love. A big square green one. Am I right?'

She nodded, but caution still pulled at her. 'Please, Paul, let's wait till after Christmas. I don't think I could stand it if everything came at once. It's exciting enough as it is, what with one thing and another. Besides,' she hesitated, then decided to be truthful. 'I'd really like an opportunity of getting the "feel" of your family towards me, first. Only a stay in your house will do that. Don't you see?'

He nodded, sobered. She was right, of course. 'Then if it's all right after Christmas let's make it a New Year do and invite the company from the rep. to our party. How's that?'

She gave in to him; he was too happy to dash any more. Besides, the New Year was a comfortably long way off – at least a dozen days off.

That night was to be her last in Aunt Cora's flat. Already some of her aunt's special treasures had been removed, and the place was beginning to acquire a bare, unwanted look. She went home unwillingly to pack her few things before going back to the maisonette she had kept locked up all this time.

As she switched the hall light on the first thing she saw was Keith sitting disconsolately on the bottom stair. In his hands was the gift she had recommended him to buy for Susaline – a long, narrow gold-paper-covered box in which stood the four bottles of perfume. Stuck up behind them was the gift token in the fancy envelope. Obviously this was all ready to show her what he had done.

She burst out laughing. 'Keith, you fool, what are you doing sitting there in the cold? Did you have any trouble getting it? Oh, it's a nice one – a good brand,' she approved, taking it from him and examining it critically. 'Nice. But for heaven's sake don't sit here. You look frozen. There's an inch of snow outside already. Here, come on in and I'll make some coffee.' She looked sharply at him. 'That is, of course, if you're alone.'

'Oh, yes,' he said in a curious dead voice. 'I'm alone all right.'

She shrugged. She didn't want any more domestic stories tonight. 'Well, come on in, then. This is my last night here, so you'd better not make a habit of sitting on that stair. The new tenants mightn't care for it. What's that you've dropped? A letter?'

He picked it up. 'D'you like the scent?'

'Yes, I do. It's a lovely gift.'

'Well, you can have it, Delia.'

269

She stared. 'What *do* you mean? Doesn't Susaline like it? You didn't tell her it was my suggestion?'

'Oh, no. She hasn't seen it. But she won't want it.'

Fear clutched at her. 'There's nothing wrong, is there? Nothing's happened to her?'

'Oh, no,' he said, still in that queer dead voice. 'She's all right ... I suppose.' He thrust the letter in her hand. 'Here, read it.'

She read it as he instructed. 'Well, what's wrong with that? She's gone north to stay with her people for Christmas. So you pack up and go, too.'

'Where does it say that?' he asked, taking the letter back from her and reading it again.

'Well, it doesn't exactly say that,' Delia admitted. 'But surely that's what she'll expect you to do?'

'No,' he said, with flat finality. 'She means just what she says. She's gone. Gone to her people, maybe. But gone, just the same.'

'Oh, don't be silly, Keith. You know Susaline, how fed-up she gets, and how impulsively she acts. Look how impulsively she acted that day when she went out in those silly shoes and fell. It might have cost her her life, too, but did she stop to think of that? No! Well, then – it's the same this time. Now don't be tiresome, Keith, and act all dramatic. Just go upstairs and write her that you'll follow on Christmas Eve when your holiday starts. If you'd told her you were giving her a decent gift she might have felt less discontented, but I bet you didn't give her any idea about this.'

'It was to be a surprise,' he said, dully. 'She said I never bought her anything. I couldn't afford to. She knew that. No, I've seen it coming for a long time. She doesn't want me.'

'You're just feeling sorry for yourself,' Delia told him sharply. 'Can't you see this is just a pathetic little feminine trick to see if you really care for her? She wants you to follow her, then she'll know for sure.'

'Does she?' He looked up, and his eyes were curiously cold. 'Well, I've followed her for the last time. She's gone, and as far as I'm concerned I don't care a damn!'

CHAPTER 18

Delia's flat was on the top floor of the block and the last at the end of the corridor. It had the advantage of overlooking a quiet side street on the far side of Chiverstock, and over the opposite roof-tops there was a fine view of the surrounding hills. It was a tiny flat – a bed sitting-room, a bathroom and minute kitchenette – but it was adequate.

She had got a lot of pleasure out of being there alone, and had been very glad, on leaving Aunt Cora's house for good, that she had kept up the rent and retained her name in the tiny metal frame outside the door.

The second day she had been in it, and roughly four days before Christmas, she ran into Keith in the square.

'Hallo, Keith,' she said, wondering if he were going to keep her talking, and almost hoping he wouldn't.

'Hallo, Delia. I hoped I'd be seeing you,' he said, and stopped squarely in her path. He was on his way to lunch, and as he only stopped for a snack, he had plenty of time to spare. Delia wasn't pleased; she was meeting Paul.

'Heard from Susaline?' she enquired, hoping he would say yes.

'No. I didn't expect to. And I'm not going up north for Christmas, either.' He set his thin lips in an obstinate line. 'What are you doing for Christmas, Delia?'

'I'm going away to friends,' she said, thankful that it was so. She was good-natured enough to want to make his Christmas bright, but he would be a gloomy companion at best.

'Oh!' His face fell. 'I had hoped we might be able to do something together.'

'I think such a plan wouldn't be right, Keith. You really ought to spend Christmas with your wife,' she said, firmly. 'Besides, what would people say?'

His lip turned up in the nearest thing to an approaching sneer that she had ever seen. 'What's the matter what they say? They're all talking about Aunt Cora's house already in the miserable street. Anyone'd think our neighbours were stainless the way they discuss what they hear coming from out walls.'

'I didn't mean what they would say about *you*, Keith,' she said gently. 'I mean, what will they say about *me?*'

'You!' He looked blank. 'What *can* they say?'

'Well, they might, for instance, say that I'm spending a lot of time with a married man while his wife's away,' she smiled, and watched him closely.

He laughed shortly. 'Well, you've done it before – so what?'

She couldn't believe it, and decided that he must be very miserable to talk in that way. It was not their Keith, hers and Aunt Cora's, to take such a selfish way.

She said, suddenly, 'Well, I must go now, Keith. I'm meeting someone for lunch.'

'Just a minute, Delia. I've something I want to discuss with you. Can you come over tonight?'

'To your flat? Oh, no, I don't think so – for the reason I've just said. 'Bye, Keith!'

She was late for lunch with Paul, but he

didn't say anything. He was so happy these days, and he believed that her face – flushed with hurrying and annoyance over Keith – was lit with excitement over him.

'I've ordered a special lunch – a preview of the turkey and plum pudding. How's that?'

'It's unlucky to have it so soon before Christmas,' she told him severely.

It was a gay lunch, marred only by a (to him) very small request which he made towards the end of the meal.

'Delia, d'you mind awfully if I ask you to pack something, well, a bit quiet to wear over Christmas?'

Her face froze a little. 'What *do* you mean, Paul?'

'Now don't take offence, my dear. You see, you *do* wear rather daring clothes, and I know they suit you, but you see–'

'Your mother doesn't like them! Is that it?'

'Stella, also,' he added quietly. 'And I do so want them to approve of you. Women are funny. To a man, clothes don't matter so much. I love to see you in gay, bright things, but women – well, they're so odd in their assessments of character–' He trailed off, miserably. He had so very much wanted his mother and sister-in-law to get on well with Delia. He had not told Delia what a struggle he had had to get his mother to write that letter of invitation, or how he had coaxed her to extend a hearty welcome to Delia. It

274

was only when he threatened to go away for Christmas that his mother had finally capitulated.

'Well, I'll have her here,' she had said, through tight lips, and a face full of disapproval, disapproval that was echoed just as whole-heartedly in the face of Stella. 'But it won't be a happy Christmas; I can see that. And no one can say that it'll be my fault. I want my sons home for the festive season, and I'll have nothing stand in my way.'

It was not the frame of mind he could have wished for, on the part of his mother, when he brought home his future wife. He had next tackled Stella, in the privacy of the tiny conservatory, which was, after all, a glass lean-to with a few sad-looking plants in pots, arranged on a slatted shelf.

'Stella, this isn't like you. Mother, I can understand. She wasn't very nice to you when Ian first brought you home, but she's accepted you now. But why should *you* be so beastly to Delia?'

'Well, what a question!' Stella had retorted. 'Why should I be nice to *that* female, I'd like to know? Why, everybody in town's talking about her. Look at the place she lives in! Look at the clothes she wears! I might very well ask my brother-in-law – why is *he* being like he is over that woman?'

With Stella in that frame of mind Paul gave it up. His brother, he found, was non-committal, but inclined to side with the women. An unpropitious beginning for Christmas, indeed.

'Will you, Delia,' he coaxed, 'will you wear something – how shall I say? – sweet and quiet? I know, that pale blue frock with the tiny frills on it.'

'That old thing! Why, I wore that before I got a new face!' she cried, in disgust. 'I'll de-glamorise myself, if you like.'

They didn't exactly quarrel, but parted on rather strained terms. And that night, when she was sitting chafing about it, on the divan that was couch by day and bed by night, a man's footsteps marched determinedly down the corridor to her flatlet, and Keith rang the bell.

'You!' She was not pleased, and he saw it.

'Well, you wouldn't come to my flat, and I did so want to talk to you, so I came to yours. May I come in, Delia?'

'Now look here, Keith, this just isn't fair. I've got a decent reputation and I don't want to lose it–' she began, with what approached the nearest show of anger he had ever seen in her.

'Good Lord!' he gasped. He put his hand on her shoulder and gently propelled her into the room. 'If you think I–' he began, then burst out laughing. 'Little Delia, get a grip on yourself. It would be just as indecent to me if I had *that* in mind, as you're making out it would be to you. For heaven's sake, girl, we've been brought up together. You're my sister, and nothing else. I want your help, and I don't leave here till I get it, because you happen to be the one sensible and helpful woman I know. And that's saying something!'

He threw his hat down, glanced around with vague approval and then flung on the table the brief-case he was carrying. He sat down at it, and passed a hand over his forehead. His face was white and tired, and he showed more signs of strain than he had during the day when she had met him in the square.

'It's a humiliating business, this. I can't expect you to see it like that, but there it is. The fact is, I've been trying to study – on my own – and I've come to the conclusion I'm a miserable flop. I brought the papers to show you.'

He turned them out of the case, pell-mell, and, wondering, she took them from him. It was a pitiful collection of examination papers and leaflets, some typewritten, some printed. The subject – freelance journalism.

'Keith! But why on earth–'

He laughed, bitterly. 'I saw it advertised. When we were waiting for the baby. I needed money badly, and fell for the assurances in the advertisements. "Earn while you learn." Well, maybe some people can.

I'm not saying they can't. But Susaline saw to it that I couldn't, even if I'd had the brains or the talent to do it.'

Delia sat down, and began sorting the papers, all thought of that other subject forgotten. They might, for all she cared, be sitting in Aunt Cora's sitting-room, with Aunt Cora in the kitchen preparing cocoa and biscuits, as had so often happened before.

'Surprised, I suppose?' His bitter voice took up the story again. 'Susaline was like that. If you hadn't got a lot of money she'd see you in hell before she'd let you have the peace to make it. She laughed at all this. Jeered at it. I asked her if she didn't want to see me get on. She said I was a poor mutt to think I could do it that way. We wrangled over it. She used to steal the papers, hide them, keep the fresh ones as they came in through the post – oh, it was hell, the whole thing. Other chaps have got an office they can work in, after the rest of the firm have gone home. I could hardly do this at the bank. So I let the thing slide.'

'Has the course finished, Keith? How long did it run on for?'

He shrugged. 'As long as you care to drag it, though they seem to like it to be over in eighteen months. I've paid for it all, and it seems a pity to waste it. I wondered...' He looked calculatingly at her. 'I wondered if you were interested enough to work on it with me, now you've no job to do. At least till you get another one. I suppose you are going to look for another job?'

'Oh, I don't know – I haven't thought yet. I'll take a week or two off while I look round, I think.' She was being evasive and he knew it. He let the subject drop.

'Well, d'you think we might work on it together? What I don't know, you might, and so on. You've always had ideas. Besides, it'd be more interesting to be able to talk it over with someone.'

It was tempting. It would take her mind off the other problems. But there was something about the thing which made her hesitate. It didn't end there. One night wasn't enough to examine the course, its possibilities, the future, his and hers, and how they would do it. He got to calling every night. By Christmas, Delia had got interested enough to decide she would take it up with him, work with him, and go through a mutual correcting of papers and swapping of ideas, if in turn he would join the night school course with her in January. The course of lectures, Delia found out, were given by an ex-journalist, and were far more useful in their way than plugging along in the dark as Keith had been doing. Together, the lectures and the written course should be of tremendous use to them both.

Keith agreed, provided he could come

there in the evenings and work with her. He had been to her flat each evening so far for nearly a week, and it had slipped into being such a natural proceeding that Delia hardly noticed anything unusual about it.

Delia went to the Faversham' house early on Christmas Eve. After an interesting week with Keith and the writing course, she had managed to smooth out her irritation with Paul, and met him with a beaming smile that produced an answering (if relieved) smile on his face. She pleased him, too, in that she had turned out a lot of her former clothes, including the blue dress he liked, to wear instead of her new ones. She had, also, left off a great deal of her make-up, and dressed her hair in a simpler fashion. Christmas, Paul felt, would be less of a trial than he had dared to hope.

The Faversham family, on their part, were doing their best to be less hostile then they really felt. But this was a concession to Paul, and not to Delia.

Delia wore soft blue; a loose topcoat and a soft woollen scarf over her bright hair, to go to the midnight Mass, and Paul, watching her covertly, decided that she had the look of a madonna about her. Perhaps it was the loose way she had done her hair, or the more discreet make-up, or perhaps the eerie light in church. He was inclined to believe, however, that just for tonight this service, this time of the year, there was a lovely softened look in her face that he had never seen before.

In that mood, therefore, neither he nor Delia was ready for the tart remarks from his mother when they arrived back at his house, cold and rather damp from the snow that was fast turning to sleet.

'If there's one thing I can't stand,' Mrs Faversham said, apparently to the air, as she slapped around getting cocoa and bread and butter, 'is people who make a show. There's many a Martha, I say, but she never gets seen. It's the Marys who get the praise because they push themselves to the fore-front.'

Ian looked up and met his wife's eyes, and said something about making a move for bed, as he'd finished all the decorations. His idea of putting up greenery was conservative in the extreme, and largely regulated by his desire to avoid damaging the wallpaper, and making the taking-down of the stuff easy. Delia looked round and wondered if she ought to say it looked nice, or hold her peace.

Paul looked irritated, but offered no comment. This was Christmas Day and not the time for bickering. Besides, his mother was always tart of tongue when she had undertaken too heavy a day and got tired.

He looked at Delia, who was leisurely folding the blue headscarf, and hoped she, too, would let those remarks go unanswered. But Delia wasn't used to his mother, and was naturally nettled.

'You wouldn't be referring to me, by any chance, Mrs Faversham?' Delia asked, but softened the words with a smile.

'If the cap fits...' Paul's mother said, and vanished into the kitchen.

'Mother would have appreciated it if you'd even offered to stay and help, instead of going out tonight,' Stella said, with marked disapproval, and murmuring a distant good-night, left the room.

'Well,' Ian said, awkwardly, 'I suppose I'll be getting along to bed, too. 'Night, both of you,' and he hurried out of the room behind his wife.

Paul frowned. While he made allowances for his mother's funny ways, it seemed to him that his brother and sister-in-law were being unforgivably rude. They had no quarrel with Delia, and they had more or less promised him to try and help keep the atmosphere happy.

'Why on earth do people have to say things like that?' he muttered, digging his hands into his pockets, and striding up and down the room.

'I didn't really expect anything else,' Delia said, doing her best to hide her annoyance. 'After all, my last visit here wasn't too happy. I don't think they like me.'

Paul looked quickly at her. This was the reaction he had been dreading. He opened his mouth to start explaining, propitiating her, preparing her for any more friction that was unavoidable, when his mother returned. She sat with determination in the corner of the settee, and looked meaningly at him.

'I'll wait while you have your cocoa if you're not too long,' she said, and though she didn't look at Delia as she spoke, the remark was meant for both of them.

Paul was nonplussed. If he let the moment go it was quite likely that his persuasion would be lost on Delia, and he probably wouldn't be able to get her to stay the holiday out. Why couldn't his mother use a little tact?

'Oh, there's no need for you to stay up, Mother,' he said. 'You look very tired. Nip off to bed. We'll wash up the cups and things and put out the lights.'

'And leave you two here alone together? I wouldn't dream of it,' his mother said firmly, and got out her knitting.

Delia's head shot up and she flushed angrily.

'Don't mind mother,' Paul said to Delia. 'She's a bit old-fashioned in her ideas.' He moved over to his mother, and leaned slightly forward so that his face was close to hers. 'It's Christmas Day, Mother, and late. Would you mind leaving us? I want to talk to Delia.'

'I'll not go and leave you two up together,' his mother returned obstinately.

'I insist on talking to Delia alone,' Paul said, losing his temper. 'Would you *mind* leaving us, Mother?'

'This is my house, Paul, and I won't be talked to like this by any son of mine, old as you are! I will not leave this room while you two are here.'

Paul straightened up, his face dark with anger. 'Then, since you won't be reasonable, there's only one thing to do. We'll go out into the street to get a bit of privacy. Slip your coat on, Delia, and let's go. I think, Mother, you'll be sorry for this.'

Delia shrugged and put on her coat. Together they went quietly out again into the night, leaving Mrs Faversham frustrated and angry, staring at the untouched cocoa.

'I really don't know what you could have to say to me, Paul, to bring me out in this wretched cold again,' Delia said, tying the scarf tighter under her chin, and thrusting her hands deep into her coat pockets. She no longer looked madonna-like, but there was a desirability about her, in her annoyance, and the way she swung along beside him.

The night air was crisp. The sleet had

stopped, and the roads were slippery and dangerous, but neither of them noticed. Paul talked, talked to Delia about mothers and their possessiveness and how it was better to let them make their little verbal thrusts and to let them get away with such remarks, rather than to make a quarrel by attempting to argue.

Delia said, at last, 'That isn't the point, Paul. I came to your home to spend Christmas, filled with the intention of being pleasant and amenable. Your mother isn't just being nasty, making those remarks. There's something behind it. If you hadn't smoothed things over, but asked her outright what she meant, you'd have got at the truth. Staying up like an old chaperone – it's outrageous! She's hinting at something, and I'd like to know what it is.'

'You're to leave it alone, Delia. I've smoothed things over. If you take mother up on anything she says when she's tired and difficult, you'll have a row in no time. And then what sort of holiday will it be for all of us?'

'That's just it, Paul. I don't think I can go on, in that house with those hostile people. In fact, I don't think I want to go back. I'd rather spend Christmas in my own flat, all by myself than go back to that atmosphere.'

His heart sank. 'I did so hope that it would go well, and that you'd consent to stay.'

'Why? Wouldn't it have been nicer if you'd just taken me out tomorrow and Boxing Day? Just our two selves?'

'You'd have liked that better, Delia?' He was torn between pleasure at her wanting the whole time with him alone, and the doubt that she'd ever get to hit it off with his family. 'I don't know what we could have done on Christmas Day – everything's dead. Besides, I did so want you to get on friendly terms with my family.'

They talked for over an hour, and walked themselves warm, and at last he got her to say that she'd go back and give it another trial, but he couldn't help noticing the mis-givings in her voice and hoped it would go all right the next day. Yet they were happy enough with each other, and it was a trifle dashing to find Paul's mother still obstin-ately sitting up, tired but determined, wait-ing. They both felt that it was a bad omen, that however much they tried to make the Christmas holiday a good one, that was how Mrs Faversham would be: obstructionist.

And that was the mood which continued during the whole holiday. Whatever was done or said, Mrs Faversham lost no oppor-tunity to make a quiet dig at Delia, although the pricks were too tiny in themselves to make an issue of. Paul noticed, though at first, for the sake of peace, he pretended not to. Even Ian and Stella got uncomfortable and tried to smooth things over, but Delia felt that it was for the sake of their children that they were trying to keep Christmas happy. But even the little ones felt that something was not quite right, and were inclined to be fretful and tiresome. It was the most uncomfortable Christmas Delia had ever had.

She had brought gifts for them all; small gifts, meant more as tokens than anything else, because she had been half afraid of being made to appear ostentatious. As it was, the adults looked at their small presents with stolid attention, then offered routine thanks and laid them pointedly aside. Delia felt that the action was a rebuke in itself. Over Paul's gifts they were enthusiastic.

Then there was Paul's mother's rudeness over Delia's praise of the food and the arrangements. 'Oh, we'd have done the same for ourselves, even if there had been no visitor,' Mrs Faversham said, in a tone of dismissal.

Determinedly, Delia kept polite and pleasant, but couldn't help reflecting that she might have done a lot better by going to spend the holiday with Aunt Cora and Sir Timothy.

Christmas Day dragged to a close, but Boxing Day brought the threatened storm. It appeared that Mrs Faversham had got rather tired of her promise to Paul to be nice to his girl-friend, and ached to get off her chest the thing that was worrying her. It was as Delia had said; that first remark on Christmas Eve had had tremendous point.

Ian and Stella had decided to take the children out for some air after a late lunch on Boxing Day. Mrs Faversham would normally have gone to her room for a rest after cooking, and Paul mentioned this.

'We'll have the gramophone on if it won't disturb you, Mother? You don't want to go out, do you, Delia?'

Delia was about to say that she'd like nothing better than an armchair by the bright fire, with some favourite records playing, when Mrs Faversham intervened, again with the remark that she wasn't prepared to leave them alone together.

There was an ominous silence. Delia sat forward in her chair, angry at once, and even Paul's expression changed.

'I think that remarks need a little explaining, Mother,' he said, through tightened lips.

'I won't have neighbours looking in and seeing you two in here alone – everyone knows my habits, and can see me in my own room, and they know that the others have gone out!'

'Well?' he asked, quietly.

She turned an outraged look on her son.

'There'll be no talk about *my* house while

I'm alive!' she told him, with asperity.

Delia said, in undisguised anger, 'And just what do you mean by that?'

'Don't talk to me in that tone, miss!' Mrs Faversham returned, acidly. 'I mean what I say; there'll be no talk about this house as there was about your aunt's house, and now about your flat! I always said that no nice girl ever took a flat in a block with a name like that—'

'A name like *what,* Mrs Faversham?'

'A name like that block of flats has got, and I'd advise you not to pursue this tone with me!'

'Mother, you'd better explain what you mean, so that *I* can follow,' Paul said. His mother ignored the warning note in his voice. Her own voice rose and became slightly shrill.

'Very well, I will! That woman,' she said, pointing to Delia, 'has the reputation of having men in her rooms – at night. There's a man been *seen* going in there and staying till quite *late.*'

There was a little silence. A silence in which Paul's face whitened and Delia's turned absolutely blank. Then her face cleared as she realised to what Paul's mother referred.

She got up. 'Why, how *dare* you?' she said, in a low voice. To Paul she said, contemptuously, 'I'm not staying in this house a minute longer – this is *too* much!'

She ran upstairs to the room allotted to her and flung her things pell-mell into her suitcase. Tears of anger and mortification stung her eyes. She didn't see Paul come in, but heard his voice behind her.

'Delia, don't go like this. There must be some explanation! Delia, please!'

'Of course there's an explanation,' she choked, scathingly. 'The "man" is Keith – Keith, who's been in my pocket since we were kids together. Your mother must want to paint me a black character badly if she has to make something out of that!'

'Yes, but why did he come? Wasn't it taking a risk, being seen by strangers letting a fellow into your flat?' His voice was not condemning, but merely the voice of one who is struggling to understand something rather obscure.

'Oh, Paul, does it matter? All right, then! The idiot's taken on some evening study and Susaline wouldn't let him do it in his own flat. He's so darn used to coming in to me, when Aunt's Cora's there, that he just followed habit. He brought the stuff for me to help him sort it out. That's all. He's been coming for four nights, four miserable nights – it doesn't seem very long to collect a bad reputation. "Man," indeed!'

She didn't notice the unconscious irony in her tone. It just struck her as being utterly ludicrous, the pair of them, Keith and herself, working very hard over those poor ink-blotted papers, while people like Mrs Faversham assumed that all sorts of wicked things were going on behind Delia's flat door.

'Why didn't you tell me all this, Delia, instead of leaving other people to talk about it and surmise the wrong things.'

'Oh, Paul, dear, you didn't want me to waste these precious hours talking about Keith, did you? We haven't had much time to ourselves since then, have we?'

He took her shoulders and smiled down at her. 'Delia, if only we could be happy together without all these upsets. Must you go?'

'Oh, I must, I must!' she said, wildly.

She flung on her coat and gathered her bag and gloves. Neither of them noticed Mrs Faversham standing in the open doorway, anger in her eyes. She wasn't going to lose what lever she had as easily as that, but she hadn't realised what a hold Delia had over her son.

'I don't believe it – a pretty story!' she said, and they swung round in surprise at the sound of her voice. 'There's no smoke without fire! You'd be advised, my son, to be careful where that smooth tongue of hers is concerned – she'd talk her way out of anything!'

Paul glowered at his mother. 'I believe what Delia says and that's all that matters. Besides, I happen to know Pemberley very well. He's interested in no other woman but his wife.'

'And where *is* his wife?' crowed Paul's mother.

'Well, where would she be? At home, I suppose!'

'She's gone up north,' Delia said, 'for Christmas.'

'Exactly,' Mrs Faversham purred. 'And you're fool enough to believe that these two precious innocents were just sitting at a table, writing!'

Delia trembled with rage. 'You're determined to turn Paul against me!' she stuttered, angrily. 'Well, if that's all Paul cares about me, that he can listen to your nasty narrow little views, he can get on with it. Excuse me!' and she walked past Paul's mother, hurrying downstairs and out of the house.

The world outside was grey and damp. Nothing looked enticing, nothing held out any promise for the future. But it was good to get away from that hard-eyed woman, who could find no good in her, and who sought so hard to wean her son away.

Paul hurried after her, shrugging himself into his coat. 'Delia, wait for me!' he called. 'You little firebrand, why don't you give me a chance to speak for myself?'

He took her arm and walked by her, slipping her week-end case away from her as he walked. 'Don't think too badly of my mother; she's a bit old-fashioned and rather possessive. She didn't mean those things; you just rub her up the wrong way!'

Delia said, 'People don't say those things without meaning them. Besides, other people are apt to believe them!'

'Well,' he retorted, 'you shouldn't lay yourself open to gossip by having Pemberley there alone with you. You might know what a small town's like – at least, you ought to by now.'

'You don't believe the story, then?'

'I'm not going to say it didn't make me wild just at first. I'm a jealous cuss, Delia, and I'm crazy about you. I don't say I liked hearing it just at first, but there – I know you, and I know that fool Pemberley. It's just like him to sit there full of himself and whatever he's taking up and not even notice you. Thank heavens,' he finished fervently.

She didn't answer but let him run on.

'It's been a rotten Christmas, Delia, hasn't it?' he murmured, pressing her arm, 'and I did so want it to be nice for you.'

'Yes, it's been rotten, but it's had its uses,' she said, thoughtfully, without looking at him.

'What d'you mean?' he asked. 'Don't let it

293

make you bitter,' he urged, as she didn't answer. 'It'll work out all right, as I told you it did with Stella. I think it would help if we got engaged right away. Show mother that gossip couldn't stop us from being together. What d'you say, Delia? New Year's Eve, as we said at first?'

It was unfortunate that he broached that particular topic just then, but he had the feeling that if he didn't bring it up tonight he would not be given another opportunity. She was, he felt, suddenly remote, and sliding fast away from him.

'When mother sees we really mean it, and when we get married, she'll come round and be nice to you, Delia,' he urged.

'No, Paul,' she said, flatly. 'That won't do. I said this holiday had its uses. That's true. It's shown me things: how rotten your mother can be, how unforgiving, and how impossible marriage with you would be.'

CHAPTER 19

One of the things that Delia felt had changed most of all was her relationship with Aunt Cora. This, of course, was inevitable, to a certain extent, but she had not quite anticipated that they would become almost strangers – polite strangers, but strangers, nevertheless.

There was a remoteness amounting almost to vagueness in Aunt Cora now. Her head was in the clouds over her new job, and as Lady Nodeleigh she had even acquired a different manner. Delia went over to the old house to help her clear up, and was too amused and surprised to actually help; she squatted on the edge of an arm of the settee and became an interested spectator.

There was a time, she reflected, when Aunt Cora would have rolled up her neat sleeves, donned an immaculate overall, and declared that she could do the job better herself. Now, of course, that was out of the question. But it was the greatness of the change that amused Delia.

Aunt Cora arrived, on that cold January day, in a magnificent fur coat, frivolous hat, and delightfully vague smile; a smile intended for sharing among all those who happened to glance her way. In her wake was the chauffeur, with one or two packages, and a hamper (for refreshment if Aunt Cora worked too hard), a diffident gentleman whom Delia knew as the solicitor who handled Sir Timothy's private affairs, and his neat and self-effacing secretary. There was some sort of odd man with them, too. He appeared to be there to help the chauffeur move things if necessary.

Delia, already there, felt she was rather like a spectator watching the players troop on to the stage. She got up and went to welcome her aunt.

'Delia, darling, how nice of you to come over and help us. We shall need all the help we can get!' her aunt exclaimed, looking round the small flat as though it were an overloaded mansion. 'Now where did I put my little list of things I felt I'd need to take away?'

The secretary moved forward with it. And Aunt Cora, who had hated all fuss and bother, kept the whole lot of them on the run the morning through. At lunch they sat down to a scrap meal (as she called it), which seemed to Delia to consist of a plentiful supply of cold chicken patties, jellies in minute papier maché cases, hot coffee, and iced cider. Then the performance started again.

Once Delia tentatively suggested that they might manage better on their own, just the two of them; Aunt Cora, she said, could give directions if necessary, and Delia would pack her little things. But that didn't suit at all. The solicitor seemed to enjoy going around making inventories for his secretary to take down in rapid shorthand, and to discuss at great length with Aunt Cora seemingly unnecessary arrangements regarding the few fittings and fewer alterations to be made. In short, Delia felt they had all determined to make a day of it.

Delia herself got rather bored towards three o'clock, and suggested that she should go for a walk and come back later.

'Oh, no, darling,' Aunt Cora protested. 'Stay until four, then you and I will go and get a nice little tea somewhere – if there's anywhere in this benighted town where such a thing can be got!'

'You used to like The Copper Kettle,' Delia murmured, and saw that Aunt Cora didn't want to be reminded of things so recently gone.

At times the old Aunt Cora still peeped through, in kind looks or words, in little shows of consideration, but on the whole the superficial society of Sir Timothy's world seemed to be laying a firm hold on her in a very short time. There was a regrettable tendency, too, to preface everything with 'Timothy says' or 'Timothy feels,' which disappointed Delia.

She tried to wriggle out of the tea engagement on the ground that Aunt Cora would probably be bored, but her aunt was adamant. 'That means,' Delia thought, ruefully, 'a pretty thorough inquisition on what happened over Christmas.'

To forestall too many questions, Delia undertook to give a free account of the holiday, which gave her scope to omit the unpleasant patches and to make it seem that it was just an amusing interlude. Aunt Cora seemed to accept it. Of Keith and his visits to her flat Delia said nothing.

Sir Timothy, it appeared, had been rather annoyed that Delia had not capitulated at the last moment. He and Aunt Cora felt they would have no peace of mind until they saw Delia safely married off, and to that end they appeared to be laying siege to her freedom in a very efficient manner. Delia saw that she could not hope to keep on putting off their invitations, and that sooner or later she would have to go and stay with them because there was no reasonable excuse (by way of engagement or marriage in her own sphere) to refuse any longer.

'Darling,' Aunt Cora probed, 'don't you like this young man, Paul?'

'Yes, of course,' Delia said, lightly. 'But I thought you'd rather see me married off in your own circle.'

'Now you're laughing at me. Naturally I'd rather see you make a *good* marriage, but don't forget,' she said, neatly dropping her little surprise parcel metaphorically into Delia's lap as she signalled the waitress for the bill, 'Sir Timothy has a lot of influence with the stage, and could put good parts in the young man's way – make him famous for you in no time.'

'You're assuming that Paul has it in him to be a great actor,' Delia remarked, and couldn't help feeling nettled at the way her aunt was determined to stage-manage her life for her.

'Oh, that doesn't matter,' Aunt Cora said, airily, as she put a treasury note on the bill and waved the girl away to keep the change. 'If the young man can't act, Timothy has enough influence to get him a well-paid administrative job in films or some such thing. There's nothing Timothy can't fix – if I ask him to!'

And then, possibly because she saw the slightest flicker of hostility in Delia's eyes, she leaned forward and impulsively put her hand on the girl's. 'Don't mind my anxiety, Delia, my dear. You see, I'm so very happy with Timothy, but only through your knowing him first did I meet him. I must never forget that. And if I seem to you like an interfering old woman, just put it down to my love for you, and my perhaps over-anxiety to see you settled as comfortably as we can manage. You mean a lot to me, my dear.'

Delia smiled a little tremulously. That was more – much more – like the old Aunt Cora.

'Yes, darling,' she murmured, 'I know. I know all that. But don't forget, will you, that one of the most precious things about being in the twenties is the freedom to run one's own life. You must have felt that, too, at my age.'

'Yes,' Aunt Cora said, with a slight twist to her mouth. 'That's just it, Delia. I did. But I made such an unholy mess of my life that I feel I just can't stand by and see you do the same thing!'

Delia and Keith joined the night school the first week in January, and had not properly got settled into their stride before Keith told her glumly one night that Susaline was coming back.

'Well, Keith, you are the stinking limit!' Delia explained. 'You went all to pieces because she left you. You wouldn't take my advice and go after her. You said she'd have to come back to you herself if she wanted you. Now she's coming you still don't look pleased! What *do* you want?'

He stared gloomily ahead at the classroom wall. The lecturer had not arrived, and under cover of the slight hubbub of the other students, they talked it over for nearly fifteen minutes. It appeared that Susaline was not coming back because she needed Keith, but rather because she had received a letter from her male cousin who danced.

'I hate the fellow!' Keith said, in a low, intense voice. 'He'll have her back at the Starlight Hall if he can, damn him! I'd hoped she'd settle down for a bit, at least, but it doesn't seem as though she's going to.'

Delia said, puzzled, 'But what's this about the Starlight Hall? I thought that all fell through when she had to give up dancing because of the baby coming?'

'That's just it,' Keith said, worriedly. 'As far as I can make out this damned cousin fellow of hers has had a job offered to him as demonstrator at the Starlight Hall provided he finds his own partner. He's making out he can't get a satisfactory one and that if Susaline practises he'll take her back with him.'

'When's she coming back?' Delia wanted to know.

'The end of this week,' Keith said, gloomily.

'Will that mean an end of your studies?' Delia asked him.

'Seems like it,' he said, 'unless I could work at your place.'

'I don't see why not,' Delia said. After all she had no one else to bother about. She had broken off with Paul so that his mother's innuendoes mattered no longer. And now that Aunt Cora was so far away there was no need to fear her misconstruction of the arrangement.

So it was agreed. They worked on happily for another three weeks. Susaline came back, not in the least penitent for her cavalier treatment of Keith, and without consulting him took up again her dancing with her cousin.

She was happy. Delia saw her once in the Square swinging along in her gay, cheaply smart clothes, her flimsy shoes with their tapping high heels quite inadequate for the severe end of January weather, and a display of far too many trinkets of the gilt and glass variety for day wear. Her happiness was a real, live thing. That angel smile beamed out and embraced everybody. She was her old self again, fit, slim, and active. She had her freedom to dance once more. She was able to wear the clothes she liked and she seemed to have taught her husband a lesson so that she now seemed to have unrestricted freedom. It all suited Susaline very well and, being Susaline, she impulsively showed her joy by buying a bunch of violets to pin on her coat and dropping the change into a blind man's tin can.

Delia, watching, had to admit that it wasn't difficult to see what the girl had which attracted Keith so much. There was something in that irresponsible gaiety that was such a tonic in this work-a-day world. It wouldn't do to have too many Susalines but one here and there did brighten things up so much. There was something enchanting in the sight of someone who could live so gloriously for today; who could push aside the sad yesterdays and leave tomorrow to look after itself.

But though Delia did not know it Susaline's tomorrows suddenly revolted and refused to be left to take care of themselves any longer. As is the way with these crises of ours it started in a very trivial manner. Susaline's cousin told her one evening that he felt too jaded to go on and sent her home. He looked jaded, too, and she wondered uneasily if it were just a matter of working too hard or whether he was sickening for something. She recoiled from the thought of illness in others and needed no persuasion to abandon the evening's practice to go home.

It was a raw night in early February and she had a swift picture of the flat inviting with its little rose-shaded lamps turned on and the electric fire glowing. If she put on an act of tiredness Keith would go like a lamb and get her something hot. He wasn't what you call domesticated, but he could and would make good coffee. It was the sustaining thought that got her home, for her feet were saturated where the cheap patent leather was cut away and the thin silk stockings were exposed to the mud and slush. She shivered a little as she let herself in to the house that had once been Aunt Cora's. The hall and the downstairs flat were brightly lit but, if she had bothered to look up outside, she would have seen that her own flat was in darkness. As it was she had that unpleasant surprise when she got upstairs: cold, dark rooms, emptiness and silence.

Susaline's temper, ever uncertain, flamed readily. She hurried downstairs again and thumped on the new tenants' door. They were an elderly couple, seedy-looking, garrulous and inquisitive. They were very interested in the young couple upstairs who were seldom in at the same time, but had so far been unrewarded with any quarrels. Now the little dumpling of a woman thrust her chin eagerly forward and asked Susaline what she could do for her.

'My husband isn't in,' Susaline said. 'D'you know if anything's happened? Was he called away or anything?'

The couple exchanged glances.

'Did you expect him to be in, my dear?'

'Of course I expected him to be in,' she snapped. 'He's in every night.'

They exchanged glances again and this time it was the man who spoke.

'He's never in at night, my dear. Didn't you know?'

'Comes in and washes. Does himself up and goes out again,' the little woman supplemented. She didn't add that he carried a brief-case. Her maxim was that too much truth spoiled the piquancy of a story.

Susaline glared. 'I don't believe it,' she stormed.

The couple looked at each other again and at Susaline.

'Come inside,' they invited.

The warm, brightly lit room decided her, though, after a little while, beside their great fire, hemmed in by their old-fashioned furniture, and bombarded by their inquisitive questions, she felt stifled. Her stockings and shoes dried on her, but, between talking, the little woman made cocoa and cut a slab of home-made cake.

They didn't get much out of Susaline for all their trouble, though she got out of them a picture of Keith using her evening's dancing practice as a shield for his own activities – whatever they were.

They heard him come in and said unnecessarily, 'There he is!'

Susaline jumped up.

'Thanks for the supper and all your kindness,' she said, and stood chatting with them long enough to give Keith time to get upstairs.

Unashamedly the couple stood at their open door, watching her go upstairs, waiting to hear what would happen.

Susaline went in quietly. Keith looked up in surprise.

'Have you just come in?' he asked.

'No, I've been in all the evening.'

'Well, the flat didn't look like it,' he said.

'Did you think I was going to stay in like a good little wife and have a nice, warm, comfortable place waiting for you?' she mocked.

'It would have been an idea,' he said. 'What happened to the dancing class?'

'I didn't stay,' she said. 'I thought I'd come home and spend the evening with you.'

'Oh, what's the idea?' he asked, suspicion written large all over his face.

'That's a nice thing to ask your wife. Any reason why I shouldn't feel like that? By the way, where were you?'

'Out … obviously.'

'Where?' she wanted to know.

'Now look here, Susaline, you go out when you want to and I don't question you. If I feel fed up with staying in every blessed night and decided to go out where I go is my business.'

'It might be if you only went out once in a while,' she said. 'The people downstairs say you're never in. That's a bit different, isn't it?'

His face flamed.

'So that's where you've been! Well,' he said, raising his voice, 'the people downstairs can mind their own business.'

They quarrelled all round the subject for a time but she could not get him to budge, and they finally gave it up and went to bed in sullen silence.

After that they played a cat-and-mouse game with each other. Keith took to opening Susaline's letters. Susaline sometimes followed Keith instead of going to dancing class, and it was by this means that she discovered that he met Delia and went to night school. What she went for she could not find out – neither could she find out where he spent the other evenings of the week because sometimes, to forestall her, Keith would stay home the whole evening and sometimes, when she guessed he was expecting her to come back early, she deliberately stayed out late.

Little by little she pieced together, from scraps of gossip in town and from her own observation, that it was Delia who had first claim on his free time, if not on his affections. Little by little Keith began to get so nerve-frayed through Susaline's spying that Delia begged him to take at least a week off from his studies because concentration or co-operation with him was hopeless. At last, in March, a final row bubbled up. Susaline faced him with it and said she wanted her freedom, with a good allowance. Keith, outraged at her duplicity, laughed in her face and said she could try for her freedom until she was black in the face. He would be the last to give it to her.

Susaline smiled secretly. 'I've got proof where you spend your evenings,' she said. 'Taking risks, aren't you?' she taunted him. 'Going unashamed to some woman's flat. A made-up piece like that Delia Grayson, at that!'

Keith stared at her open-mouthed. Then he laughed shortly.

'You've been thorough, but not thorough enough. The idea of having an affair with Delia Grayson is just plain barmy. We've sat at opposite sides of the table writing. Every minute I was there the window was uncurtained, in full view of all her neighbours. If you can make something out of that, do so.'

For the moment Susaline looked nonplussed. Then she let him have her final barb.

'You poor mutt; I can make something out of it and I will. Studying with you indeed! Can't you see that Delia Grayson has been in love with you for ages – since long before I came along, anyway?'

CHAPTER 20

After Keith gave up his night school work and private study with Delia in the flat, she found that time hung heavily on her hands.

Since Christmas she had had an absorbing occupation. She had had no need to find another job up to the moment and had found it restful to live on her savings these last few weeks. It hadn't been so expensive, after all, since Aunt Cora had insisted on paying the rent of the flat for the next twelve months as Delia had refused the proposed allowance.

Soon, Delia supposed, she would have to look around for another job, if only for something to do. She, too, had abandoned the writing course, for, like Keith, she found it a thankless job struggling alone with it. She had not seen him since his row with Susaline – in fact, she didn't know there had been a row. Life was just a blank, and it was in this mood one evening that she turned up her old diary of Cornwall.

That lovely holiday was lived again by going over those brief notes, but the important factor for her was a promise she had written down as a reminder – a promise to Paul that she would go and see him in his first big part. Acting on the spur of the moment, she went to the telephone and rang up the theatre. He would, she judged by the time, be just getting ready for the evening performance. His voice answered her.

'Oh, it's you, Delia. The stage door man said he recognised your voice, but the description he gave of you wasn't flattering.'

Delia listened intently to see if, woman-like, she could detect any pleasure or excitement in his voice at her ringing up, but there was none. He was just nicely friendly. She did not know that for days he had been on the point of telephoning to her.

'Paul,' she said, 'six months ago I made you a promise to come and see you in your first big part. The weeks have gone by so quickly. Am I still in time?'

'No, just a fortnight too late,' he said, 'but you are in time for something else – that's if you can come down tonight. Of course, it may come to nothing, but, as a matter of fact, there's a film chap coming here tonight. I seem to have had such good notices these last two weeks that it's roused the film wallahs.'

'Paul, darling, how perfectly marvellous. Of course I'll come – but I'll have to make some speed, won't I?'

'You've got half an hour,' he told her.

Sitting in the front row of the stalls Delia watched Paul through new eyes. Even she, who knew his work so well, was agreeably surprised. He had a finish which surprised her, and an easy confidence and enjoyment in his work that found its way over the footlights and communicated itself to the audience.

It was an enjoyable evening, marred only by the fact that the Faversham family were sitting two rows behind her. During the interval, as she gazed around to see if she could spot the film man, she looked right into Mrs Faversham's face. Paul's mother, Ian and Stella had undoubtedly seen her already. They steadily looked right through her and ignored her stiffly inclined head in their direction.

After she had got over the first surprise at seeing them there Delia could hardly suppress a rueful smile. How like Paul! He must have known his family were coming and yet he had, with complete lack of tact, given her by far the better seat – or was it because he still cared? She hardly thought so, and was in no mood to surmise.

At the end of the show she lost no time in getting round to the stage door, hoping to reach it before the family. But they had got there first by the simple means of foregoing the end of the play. Because they were there, and because Paul was already surrounded by crowds of congratulating people, she stayed long enough only to say a few words to him, to smile into his eyes and wish him luck, and then to allow the press of people to edge her away from him.

She noticed his family had taken up a stand, a firm stand, behind him. They wanted to be in on it when the film man spoke. Delia hadn't spotted the film man, but he had seen her and watched her exit thoughtfully. With remarkable tactics he got Paul to himself and cheated Paul's doting relatives of hearing the few encouraging words that he had to say. Then he went on: 'Who was that lovely girl who came up and spoke to you?'

'Which one?' Paul asked. He had a confused idea of so many attractive women who had made it their business to come up and speak to him that night.

'Copper-coloured hair,' the film man said, enumerating swiftly. 'Wide, dark eyes, a haunting expression, good carriage – my stars, she's got everything. Photogenic! Knew how to dress, too. I could make something of her.'

'Oh,' said Paul, flatly. 'That's Delia Grayson, the girl I hope to marry.' But there wasn't much hope in his voice.

The film man shot him a curious look but said no more. But when he was leaving he repeated, 'Remember that girl – bring her with you when you come.'

Toward the end of March Keith phoned Delia and said, 'I'm lonely and fed up. Let's go out together somewhere.'

'Where's Susaline?' Delia countered.

'Oh, dancing, I suppose,' he said, carelessly.

'I don't think so, Keith,' she said. 'It's one thing to study here with you but another to start going out with you.'

'You went to night school with me,' he protested.

'Well, that's with lots of people,' she said.

'For heaven's sake, Delia, what's the difference between the crowds at night school

312

and the crowds at a theatre?'

She was silent.

'Well, Delia, if you like, I'll try and find Susaline and tell her what I'm going to do, if that'll make you happy. But, believe me, Susaline won't care a hang either way.'

'All right, then, Keith, if you'll do that.'

He arranged to meet her in the Square. She looked curiously at him as they met.

'Did you tell Susaline?' she asked.

His glance slid away from her.

'No, I couldn't find her but I left a note. Same thing.'

She started to protest that it was not the same thing and then realised how childish it would sound. After all, as he had said over the telephone, what was the difference between this and night school? He gave her no time for reflection but thrust into her hands a bunch of primula and a box of chocolates.

'Come on,' he said, 'we'll miss the start of the big picture.'

'I thought we were going to the theatre,' she said.

He didn't stop, but said hurriedly, as he steered her across the road, 'Sorry, Delia, but they're all booked up. The King's is the best I can do. It's a good picture. What's the difference?'

She didn't answer. To point out that the pictures were in darkness and the theatre was not entirely savoured of bickering. So she let him have his way but it was, for her, by no means a comfortable evening.

There was, too, a new element about him tonight. She couldn't pin it down to anything in particular beyond one or two seemingly unimportant details. He usually came to meet her with an old felt hat pulled well down over his eyes and his overcoat shrugged on dejectedly. Yet, tonight, he had obviously taken pains with his appearance. There was almost a jaunty air about him; an air of a man being out with his girl friend.

There was, too, an air of being conscious about her. On other occasions she had been nettled by his not even looking at her. She might have been a man or an elderly woman; someone to talk to but not someone to really look at. Now it was different. He looked at her intently, as if he was seeing her through new eyes, and the obvious approval in his face made her pulses race.

This was the Keith she had always dreamed of seeing. In this new mood there was something disturbing about him; something vaguely exciting and somehow, though she hesitated over the expression, not exactly *good*. She tried to shrug the thought away. Reasonable for the warning note to come about a stranger, but this was Keith, Keith whom she had known all her life.

But it persisted. It persisted even though he was clever enough to leave her at the main entrance to her flats after the most perfunctory and friendly good-night.

She went straight to bed. But the thoughts that had struggled for expression all the way through the film performance now began to take shape in her mind. What had made Keith change? What had made him suddenly see her as a woman and not as just as friend, a lifelong friend who evoked no sort of interest in him whatever beyond the needs of their mutual work?

Could it be that Susaline had left him again? She hardly thought so. Besides, he would have told her if Susaline had gone. It was the first thing he said when he came to her on those occasions. Indeed, sometimes she wished he wouldn't be so anxious to come to her with that particular trouble. The subject of Susaline had long ago become boring to her.

No, it was something else, and though she thought all round the subject for hours, far into the small hours, she could come to no satisfactory conclusion.

One thing that worried her more than all others was her own attitude to Keith now that this change had come over him. She found him dangerous, disturbing, but she also found herself wanting to see what else happened. This was the Keith she had always longed to discover, in those days before he met Susaline, and he was free to pay attentions to herself. She had dreamed of him looking at her as he did tonight, of being aware of her, of buying her things like flowers and chocolates, of making himself so spruce to come out and meet her for the evening. But it had never happened, then.

Of course, she admitted fairly to herself, in those days she hadn't looked so prepossessing herself. That was before she had paid that fateful visit to the beauty parlour. She had been so very ordinary. Who could blame Keith for not getting excited about her?

But then, came the instant answer, he hadn't become excited about her when she did look glamorous enough to arouse (and maintain) the interest of half the unattached men in town. She struggled to remember his exact words when he had first seen her fresh from the hairdresser's and facial expert's hands.

He had stared at her for a blank second. Then, 'Good lord, what on earth have you done to yourself, Delia?'

She had explained. 'Why shouldn't I, Keith? Other women do, and the earth doesn't stop revolving!'

He had screwed his face up in unrestrained disapproval, the expected disapproval of a brother for a favourite, clean-scrubbed sister. 'Disgusting! Don't expect to be seen around with me with all that muck on your face!'

She turned over in bed and buried her face in the pillow, forgetting for the moment the thick layer of night cream she had not long applied. There was one decision and one decision only to which she could come. She knew it, and faced it squarely. She mustn't see Keith again.

It was all right in the old days, but to see him now – after he had shown so clearly that, whatever the cause, he now felt that way about her – would be the sure way to court disaster. She shuddered. 'It's beastly of him, beastly! Why does he have to do this now of all times?'

Twice he rang up at her flat, and each time she made an excuse not to see him. Once she had another date with a man she had not seen since she left Sir Timothy's office. She had made it specially so that she would have a legitimate excuse, but after going out with the man she wished she hadn't. It had been very boring. The second time she simply said she wasn't free, but didn't bother to make an appointment. She felt frustrated, and began to think of going out of town. She began to dread the telephone ringing, and once, when it rang at about the time Keith rang, she didn't answer it, then was tortured for the rest of the evening in case it had been Paul.

But Keith didn't bother to use the telephone any more. He strode down the long passage and knocked at the flat door, taking Delia by surprise. Before she had had time to realise that it might be him, she had naturally opened the door, and he gently propelled her in before him, as he had on that other occasion before Christmas when she had protested about his presence there.

'You've been putting me off, Delia? Why?' he began, and she was quick to notice the new masterful tone in his voice.

But because he was, after all, just Keith and not a stranger, she was able to answer him in a more or less normal tone. 'Because I didn't want to see you,' she said, calmly.

'But why, Delia? Not afraid of me all of a sudden, are you?'

'Good lord no, Keith! Don't flatter yourself. But I have asked you to consider my reputation and not come to my flat. If you really had any consideration for me, you'd do as I ask and keep away. There's been talk, you know.'

He smiled, and flinging his hat on to a side table, he sat down easily on the divan and pulled her down beside him. 'Who cares?' he asked, easily.

Delia frowned. He wasn't even as easy to deal with as he had been once, and she found herself wishing that he'd start talking about Susaline.

'Where *is* Susaline, by the way?' Delia asked, suddenly.

'Dancing,' he said, calmly. 'But don't let's talk about Susaline. Let's talk about us.'

It was the usual line, the line of the all-conquering male, and although she felt disappointed that Keith, of all people, should not attempt to use any different line of talk to her, it did at least make him a little easier to deal with.

'All right, if you think we shall be at all interesting,' she smiled. 'I should have thought that after knowing each other all our lives we'd find no more to say.'

'Would you?' he asked softly, and leaned a little further towards her.

Against her will her heart began to beat faster. She was conscious of the clean fairness of him, of the smell of his soap, the freshness of the non-scented hair oil he used. His linen was so clean, everything about him neat as a new pin. Just as he had been when he was courting Susaline, and, indeed, the string of young women before Susaline's time. Delia thought wildly, 'I wish he hadn't shaved, that he hadn't been quite so bandbox – it would have made it easier!'

He said, softly: 'You know, Delia, you've gradually become such a lovely woman that even I – used as I am to seeing you around – have to sit up and take notice! How d'you do it? And why haven't you been snapped up by some other fellow, long ago?'

'Don't be silly, Keith! That sort of talk

doesn't suit you! Just what *did* you come for tonight?' she retorted.

'To talk to you,' he replied, in no way put out by her brisk tones. 'I can't get any sense out of you on the telephone, or I would have suggested another evening out. I enjoyed that last one. Didn't you?'

'It was all right. But I prefer going to Night School with you. You're more interesting in working mood than at the pictures.'

Instantly she was sorry she had said that. He took it the wrong way. 'I can *be* more interesting,' he smiled.

'I didn't mean any such thing,' she said, hastily. 'I meant I preferred your company at work. Otherwise, you seem to be just like any other young man. And those are ten a penny – free!'

She thought that would make him sit back and look sulky as he would have done not long ago. He had in those days taken offence so easily. Now, however, he seemed to be a different person. He just smiled silkily at her, but not from his eyes.

'The kitten shows her claws,' he said, and came a shade closer. 'As to being free, for what? You don't want marriage, Delia. You could have had marriage scores of times with any of these fellows who've been dancing attendance on you. No, you want a good time, or why else would you have strung along with me since I've been married?'

She attempted to thrust him away. 'Well, there's gratitude,' she burst out in disgust. She was surprised that he should say that, even allowing for the alteration in his manner just lately. 'You wanted someone to talk to about your rotten choice of wife, and you came to me, and I honestly hadn't the heart not to listen to you. Is that all I get for it?'

'Oh, no,' he murmured. 'That's just it. You're going to get your reward, Delia. The reward I imagine you've been waiting for all this time.'

Before she could protest, he had tightened his arm round her and pulled her to him. His lips, thin and well shaped, but purposeful now, fastened on hers, and he kissed her.

She didn't resist, not because she liked it, but because there flashed into her mind a question she had asked herself all those months ago in Cornwall. Would she have said yes to Paul if she could have compared his kiss with that of Keith? Well, now Keith was kissing her, and purely from the vantage point of experiment where Paul was concerned, she felt she had to make no protest. To experience it and to judge accordingly.

Her first reaction was of surprise and then anger. To herself and Aunt Cora, Keith had always been upright, beyond reproach. It had been so firmly ingrained in both of them that it had become a sort of cult. Now, with this first kiss of Keith's, that illusion was shattered once and for all. It was not the kiss of a man who loves a woman. It was at once hungry, passionate, and vaguely insulting.

She struggled to push him away, but he wouldn't release her. He did, however, take his lips from hers and look sheepily into her eyes. 'What's the matter, Delia?' he murmured. 'Can't you take my brand of kisses? Or should I have gone slower about it, crept up on you so to speak?'

'Keith, you're horrible!' she spat out.

He raised delicately shaped fair eyebrows, but made no attempt to move. 'You woman!' he said, mildly. 'Here's you been chasing me for ages, and now I've let you catch me you don't like it. There's Susaline howling for her freedom, but what would she do with it if I gave it to her? It seems to me, in my limited knowledge of the ways of women, that the way to deal with them is to continually say "no." They either come round and accept it, or they fight like truculent kittens and are infinitely interesting. I think you're going to fight all the time.'

'You're right, I'm going to fight, but not all the time, because there won't be any time after this. You get out of my flat before I ring down for the porter to put you out!'

He ignored that. He raised puzzled eyes to hers. 'You know, Delia, I just don't understand you. You've been wanting this all the time. Even Susaline saw it. It was she who opened my eyes to the fact that you're crazy about me. After all, you have been no more than a sister to me – a fellow can't be blamed if he isn't very interested in a girl he's known all his life. But when his own wife ups and says that said girl is in love with him, well – that's something! Don't you agree?'

Delia's face flamed in fury. She could cheerily have knocked Susaline down for saying such a thing. It would have been bad enough for Keith to see her feeling for him himself, but to be woken up to the fact by Susaline of all people...

'Look, Delia, don't let's fight. I'm not asking you for anything impossible or indecent. You know me; I'm not that kind of a man. I'm not the kind to drag women through newspaper publicity, either – you know what I mean. I'm not giving Susaline her freedom, because I don't believe she honestly wants it. At the same time, I'm not going to insult you by doing anything you don't want. But you do want me to love you a little, don't you? Yes, I can see you do. I've been a blind fool not to see it all along. Well, I could come here sometimes and pet you and make you happy, and who's to know? Who will come to any harm by it? Delia, what d'you say?'

She closed her eyes in panic. She had

never panicked before. She had always known how to deal with men. But this new Keith was such an unknown quantity he might well have been a stranger. She wondered for a moment whether he had been drinking, but discounted that immediately. She could tell he hadn't. But it might well be that hearing from one woman that another was in love with him was enough of an overwhelming thing to affect him as strong drink would do.

'I must think … I must use guile … I must be clever with him…' she told herself, and struggled to keep her composure.

He kissed her closed eyelids, and she opened them suddenly. It must stop, now, before he got any more difficult.

She laughed a little, and leaning towards him, brushed her lips lightly against his cheek and got up. As she expected, the action disarmed him and he let her go.

'You know, Keith, I am a fool, but just at first I was scared. You looked such a brute when you first came in.' She got cigarettes for both of them and came and sat down again. Easily. As she would have in the old days. She lit them both and asked if he wanted a drink. He shook his head.

'Let's talk this over and see how it'll work. You sure Susaline won't make trouble if we – well, just love each other a little?'

The wary look fled from his face and he

entered the discussion animatedly. She let him put his arms round her, kiss her once or twice, and when she protested she was tired and would prefer it if he came the next night, he went without too much difficulty.

When he was at last outside the door and she had shut it on him, she stood staring stupidly at it, and then she felt the reaction. She realised she was trembling all over and that her legs would scarcely support her. With difficulty she bolted the door and slipped the chain on, and somehow stumbled over to the armchair.

How long she sat there she didn't know. Finally she managed to get herself a drink and that steadied her. She realised that it was late. She was tired, but she knew she wouldn't sleep that night. But she must rest.

She crawled into bed. At first she thought she'd run away to Aunt Cora, but put that idea out of her head. It was feeble. Childish. Aunt Cora would say she had asked for it. No, that wouldn't do.

Paul? How could she? What would he say when she told him how it all led up to it? Besides, she didn't want any trouble between the two men.

But somehow she must get away from here, somewhere where Keith couldn't find her. That meant giving up the flat. Plans chased round in her head. Aunt Cora had paid the rent for a year and that complicated things. Plans … she discarded them almost as quickly as they came. None were any good. And she had invited Keith to come tomorrow night. He would come, she knew.

Just before dawn she made up her mind and then went to sleep. Melita. Melita and James. She would pack a bag and go early tomorrow morning for a brief spell of safety and time to think. She would go to Cornwall.

CHAPTER 21

Melita and James were at the station in the car. With them was the baby, a bonny child of some seven months, who crowed and laughed as though the whole thing were great good fun. Delia was grateful for the presence of the child; it gave an opportunity for everyone to talk a lot of nonsense and to make it a frothy, gay meeting, rather than the quiet one dominated by searching looks and a polite refrain from awkward questions, which Delia had expected and dreaded.

Melita said, as they collected her small quota of luggage and started off, 'We got your telegram only a few hours ago. Bit dramatic, eh?' and laughed a little uncertainly.

'Look here, you two,' Delia began urgently, but James cut in.

'If you're thinking of apologising for springing this visit on us, Delia, please don't. We said when you went last October that whenever you wanted to come down we'd have open house for you. That's a promise we meant. So let it go. If Melita's inquisitive, put her in her place. You've my permission to do so.'

Tears stung Delia's eyes, and for the moment she could do no more than stammer incoherent thanks. But later, when she had recovered a little, she said:

'I'll tell you why I came down here. It was to get your help, both of you. If you can't give me help and advice, at least I shall be safe with you here and have time to think it all out for myself. At the very least, Cornwall's healing. I must have time to think.'

They didn't press her then to tell them about it, but waited until she was ready to talk, and that wasn't until the end of a long and satisfying day punctuated with fun with the baby, a jolly, fat, healthy child, and walks into the village with Melita on shopping expeditions.

'Isn't it a funny thing?' Melita said. 'Since the child arrived I never seem to be able to think up a coherent shopping list. I'm always popping out for something or other at the last minute!'

She laughed a lot more now Delia noticed.

There was an infectious gaiety about her that made her good to be with. It struck Delia that James, too, had changed a lot. Although no one could accuse him of infectious gaiety, at least his manner had eased considerably, and he had lost that drawn haggard look, and that tendency to be cutting of tongue when you least expected or wanted it. Could it be the baby who had achieved this change? Or was it that the presence of the baby filled an alarming and widening gap in their lives and took away the consequent fear of their marriage coming to grief?

There was a different atmosphere in Haley's Gap altogether, Delia noticed, and was glad of it. People visited them more, and instead of remaining aloof from the village, Melita flung herself madly and joyously into everything, from a responsible position in the village institute to playing the organ in the sailors' mission on Sundays. The baby was left comfortably in charge of the 'Nannie,' which was the glorious title given to the fifteen-year-old from the village, dressed elaborately in a navy uniform several sizes too large for her; a child who swelled with pride each time she went out with the enormous cream and chrome bassinette and styled herself a 'member of the doctor's household'.

That night, with Melita comfortably curled

up on the end of Delia's bed, the story of Paul and Keith came tumbling out. Delia hadn't meant to tell Melita; six months ago Melita would not have appeared an attractive audience to her. But now, the new Melita had some sort of understanding which drew from the reluctant Delia those things she had decided to keep to herself.

'I didn't think Keith was a stinker like that, Delia,' Melita said, slowly. She, too, had known him long before he met Susaline. 'Still, you never know. I must say I think you were a bit of a nitwit to encourage him to your flat to work but still – even when I was there, he just treated you as a sister. I can't honestly say I blame you.' She smiled, a bright, warm smile. 'The trouble with you is you're too kind. That fellow needed a kick in the pants rather than a helping hand.'

Delia said, 'I wonder what he'll do tonight when he finds the flat closed up and me gone?'

'Will he guess you've come down here?' Melita wanted to know, and brought a look of alarm to Delia's face. 'But he wouldn't have the nerve to follow you. Besides, he couldn't – there's his job. He couldn't just down tools and leave that, could he?'

'No-o,' Delia said, slowly, 'though I some-times wonder if in a mad, fed-up mood he'd throw it all up. No, I don't think he would, though. At rock bottom he's too conventional to give that up.'

The next day Delia wrote to Aunt Cora and told her that she was tired of town and had gone down to visit Melita. 'I had to tell her, Melita, in case she called at the flat and was alarmed at my absence. We haven't quite got used to the idea that we're now living in separate camps.'

'Why don't you let Aunt Cora marry you off if you're really not keen on this Paul?' Melita asked, curiously.

'Would you if you were me?' Delia asked.

'I don't know,' Melita answered, slowly. 'You see, even if I wasn't in love with my first husband, at least I thought I was, and that meant that there was no room for anyone else in my thoughts. Now, with you, it's different. There doesn't seem to be any fellow that takes up every waking moment. At least, not now that Keith has shown the cloven hoof, so to speak. I did begin to wonder how it would all turn out, to tell you the truth, when I saw how crazy you were about him. But now you seem to be … just empty.' Melita looked slightly apologetic as she said it. But Delia knew it was the truth.

That was what she was … just empty.

She stayed in Cornwall nearly a month. At first it was just for the rest and the pleasure of being with James and his family. Then, when the coach tours resumed their season's programme, the holiday resolved itself into a sort of pilgrimage – a revisiting of just those places which she and Paul did together in the same order.

Delia couldn't have said what made her do it. It wasn't exactly nostalgia for Paul, but rather a curiosity. A trial to see if she could recapture those feelings she had experienced then. And it came about by her walking down to James's own cove, at the foot of the little harbour, on just such a night as she and Paul had done it together. She remembered his kiss, and now – in view of her being able to compare it with that of Keith – she realised, with a sense of shock, that all along she had been following the wrong track, chasing the wrong shadow. Whatever the circumstances, Paul would never have behaved as Keith had done. If he had been unhappily married, he would have kept the knowledge to himself, not taken advantage of an old friend's kindness and company, first by whining and impinging on her free time, and then by playing so devastatingly on her affections.

That started the whole idea of the pilgrimage, and by the time she made the trip to Land's End she knew the truth. Oddly, when she and Paul had gone there together, it had been a grey day of mist and damp, but today, with the fresh green grass and the spring flowers starting from banks and roadsides, the whole earth seemed full of new promise. As she left the main cluster of tourists to look across the blue of the channel, her heart leaped; the Scillies were plainly visible.

'First time for months,' a man said, near at hand. 'Hardly ever able to see 'em with the naked eye,' and Delia turned to see the driver of the coach, standing by her, looking as enthusiastic about it as if he had caused the phenomenon himself, unaided.

She nodded. 'It's an omen, a good omen,' she murmured, and moved away.

The place was full of memories for her. The tiny café where Paul had taken her to tea, from thick white mugs; where huge slabs of shop-cake had gone down as well as if they had been delectable fancies from Aunt Cora's kitchen. There they had seen the extremely thin tourist who furtively ate tomato sandwiches out of a brown paper bag, despite the notice on the wall which forbade one's own food to be eaten on the premises.

She walked over the bluffs by the tiny path until Sennen Cove could be seen. The old fisherman was still there, inveigling tourists to sit in the chair – a rocklike formation exactly the shape of an armchair – and tempting them to look down into the churning waters at a needle-rock known as the Irish Lady.

Delia smiled as he came forward, and she let him go through the performance again. An old man with white grizzled hair and skin like tan-stained leather. His teeth were now yellow fangs, and his bright blue eyes were mere slits in the maze of wrinkles that formed his face. The Irish lady, who sang to the drowning men... Last time Paul had been with her, and this same old man had said: 'This time next year there'll be three on yer – a little'un maybe.' Well he was wrong. Or was he? This time next year he had said; that was late October again, six months and more ahead. A lot could happen in that number of months.

Suddenly Delia was all impatience to get ahead. While she listened dutifully to the story of the great rock that was supposed to be like Queen Victoria's profile, she was working out how many more tours she had to make to complete the pilgrimage. There was still Lamorna to do, but she decided she would rule that out, or at least, merely go there to look; she couldn't undertake that dreadful cliff climb without Paul to hang on to. Lamorna, Mousehole and ... Polperro.

'Aren't you tired of going about alone?' Melita wanted to know that night. 'We'll come with you if you're lonely.'

Delia said, 'I'm only doing two more tours, then I'm going back to Chiverstock. There's something I've set myself to do ...

alone, I'm afraid, Melita ... and then I'm going back to find Paul.'

'Darling, I'm so glad!' Melita sounded whole-heartedly sincere. 'Is it all right? Will it work out, d'you suppose?'

'I don't know,' Delia said, slowly, but she couldn't disguise the excitement in her voice. 'That's what I've got to find out.'

The sun blazed high overhead, in a sort of advance taste of high summer, the day she went to Polperro. It was phenomenal weather. Tourists wore summer frocks and carried light coats. 'I wish Paul were here,' Delia murmured, and played with the idea of writing suggesting he came for a week-end. But how did she know that he'd be free to come, or that he'd want to if he could? Also, there was a nagging anxiety about the safety of his letters addressed to his home; his mother had been so bitter, so ready to break them apart, Delia was doubtful as to just how far Mrs Faversham would go in order to keep Delia from her son.

This was where the anchor had been bought. She didn't go near the shop in case there were other anchors on chains; she wanted to feel that hers was the only one and not just a trinket made up ready to catch tourists.

'So you're leaving us tomorrow, Delia?' James said that night. 'We'll be sorry to lose you, though just lately you've taken to going off like the wild cat that walked on his wild lone.'

Melita said, 'Ah, there was a purpose behind it!' and laughing, looked mysterious, but excited, too. 'Oh, Delia, I hope it turns out all right, I *hope* it works!' and getting up, impulsively kissed her. Delia's eyes were bright with unshed tears.

'You're darlings, both of you, and I want you to know how much I appreciate the way you've both left me to myself to work it all out in my own way. I couldn't have asked for anything more. And if it does turn out all right, I promise you, you'll both be the very first to know.'

On the train back, the next day, she paused and thought for the first time of the possibility of her being unable to see Paul. It was an unwelcome thought, and she couldn't have said what put it into her head.

'What shall I do if I can't see him and don't know where to find him?' she panicked, as the miles were eaten up and she was being rushed towards Chiverstock. 'I can't go back to the flat – I don't want to!'

Commonsense came flooding back, however. There was no need to fear a meeting with Keith, on a week-day, when he would be at the bank. She must go back to the flat to collect other things she'd need. More or less she'd made up her mind to give the place up, and if she could come to no agreement with Paul, if he no longer wanted her, she'd go elsewhere, to some other town – county, if need be – to live and work. Chiverstock was too full of memories to be of any use to her now.

She felt better when she had made her decision. She even allowed herself the promise of a visit to Aunt Cora before she finally went away, and that settled her completely. She had a tidy mind and liked to leave no loose ends.

Chiverstock was clean-washed with spring rain when she arrived at the station and left her baggage in the waiting-room. It was necessary to go through the square to get to the theatre, but it was an effort. She would have to pass Sir Timothy's window, the bank, the solicitor's where Paul's brother worked, and the Starlight Hall. Here she got her first shock.

Outside was a new hoarding, with two blonde figures dancing in each other's arms. It was merely a month ago since she had been here, yet already the Starlight was boosting its new exhibition dancers – Keith and Susaline Pemberley.

'How long's that been going on?' she asked blankly, as she became aware of the doorman staring curiously at her.

He came over. 'New on tonight. Don't know how they'll turn out yet, but shouldn't be surprised if they aren't a big attraction.

Young chap works over at the bank,' he said, jerking a thumb. 'Married, they are. Never did care for married couples working together – too many rows. Still, she fell out with the dark chap she had so it might turn out all right.'

He went back to his gloomy survey of the square and Delia walked on. Why had Susaline quarrelled with her cousin? The nature of her? Probably. But looking back, she recalled that when Susaline had first come home to meet Aunt Cora, she had been trying to coax Keith to go in for dancing with her. Was this the thin end of the wedge at last? Or had he decided it was the only way to keep his wife?

Delia grinned twistedly. Well, at least he could dance better than write. Even she, at her most kind and encouraging, could hardly say with truth that he showed any flair for writing. He was too persevering and hadn't the imagination or the 'feel' for words. But he had always been a good dancer.

At the Repertory Theatre she got shock No. 2. New bills were up here also, and Paul's name was missing.

Her heart sank. This, then, was the premonition she had had on the train. Paul had gone. Gone without attempting to get in touch with her. Or had he?

She thought quickly. The only way he could have communicated was by telephone or letter at the flat. That, then, must be the next port of call.

Somehow, after Melita's bright house, in that lovely corner of Cornwall, the flatlet looked desperately dreary and conventional. This wasn't home; it couldn't be, ever. For the first time she was glad she had decided to leave it.

She put off the moment to look in the box behind the door. When she did, it was as she had suspected; there was, among that collection of bills and receipts, no letter from Paul. There was, however, one from Aunt Cora, written before she could have received Delia's from Cornwall.

In it she said briefly that Sir Timothy had had to go abroad on business, and had decided that she should go with him to visit places she hadn't yet seen. They would be gone six months. Timothy, she said, had decided to take a new partner, to carry on while he was away; a brother of the partner who had died before Delia's time. An admirable man, she enlarged, who could be entrusted with the business while they were away. Aunt Cora bubbled happily through the four closely written pages, unconscious of the piling up of unpleasant surprises to which she was contributing.

Delia slumped down in a chair. Paul had gone. Aunt Cora had gone. There was nothing left, now, then.

Yes, there was. There was still one opening, though a slender one, of finding out what had happened to Paul. She picked up the telephone receiver and dialled his brother's number at the office.

'Mr Ian Faversham is engaged,' she was told, and when she persisted in her desire to speak to him, either by hanging on the line or ringing again at intervals, they reluctantly fetched him.

'Well, Delia?' Ian's voice was cold.

'I want to know where I can find Paul,' she said, coming straight to the point. 'There's something I have to say to him. Let me have his address, Ian, will you?'

'He doesn't want to hear from you,' Ian said.

'Did he say so?' Her voice was desperate.

'I don't know much about it, except that I'm afraid I'm not at liberty to pass on any information about my brother's movements.'

He was about to hang up, but she said quickly, 'Why can't I know? Surely it's for Paul to tell me whether he wants to hear from me or not?'

'Well, what do *you* think?' Ian countered. 'He had plenty of opportunity to write and tell you himself, if he'd wanted you to know.'

'No harm can come of giving me his address,' she pleaded.

'I can't waste any more time, Delia. If you aren't satisfied with what I've told you, I suggest you go and see my mother.' With that he replaced the receiver.

Mrs Faversham was the last person that Delia wanted to see, but it seemed her last hope. If the woman wouldn't tell her over the telephone, it looked as if a personal visit was the only thing left.

She dialled the Faversham house quickly, before Ian had had time to telephone and warn his mother that Delia had been enquiring. But it was obviously all arranged between them. Stella answered the telephone.

'If you want any information you'd better come and see my mother. She isn't talking to you on the 'phone.' The receiver was replaced immediately.

Delia frowned. It seemed rather vindictive of them to want to go to such lengths, but there was this hope; that, once there, she might stumble on something that would give her a lead as to where he had gone. If, as she suspected, it was the film job that was offered to him, she didn't even know the company's name.

'What a fool I am – why, the theatre would have told me!'

She telephoned the box office first, but they weren't able to help her. It seemed that Paul had not left the company because of any other offer of work, but simply because he had fallen out with the manager. They were unfriendly, unhelpful.

Wearily, she took her few things, packed, down to the booking office of the station, and made the few arrangements for again locking up the flat. She got in touch with Aunt Cora's solicitor and told him she was leaving it for good, so that some new tenant could be found, and the rent Aunt Cora had paid adjusted. There was nothing left, then, beyond that unpleasant visit to the Faversham house, to keep her in Chiverstock.

The Faversham women were waiting for her, in the sitting-room. Around Paul's mother's mouth was a grim smile playing.

'So you expected me to give you my son's address, did you?' she said, with every evidence of enjoyment at the coming interview. Stella had a grim, cold look that Delia didn't understand, and didn't attempt to worry over. Stella, it seemed, was content to let her mother-in-law make the pace and to tag along behind.

'Frankly, no,' Delia said. 'But since I couldn't get it from anywhere else, it was worth a trial.'

'Well, you won't get his address,' Mrs Faversham said, 'but I will tell you what happened. I think you'll like to know. My son's going to be famous. Rich and famous – and you'll have no part in it. You just can't reach him.'

Delia listened in silence.

'And I'm glad – glad that he's free from

the like of your sort!' There was withering contempt in Paul's mother's voice.

'Save the insults, Mrs Faversham, and just tell me where he is,' Delia said, quietly.

'I'll tell it in my own way,' Mrs Faversham said, bridling, 'and I'll thank you to keep a still tongue in your head, miss!'

Paul, it appeared, had got his film offer. 'A fine contract, and it took him away – right away – at once!' his mother said, with satisfaction. 'What did they call it, Stella? Ah, that's right – on location.' She paused for effect. 'To Africa.'

'To Central Africa,' Stella added.

'When are they sailing?' Delia whispered, after a pause in which she drew breath and made a lightning effort to realise that Paul was probably no longer in the country. Mrs Faversham watched her greedily, and seemed faintly disappointed.

'They've sailed,' she said, harshly. Stella darted a quick look at her, but Delia was too shocked to bother over such a detail. For her it was a thing of wonder that Paul's mother could hate her so fiercely and want to watch her being hurt like this. 'He's gone right away, and it's your own fault!'

'What d'you mean, Mrs Faversham?'

'Mother!' Stella warned softly, though for what reason Delia couldn't guess.

'I won't be silenced! She *shall* hear!' the older woman snapped. 'He did try and see you, though I warned him he'd better not. He went to the flat, and found that nasty Mr Pemberley knocking. He seemed to imagine you'd be – er – expecting him!' She bared her teeth with pleasure. 'Naturally, my son didn't think it necessary to wait any longer to say goodbye to such a creature who had men in her rooms at night!'

'Mother, you don't know for sure–' Stella began, nervously, but Mrs Faversham cut her short.

'I don't *have* to know for sure! Look at her face, her guilty face? That's confirmation, if nothing else is!'

Delia got up, and silently walked out. She hardly noticed what they were saying. For her the essential thing was that if Paul had indeed run into Keith on her doorstep that could only have been the night she had left for Cornwall, now a month ago. Too late…

She stumbled out of the road in which Paul had lived and took a bus back to the square. It was too soon for her train, the train she had decided to take to London, in the event of her not being able to contact Paul. London seemed a large enough, a remote enough, impersonal enough place from which to make a fresh start. There no one would know her. And she would know no one. All she asked, now, was for work. Hard work, in which to forget…

She walked round the Square, almost unseeingly. Yet it was all imprinting itself on her brain in the brilliant spring sunshine: the Georgian houses, the shops, the green, railed-off patch in the centre with the memorial; the cinema where she had gone with Keith, and hated it so; the rep., the Starlight Hall, the café ... and the lane in which was The Cellar.

'Just a farewell visit,' she whispered to herself, crossing the Square, and letting her feet take her, almost against her will, to that place where she and Paul had first become friends. 'I know I shouldn't do this, but I must ... I must have some memory to take with me. It's got to last for so long.'

She went slowly down the steps, and past the little cash-desk and the kitchen door, into The Cellar itself. She took in everything, even to looking back at the kitchen door for a sight of Miss Ann.

And there stood Miss Ann, mouth open, eyes popping, wildly gesticulating. Miss Bessie appeared, and also gaped.

Delia nodded and smiled. 'I've been away,' she explained, thinking that their surprise was due to her long absence.

'Look who's here,' Miss Bessie whispered, then again gesticulating behind her, fetched Miss Lou.

'Oh! Oh, my goodness!' Miss Lou gasped. 'Well, I never did – now it'll be all right!'

'Sh-h-h!' the other two hissed at her, and

with a great air of conspiracy they huddled together, pushing Delia forward, and pointing. 'The usual,' they said, in chorus, nodding and beaming. 'The table in the alcove!'

Delia smiled. 'Might as well,' she sighed, wondering how she could get through a lonely lunch in this place at their own favourite table.

She wandered over to it, and pulled back the curtain. There was a man in there, a man who got up with a wondering face, and a look of complete unbelief in his eyes.

'Delia!' he breathed.

'Paul!'

She let the curtain swing to behind her, to the disappointment of the three sisters who clustered in the doorway, and one or two customers whose interest had been aroused by the little pantomime. Paul took her in his arms, and for the moment Delia forgot everything: The Cellar, his mother, the posters in the Square, the drenching belief that she had lost him. All subsided into a vague mist, and she felt herself drift in the thrill of his embrace.

When at last he let her go and they sat down (still grasping hands as if reluctant to let each other go for fear of another separation) they stared at each other for a full minute, then let go a barrage of questions, both at the same time. Into the storm of hows, whys and whens, Miss Lou triumphantly bore down on them, with covered bowls of chicken broth. 'Special!' she hissed, and noted with approval their happy faces.

'Paul,' Delia managed to get out at last, 'your mother said you'd already sailed with the film company.'

His face darkened with anger. 'I don't sail for two days. She knew that,' he said.

Between questions, half-finished answers, and the special lunch which Miss Lou insisted on their clearing up while it was hot, Delia told him what had happened since she returned from Cornwall. He was angry, but his anger lost its heat in the miracle of finding her again.

She said, 'Don't you want to know about Keith?'

'I'm afraid I made a mess of his face that night outside your flat,' Paul grinned, 'but it doesn't seem to have stopped him taking up a dancing career with that wife of his!'

She repeated her question.

'No,' he answered, 'I know.' He smiled. 'It didn't matter, anyway, Delia. I knew there was some reasonable explanation – knowing you as I do.'

'But how did you know?'

'Like an ass, I tried everywhere to find you, except James and Melita. I didn't think of them till this morning. I had a brief but pithy trunk call with Melita who told me most everything I wanted to know.' He smiled into her blank face. 'So, you see, my trouble wasn't to know what you were doing, but where I could pick you up. You weren't at the flat. I was stumped.'

'And you came here – why, Paul?'

'Sentimental journey, I suppose,' he smiled, 'and to think. I might have missed you altogether!'

'But you didn't, Paul, I'm going to miss you. How long will you be away?'

He looked at her throat, at the slender silver chain, the end of which vanished behind her dress. 'The anchor?' he hazarded.

She nodded.

'You still wear it, then, Delia?'

She nodded again.

'Melita told me about your going over the ground we travelled, Delia. Why did you do that?'

'To find the answer to a question, Paul.'

'What did the pilgrimage tell you?' Everything hung on her answer and he waited, hardly daring to hope, despite Melita's rather precipitate assurance that Delia was crazy about him.

'That I've been an awful fool, Paul, and that it was you I loved all the time.'

Miss Bessie, having won the lots they drew in the kitchen, proudly sailed in at this point with the coffee; coffee with cream floating on the top.

Paul said, 'Does that mean you'll come to

Africa with me? We can be married on the boat, you know. And there's a bit of news for you that I think you'll like,' and he told her what the film man had said, that night at the theatre.

'I don't care about that, Paul. I'm so sick of the glamour that Aunt Cora wished on me, though I suppose I'll have to keep it now.'

'Then you don't want to marry me?'

'It isn't that. It's ... well, I do seem to have been a disturbing influence in many lives, don't I? It wasn't any fault of mine, but there it is. Now everyone seems to be settled nicely – Aunt Cora and Sir Timothy, James and Melita. Even Keith and Susaline'll rub along, with their dancing, now I'm not around. Will I be doing the right thing, going into your life? Will I be a disturbing element wherever I go?'

'Maybe,' he grinned, 'but it's the kind of disturbing element I like! Oh, Delia, darling – stop arguing. Let's get married and take a chance. We love each other. We're going into a new world – the film world – where we can travel and work together. We can leave Chiverstock and its narrowness behind, and forget all the unpleasant memories. We'll just take the memory of that month in Cornwall with us, and when we come back, it will be to Cornwall, and not to Chiverstock. What do you say?'

He paid the bill in a dream, and they said

an incoherent goodbye to the three sisters, who, still in a huddle, but a very excited huddle, neglected their other customers to watch Paul and Delia go.

'I knew it would be all right,' sighed Miss Lou, the sentimental one.

'I said so all along,' Miss Bessie asserted. Paul was her hero and special pet. 'True love never runs smooth.'

'Such a handsome man,' breathed Miss Ann, dreaming of her long-lost youth.

'She's lovely, too,' murmured the other two, as Paul and Delia reached the top of the steps, stood for a second silhouetted against the strong sunlight of the Square, before stepping forward out of sight of the watchers below into their new life together.

The publishers hope that this book has given you enjoyable reading. Large Print Books are especially designed to be as easy to see and hold as possible. If you wish a complete list of our books please ask at your local library or write directly to:

Magna Large Print Books
Magna House, Long Preston,
Skipton, North Yorkshire.
BD23 4ND

This Large Print Book, for people
who cannot read normal print,
is published under the auspices of

THE ULVERSCROFT FOUNDATION